Praise for *Suspense and Sensibility*

"The author smoothly combines characters from *Pride and Prejudice* and *Sense and Sensibility* while remaining true to Austen's originals."
—*Publishers Weekly*

"No evil is a match for the witty and happily married Darcys."
—*Kirkus Reviews*

"A page-turner."   —*The Republic of Pemberley*

Praise for *Pride and Prescience*

"Thoroughly 'light and bright and sparkling,' in the best Austen tradition with a dollop of murder and mayhem to leaven the whole. A delight."
—Stephanie Barron, author of the Jane Austen Mystery series

"Well crafted...Bebris works her own brand of Austen magic, whetting the reader's appetite for a sequel. Taking a lighter approach than Stephanie Barron's sleuthing Jane Austen series, this one should appeal as much to Regency readers as to Austenites."
—*Publishers Weekly*

"Mannered prose, Regency backdrops, moody country houses, and delightful characterization place this new series high on the to-buy list."
—*Library Journal*

Forge Books by Carrie Bebris

Pride and Prescience

Suspense and Sensibility

North by Northanger

Suspense and Sensibility

OR, FIRST IMPRESSIONS REVISITED

———◆———

A Mr. & Mrs. Darcy Mystery

Carrie Bebris

A TOM DOHERTY ASSOCIATES BOOK

NEW YORK

This is a work of fiction. All of the characters, organizations, and events portrayed in this novel are either products of the author's imagination or are used fictitiously.

SUSPENSE AND SENSIBILITY

A Forge Book
Published by Tom Doherty Associates, LLC
175 Fifth Avenue
New York, NY 10010

www.tor-forge.com

Forge® is a registered trademark of Tom Doherty Associates, LLC.

Library of Congress Cataloging-in-Publication Data

Bebris, Carrie.
    Suspense and sensibility, or, First impressions, revisited : a Mr. & Mrs.
Darcy mystery / Carrie Bebris.
        p. cm.
    A sequel to Pride and prescience, or, A truth universally acknowledged,
which was a sequel to Jane Austen's Pride and prejudice.
    ISBN-13: 978-0-7653-1844-2
    ISBN-10: 0-7653-1844-X
    1. Bennet, Elizabeth (Fictitious character)—Fiction. 2. Darcy,
Fitzwilliam (Fictitious character) —Fiction. 3. Married people—Fiction.
4. England—Fiction. I. Title: First impressions, revisited. II. Austen, Jane,
1775–1817. Pride and prejudice. III. Title.

PS3602.E267 S87 2005
813'.6—dc22

                                                            2004056304

Printed in the United States of America

D 0 9 8 7 6 5 4

For my sister, Dorothy,
and my grandfather, James Diliberti

Acknowledgments

Many people have contributed to the creation of this book in ways large and small. I particularly wish to thank:

My family, as always, for not only understanding my need to sequester myself away to invent conversations with imaginary people in faraway times and places, but also for encouraging me to do so.

Eliza Diliberti, Victoria Hinshaw, Anne Klemm, and Dorothy Stephenson, for criticism in various stages of the book's development. James Lowder, for Latin translations and other shared wisdom. My editor, Brian Thomsen, for his insight and guidance. And Natasha Panza, his extraordinary assistant, for her adept attention to a thousand details.

Members of the Beau Monde chapter of Romance Writers of America, for generously sharing their knowledge of Regency England. Also, my fellow members of the Jane Austen Society of North America, for their continued support.

Jane Austen, for creating Harry Dashwood, Kitty Bennet,

and the Darcys. William Shakespeare, for quotes used in Sir Francis's dialogue.

Finally, my readers, for their praise, questions, and feedback. And for their wanting, like me, to spend just a little more time with the Darcys.

"My good opinion once lost is lost for ever."
—*Darcy to Elizabeth,* Pride and Prejudice

O wad some Pow'r the giftie gie us
To see oursels as others see us!
—*Robert Burns*

Prologue

"There is, I believe, in every disposition a tendency to some particular evil, a natural defect, which not even the best education can overcome."

—Darcy to Elizabeth,
Pride and Prejudice, *Chapter 11*

1781

*D*amn this mortal coil."

Sir Francis Dashwood muttered the words under his breath, though he had no audience. He sat alone in his bedchamber, surrounded by the opulence he'd enjoyed all his life but experiencing the poverty every man knows when his years on earth run out. Time was no longer his to command. Once he'd had it in abundance, spent it as liberally and recklessly as any other commodity in his possession. Now it was in dreadfully short supply.

Servants had left a simple meal on the bedside table. The sandwich went untouched, but the glass of brimstone he drained in two swallows, relishing the familiar taste of the sulfur-laced brandy.

He stared at his reflection in the ornate gilded mirror across from his bed, resenting every wrinkle that etched his ruddy face. Where had that faded hair come from? The liver spots on his hands? The slight tremble that seized his fingers? Eyes watery with age stared back.

As a young man, he'd reveled in his vitality. He'd mocked mortality along with morality, dared death and the devil to catch him if they could. He'd lived each moment to its fullest, leaving no desire unindulged, no curiosity unexplored. And he harbored no regrets. If he had his life to live over again, he would change nothing. It had been a good run.

But it was not enough.

Fiery orange light slanted through the window to stripe the floor. Sunset might claim the bleak late autumn landscape of West Wycombe Park, but it would not claim him so easily. No, he would not go quietly into the darkness. His spirit was too strong to meekly concede the battle his body waged with time.

He gazed beyond his own image in the glass, to the reflection of the portrait that hung behind him. That, too, was an image of himself, but at one-and-twenty. The painter had captured him in the full vigor of youth. Just as the adventure that had been his life was beginning.

Inside, he was still that young man. Yet now he scarcely had the strength to even rise from his bed.

He twisted the sheets with arthritic hands, cursing his physical weakness, cursing the corporeal shell that could no longer keep up with him. He cursed the mirror that bore witness to his frailty. He'd paid handsomely for the artifact, one of many treasures that he'd acquired in his lifetime. He'd been drawn to it by the images of ancient Greek champions that adorned its frame, but now they seemed to taunt him with their puissance. Tonight, he would gladly trade the mirror—nay, his whole estate—to inhabit once more the body of a young man, to again take health and strength for granted.

He could not tear his gaze away from the reflections: Two images of the same man, separated by mere inches but a gulf of more than fifty years. Dawn and twilight.

He wanted another sunrise.

His vision grew cloudy, as it often did now at the end of the day. The dual images of himself became less distinct, fading at their edges and drifting toward each other. He blinked rapidly and rubbed his eyes, trying to stabilize the view, but in vain. His eyesight, like the rest of his body, was failing him.

This last failure, however, was welcome, for after another minute, the two images merged completely. Despair fled, replaced by satisfaction.

Slowly, a smile spread across his face. He was a young man once more.

If only in the mirror.

One

"If any young men come for Mary or Kitty, send them in, for I am quite at leisure."

—Mr. Bennet to Elizabeth,
Pride and Prejudice, *Chapter 59*

1813

Elizabeth Bennet Darcy tried very hard to concentrate on the letter in her hand, but the intrusion of her own thoughts conspired with the fine prospect outside her window to distract her.

When the post arrived, she had withdrawn to her favorite sitting room at Pemberley. Such had become her morning custom in her few months as mistress of the house. The room, she understood, had also been a favorite of her husband's mother, and Elizabeth suspected the late Mrs. Darcy had shared her opinion that it offered a view of the river and valley superior to any other in the house. Today, though patches of snow stubbornly resisted the caress of the late winter sun, the smell of damp earth nevertheless carried the promise of spring.

Fitzwilliam Darcy's ancestral house bore the imprint of so many generations that Elizabeth had not yet found her place here. Home was anywhere her husband was, and Darcy had

15

done much to ease her way, but the greatness of his estate required her adjustment. She did not want to depart Pemberley before she truly felt settled. But family duty beckoned, and they were obliged to answer.

She left the window, returned to her desk, and read once more the cross-written, blotted lines. As she contemplated her response, Darcy entered. His tailcoat, leather breeches, and top boots indicated his intent to go riding.

"Good morning, again." Darcy kissed her cheek. "I came to invite you for an airing."

She set aside the letter with a heavy sigh.

A frown creased his forehead. "Perhaps instead I should enquire what I have done to merit such a reception? I realize riding was never your favorite pastime, but I do not recall your ever greeting the suggestion with despondency before."

"It is not your invitation that dismays me." Under her husband's influence, she'd developed greater interest in riding, though in truth, it was the company more than the activity that appealed to her. She looked up into his face and smiled wistfully. "I am afraid, sir, that you have committed crimes of a more grievous nature."

"Indeed?" He set down his hat and leaned against the edge of her desk. "Name the offenses."

"Like a nursery-tale knave, you have carried me off to your secluded castle and kept me to yourself for nigh on three months, with no thought of returning me to the companionship of my family."

"Are you not enjoying our privacy at Pemberley?"

"I did not say I was the one harboring objections."

After the turbulent events that had marked the first few weeks of their marriage, Elizabeth and Darcy had both relished their retreat to Derbyshire. As Darcy's seventeen-year-old sister, Georgiana, was the only other resident of Pemberley, they'd enjoyed a quiet transition to married life. Now that March had begun, however, their idyllic sequestered state seemed destined to end as society made its claims upon them. "Do you think my equestrian skills can bear the intense scrutiny of a trot through Hyde Park?" she asked.

"Where London society rides to be seen?"

He tactfully avoided further response to her query, but his silence formed reply enough. She arched her brows, merrily daring him to put his thoughts into words.

He cleared his throat. "Perhaps it is best that we have no plans to visit town any time soon."

She laughed. "You know that you need not spare my vanity. I harbor no illusions about the quality of my horsemanship—my goal on any outing is simply to sit a mount without embarrassing myself." She gestured toward the letter. "Unfortunately, our rides may indeed take place on Rotten Row in the near future. I have received another note from my mother this morning. She reminds me again what a wonderful thing it would be for us to sponsor a London season for Kitty."

"Have not Jane and Bingley already committed themselves to that noble cause?"

"Mama now fears that, given Jane's delicate state of health, the excitement of escorting our sister to balls and concerts might overtax her."

"But the Bingleys do not anticipate their new arrival until September."

"Surely you cannot seriously expect my mother to defer the pleasure of fretting over Jane's condition? She has but six months remaining in which to describe her anxiety to all her acquaintance."

"Ah, yes—I had forgotten about her nerves."

"My father would envy you, for I am sure he is continually reminded of them." Elizabeth suspected her father spent a good deal of time in his library of late to minimize the reports of her mother's daily visits to Jane. Mr. Bennet cared about his eldest daughter, of course, but didn't require updates as detailed or as frequent as those Mrs. Bennet was inspired to provide. Simply show him a healthy grandchild and safe new mother at the end of it all, and he would be satisfied. "Perhaps we ought to take pity on him and invite him to London along with Kitty."

"You have agreed to this scheme regarding Kitty, then? When did you intend to tell me?"

"I have agreed to nothing yet. You know I would much rather remain here at Pemberley with you than leap into the social whirl of town—"

"But Kitty has been out for three years now, and Hertfordshire holds few prospects for her," he finished. "A London season would improve her chances of meeting an acceptable young man."

"Precisely. And it sounds as if Jane has her hands full enough dealing with my mother. Besides, you know how disposed Jane and Bingley are to always think the best of everyone. When it comes to assessing potential suitors, you and I would prove more discerning chaperones for Kitty."

"True." Darcy's face clouded.

She knew he thought of Bingley's sister Caroline, whose own recent courtship could have profited from greater vigilance. She attempted to divert his musings. "Georgiana would benefit, as well."

"You wish to marry off my sister along with yours this season?"

"Only if she herself wishes it." Georgiana, unlike Kitty, possessed an inheritance sizable enough to grant her comfortable independence should she choose never to wed. "I meant that she might enjoy Kitty's companionship since they are so close in age."

He leaned over to drop a light kiss on her forehead. "Write to your sister. Shall we invite Mary, too, while we are about it? Complete our whole family's husband-hunting at once?"

"I shall ask her, but I doubt she will accept." Elizabeth's other unmarried sister, critical of the frivolity of society's elite *ton*, had already expressed disdain for the whole enterprise.

"Besides," she added, dipping her pen, "if all five of us sisters married within a twelvemonth of each other, my mother's joy would be too great for anyone to bear."

Two

His person and air were equal to what her fancy had ever drawn for the hero of a favorite story.

—Sense and Sensibility, *Chapter 9*

*W*ill there be any eligible barons there, do you think?" Kitty, the comb in her hand all but forgotten, gazed expectantly at Elizabeth in the dressing table mirror. "Or an earl? No—a duke! I would so love to meet a duke tonight! Might one be there?"

"I daresay there might. But mind, you shall not speak to any gentleman to whom you have not been properly introduced."

"Of course, Lizzy, of course. But Mr. Darcy knows everybody, doesn't he? Surely he must know a duke or two."

In truth, Elizabeth was not at all certain who would be present tonight or how many people Darcy might know. They were engaged to attend a party at the home of some new acquaintances, Sir John and Lady Middleton. "Mr. Darcy does not know everybody. Why, he met Sir John only this week, and they have been members of the same club for years."

"Oh, where is the maid? We'll be late if she doesn't dress my hair soon!"

"She is still ironing your gown." Elizabeth pitied her lady's maid, so intense was Kitty's excitement this first week of her first London season. Her sister hadn't been demanding in an imperious sort of way, so much as desperately afraid of missing something if she paused a moment to catch her breath. But the servant had borne Kitty's flurry with patience and good humor. "If you had not changed your mind so many times about what to wear, we would not be in danger of arriving late."

Three dresses, donned and discarded, lay on the bed. Pink had given way to white, then lavender, before blue was determined the most flattering. Kitty regarded the rejects dubiously. "Perhaps the lavender after all—"

"Kitty!"

A gentle knock on the door interrupted them. Georgiana entered, fetchingly attired in a dark green tunic over a white gown trimmed with gold ribbons. Kitty gasped.

"Oh, dear! My blue gown has gold ribbons!"

"I shall change," Georgiana offered.

"No, no—you are already dressed." Kitty bit her lower lip and considered once more the pile of cast-off silk and lawn. "I will wear the pink instead."

"The pink is most becoming," Georgiana said. "I think it is my favorite of yours."

"Truly?"

The suggestion carried: Pink was now the gown of choice. Darcy's even-tempered sister had a soothing effect on Kitty, for which Elizabeth was grateful. Perhaps Georgiana's presence would also spare the maid the trial of every hair ornament in Kitty's jewelry box before they could depart.

Elizabeth left the younger girls and withdrew to enjoy a few moments' peace in anticipation of the evening ahead. At her own dressing table, she tested her headdress to ensure it was secure, then slipped on her gloves and went in search of Darcy. She found him in the hall, hat in hand and wearing his greatcoat. He glanced at the tall case clock, whose hands indicated that the Middletons' soirée had already begun.

"Is your sister ready?" he enquired.

"Not yet. She was having a gown crisis, but I think disaster has been averted."

A look of concern crossed his countenance. "Your mother provided her with numerous new gowns for the season. What misfortune befell them?"

"The unknown preferences of a duke."

Concern gave way to confusion. "Which duke?"

"Any duke. She has high hopes of meeting an unattached peer tonight and turning his head. All chance of her future happiness, therfore, now rests entirely on several yards of pink silk and lace trim."

"I pray they are up to the charge." He looked again at the clock, then cast an impatient glance toward the staircase. "She shall not meet anyone if we never leave our own townhouse."

"The soirée will last for hours, and I am certain we will not be the only guests to arrive late. Most of the *ton* does not share your strict definition of punctuality."

"They might form a more tolerable group if they did."

"But then who would take note of them? One cannot make a grand entrance to an empty room."

"Precisely why I prefer to arrive in a timely manner, before an affair becomes crowded."

Her husband, she knew, did not care to draw attention to himself, nor to endure the tiresome company of those who did. He favored small gatherings of intimate friends over large assemblies of near-strangers, intelligent conversation over mindless gabble. His willingness, therefore, to sponsor Kitty for a full London season demonstrated affection for Elizabeth surpassing any that mere diamonds or other baubles could represent.

Tonight's event, she suspected, would be just the sort of crush Darcy dreaded. She'd heard that the Middletons' parties were always crowded affairs, the length of the guest list inspired more by the baronet's gregarious nature than a realistic understanding of how many people his rooms could comfortably accommodate. Sir John, who had eight children of his own, took great pleasure in gathering young people together and wanted to include everybody in everything. Upon meeting Darcy and learning that he and Elizabeth had two young ladies in their charge, the baronet had insisted that the four of them attend Lady Middleton's soirée.

She wondered whether Darcy realized what he had gotten himself into by accepting the invitation. "Have you any idea how many guests the Middletons expect?"

"Sir John called tonight's party a small get-together, so I anticipate a pleasant evening."

Poor Darcy.

She wrestled a few moments with her conscience over whether to warn him of the probable scene ahead, but decided against spoiling his night any sooner than necessary. "Did Sir John say whether his eldest sons would be there?" The Middletons had two sons in their early twenties—John, named after his father, and William.

"They will. They have no titles, however—will Kitty still wish to meet them?"

"Kitty wants to meet every eligible young gentleman in attendance."

He regarded her warily. "Elizabeth, I trust your sister will comport herself in a dignified manner?"

"Of course she shall." She prayed.

Since the elopement of their youngest sister, Lydia, last August, Elizabeth and Jane had worked hard to curb Kitty's more foolish tendencies and check the undisciplined behavior in which she'd been allowed to indulge with Lydia. Kitty now, her sisters hoped, comprehended the difference between cream-pot love and genuine regard, and understood that genteel conduct solicited more respectable attention from gentlemen than did brazen flirtation.

"Kitty has learned from Lydia's poor judgment, and benefits from the steadier influence of our company," Elizabeth added. "Sometimes entire weeks pass without a single mention of officers or red coats."

"Yes, it seems she has moved on to dukes."

"You cannot fault her for harboring the same aspirations as every other young lady in town." A servant arrived with Elizabeth's wrap and helped her drape it over her arms.

"Georgiana anticipates the evening more soberly."

"Your sister has experienced previous London seasons, so the prospect of a society affair does not hold the novelty it does for Kitty. Yet despite her natural reserve, I believe Georgiana, too, looks forward to increasing her limited acquaintance this evening."

"Her present circle is quite large enough."

"Darcy, you have shielded Georgiana from the fashionable world since the day she came out. You cannot sequester her forever."

He turned, avoiding her gaze by inspecting his appearance in the trumeau mirror. "I do nothing of the sort."

Behind him, she raised a brow. He saw the accusation in her reflection.

"I merely restrict her exposure to men whose motives or merit I question," he clarified, setting his hat down on the table to adjust the shoulders of his coat.

"That is to say, any men at all."

He faced her and shrugged. "Am I to blame if all the gentlemen one encounters these days are rowdies who lack purpose? Or worse—rakes and rogues who engage in less than noble behavior?"

She sighed, knowing that a single conversation could not surmount Darcy's natural protective instincts toward his sister, nor his self-reproach for what he considered an inexcusable failure of watchfulness on his part. When Georgiana was but fifteen, even before she was officially out in society, she'd almost eloped with a fortune hunter—the same ne'er-do-well who had eventually seduced Lydia. That another, more sophisticated friend of theirs recently had been similarly deceived by another "gentleman" only increased his mistrust.

"Not every potential suitor is a secret scoundrel, Darcy. Honorable men yet exist."

"I should like to know where." Though he spoke lightly, she could read disillusionment in his eyes.

"I found one."

She crossed to the table, lifted his hat, and placed it on his head. As she met his gaze, she offered a playful smile. "Unless you really married me for my vast fortune?"

"Nay," he said, taking her hands in his as she lowered them.

"My superior connections?"

"Mistaken again." He held her gaze and returned her impish grin. "In fact, I believe it was *you* who drew in *me*."

"Indeed? I had no notion of my own talent for scheming. To what do I owe my success?"

"Your honeyed tongue. Who could resist being told that he was full of arrogance, conceit, and selfishness? Or that he was the last man in the world whom you could ever be prevailed upon to marry?"

"With enticements like that, you must have wondered that no one had whisked me to the altar already."

"I wondered only whether I could change enough to lure you there myself."

She studied him a long moment, grateful that they had found their way past early misunderstandings and to each other. "First impressions are not always accurate reflections of one's character, are they?"

"No. Thank heaven."

They arrived at the Middletons' quite late, even by fashionable standards. Kitty practically leapt from the carriage when it came to a stop in Conduit Street. They entered to find the formal receiving line ended and their hosts circulating among the guests.

To Kitty's obvious delight and Darcy's equally evident despair, the event was indeed a squeeze. The rooms were packed so full of people that Elizabeth wasn't sure how anyone managed to converse, let alone dance. Yet strains of music from the next room indicated that couples made a noble attempt amid all the noise and heat.

"Have you ever seen so many people of consequence in one place?" Kitty exclaimed. "And so many gentlemen! Elizabeth, surely there is someone here to whom you can introduce me?"

Elizabeth scanned the room but saw not one familiar face. Luckily, she was spared the necessity of replying with a disappointing negative by the approach of an older man with a ruddy, genial countenance. "Is this our host?" she asked Darcy.

"Indeed."

"Mr. Darcy! I'm glad you are come!" Sir John clapped Darcy's shoulder heartily, suggesting an acquaintance of years rather than barely a se'nnight. "I was just talking with Carville and Hartford about organizing a shooting party, and you must promise to be among our number."

"I would be honored, though my skills could but poorly complement any party led by you."

"Nonsense! I can tell by the look of you, you're a fine shot."

"Fair," Darcy demurred. Though he enjoyed shooting and hunting, he was not a man who liked to boast of his skills or recount every detail of his last chase. "However, they tell me at the club that you are a sportsman without equal."

"Whether that is true or not I shall leave to the judgment of others, but I can think of nowhere I would rather be than out of doors with my hounds." He smiled broadly at the women. "These lovely ladies must be your wife and sisters."

"Sir John Middleton, may I present my wife, Mrs. Darcy, her sister, Miss Catherine Bennet, and my sister, Miss Darcy."

"Charmed!" The baronet, to Elizabeth's relief, bowed rather than offer the same effusive welcome Darcy had received. "Please, you must come with me to meet Lady Middleton. She will not want to defer the pleasure of your acquaintance another moment."

They found their hostess in the card room, attempting to complete a rubber while half-listening to the whines of a girl about six years of age. A flustered nursemaid was trying to discreetly steer the girl from the room, but Lady Middleton's distracted murmurs only encouraged the child to continue her campaign to be allowed to remain.

"Marguerite, what are you doing out of the nursery?" Sir John gave the child a playful pat on the head as if rewarding one of his hounds. He turned to the Darcys with a smile. "My youngest," he said, as if birth order provided sufficient explanation for the child's presence.

"I'm sorry, sir." The nursemaid tried to take Marguerite's hand, but the child jerked her fingers away. "She dashed out the door and down the stairs before I could stop her."

Sir John rubbed the underside of Marguerite's chin. "Don't want to miss the party, do you, little dove?"

"Let me stay, Papa! I want to stay! Make Mama let me stay!"

Elizabeth generally liked children—indeed, she cherished hopes of having her own before long. But allowing such a young girl at a formal society function was an indulgence she'd never witnessed before, and for good reason. Marguerite's pleas and cajoles so distracted both parents that Lady Middleton could scarcely focus as Sir John made a rather disorganized introduction to the Darcys.

"It is a pleasure—hold still, please, Marguerite—to meet you, Mrs. Darcy," Lady Middleton finally said to Georgiana.

"No, no, my dear," Sir John interjected. "That's—in a moment, dove—that's *Miss* Darcy. The other ladies—I said one moment, my little angel—"

"Lovely to meet you all. I have been dying to make your acquaintance for ages, ever since Tuesday." Lady Middleton turned her attention back to her cards. "Marguerite, do cease tugging on my arm."

Whilst the Middletons were thus besieged, three gentlemen entered the room. Two of them appeared very much alike: large, athletic young men who looked like they could sit a horse or box in Jackson's Rooms with equal skill. They wore close-fitting single-breasted coats—one claret, one brown—and fair hair carefully styled to appear as tousled as if they had just come in from a foxhunt. The third gentleman wore his dark locks in the same mode, as deliberately arranged as his cravat. He had a more slender but no less vigorous build, his broad shoulders and narrow waist shown to advantage by a blue dress coat so up-to-the-minute in fashion that it could have been cut that morning. Tight-fitting pantaloons and silk stockings revealed muscular legs, and his polished shoes competed with the chandelier for shine.

By all appearances, they were typical London bloods, all three—aristocratic gents with too much time and money, and little ambition to do anything productive with either. Elizabeth dismissed them without another thought, until she heard Kitty sigh beside her.

"Look at them, Lizzy—pinks of the *ton* if ever I saw one." She sighed again. "Oh, they're coming this way!" Kitty looked as if she might swoon with the effort of keeping her excitement in check. "Quickly—is my hair still in place?"

"At least as well as theirs."

The gentlemen reached Lady Middleton's table. "Mother," said the young man in brown, "Lady Carrington is looking for you. We left her in the dining room."

"Thank you, William. I shall go to her directly I finish this rubber."

"William, tell Mama to let me stay!"

William looked somewhat amused by his sister's demand, but the other fair-haired gentleman cast her an impatient glance. "Marguerite, ought you not be in bed?"

"Go away, John. You are always such a spoiler!"

"A soirée is no place for children."

Marguerite was on the verge of another retort when the third fellow intervened to diffuse the family squabble. "Miss Marguerite, if I asked your mother very sweetly, do you think she would honor me with an introduction to this gentleman and the pretty ladies with him?"

"They are only a Mr. Darcy and his sisters. Mama, if you do not let me stay, I shall scream. I shall!" Her shrill voice already carried above the din.

"Nonsense, child. You will behave like a proper young lady while Nurse escorts you back upstairs." Lady Middleton turned to the Darcys as the nursemaid stepped forward once more to take her charge. "Forgive me. These are my sons, John and William Middleton, and their friend Mr. Harry—Henry— Dashwood. Gentlemen, this is Mr. Fitzwilliam Darcy, his wife, and their sisters—"

"Nooooooo!"

Marguerite's shriek brought the burbling room to abrupt silence. Lady Middleton gaped at her daughter, her expression flashing from horror to embarrassment to anger to self-consciousness in rapid succession. Marguerite regarded her mother warily, realizing too late that even mothers worn down by the demands of seven previous children have thresholds of tolerance that cannot be crossed.

"Now that you have caused a scene, we need not indulge you further to avoid one," Lady Middleton said quietly.

The young nurse, whose further attempts to lead her charge away had occasioned the outburst, apologized profusely to her mistress and reached for Marguerite.

"I think you have sufficiently exhibited your ability to control the child," Lady Middleton said to her servant. She took her daughter by the hand. "We are going upstairs. Now. And if you want Nurse to keep her position, you will stay in the nursery and behave yourself for the remainder of the night."

Those at the card tables went back to their games of whist and lottery, but awkward silence lingered in the air.

"Mr. Darcy, was it?" Mr. Dashwood stepped toward them. "I believe I've heard of you down at White's. You have an estate in Derbyshire, do you not?"

Darcy bowed. "Yes, Pemberley. Near Lambton." He studied Mr. Dashwood. "Your name sounds familiar to me, as well."

"Perhaps you are thinking of my father, Mr. John Dashwood—a longtime member of White's."

"Of course. How is your father?"

"He passed away last autumn."

After Darcy and the rest of their party offered condolences, Sir John cleared his throat.

"Mr. Darcy, if your wife will excuse us, Carville and Hartford are in the billiards room, along with some other gentlemen I would like you to meet. You must hear Hartford recount his last foxhunt. What a tale! To tell it properly takes a full half-hour."

"Half an hour?" Darcy stammered.

"At least."

He turned to Elizabeth, his expression revealing to her alone the felicity he anticipated. "Can you get on without me for a while?"

"We can survive." She suppressed a wry smile and lowered her voice so that it reached only his ears. "Will you?"

Before Darcy could respond, their host addressed his sons and Mr. Dashwood. "I'm sure you fellows will attend to the ladies?"

"Of course, Father," answered William.

Darcy departed with the baronet to enjoy Hartford's regaling account, and William immediately fulfilled his filial obligation by asking Georgiana to dance. She accepted, and the two went to join the reel just beginning.

John Middleton suggested that perhaps the two remaining ladies might care for some refreshment. Though not hungry or thirsty, Elizabeth welcomed the opportunity to move to another room of the house. No sooner did the party pass through the doorway, however, than Mr. Middleton spotted a chap he simply had to speak to about a horse, or a hound, or something or other, and would the ladies please excuse him? He abandoned them before they could answer, leaving Elizabeth and Kitty in the sole custody of Mr. Dashwood.

Elizabeth half expected him to drop them as quickly as Mr. Middleton had, in search of more fashionable people with whom to while away the night. However, he offered his arm to Kitty, who almost tripped over her own feet in her eagerness to accept it, and proved himself most attentive as he steered them through the crowded rooms.

"So, why haven't I seen you at Almack's yet this season?"

"We have only just arrived in town," Kitty replied. "And Mr. Darcy doesn't like Almack's."

Mr. Dashwood laughed. "None of us likes Almack's."

"Then why does everybody go there?"

"Because everyone *else* is there. And to talk about how much they dislike it. The only thing more fashionable than being seen at Almack's is complaining about it."

"Oh." Kitty's gaze bordered on worshipful every time she looked at Mr. Dashwood. "Well, then, if I am fortunate enough to go, I shall object the whole while."

Mr. Dashwood laughed again. "I should wait until afterward, were I you. The last feathers you want to ruffle in London are those of Almack's patronesses."

"Why is that?"

He stopped, regarding her with a look that was half surprise, half amusement. "My—you *are* new in town, aren't you? Admission to Almack's is decided by seven ladies who guard its vouchers more fiercely than dragons their gold. Their influence in society extends well beyond the walls of their assembly rooms. Cross one of them, and you might as well go back to the country for the rest of the season."

Kitty absorbed this intelligence with the solemnity of an acolyte being indoctrinated into a new religion. Had Mr. Dashwood revealed that the *beau monde* subscribed to an official creed, she would have memorized it.

They moved on. Mr. Dashwood greeted numerous acquaintances, appearing to know nearly everyone. As they passed two fastidiously dressed dandies, he nodded in acknowledgment. "Albertson. Leopold." They bowed in response.

"Those jeweled buckles on their shoes look absurd," he said when they had passed out of earshot. "But I shall have to ask them who designed their waistcoats."

Kitty turned round to get a second look at the shoes, but another party had closed in behind them, blocking the view. One could still glimpse Albertson's chest, however. "Your own waistcoat is more flattering," she said.

He stopped to look her full in the face, assessing her sincerity. "Truly?"

"At least—well, I think so anyway." A flush crept into her cheeks. "But what do I know about gentlemen's clothes?"

"Enough to know your own mind. That puts you ahead of

half the ladies in this room." He took her arm once more and continued leading them toward the dining room. "I'd be careful about expressing it, though. You wouldn't want to let on that you can think for yourself."

"Is that a liability in a woman?" Elizabeth asked.

"In some corners of the Polite World, that is a liability in anyone. We are a frivolous, mindless lot."

Kitty continued to gaze at Mr. Dashwood as if he were the first gentleman she'd ever encountered. Indeed, she seemed to be concentrating harder on making conversation with him than Elizabeth had ever seen her focus on anything else in her life.

"Are you in London for the whole season?" Kitty asked.

"I live here most of the year. I have a house in Sussex, but I haven't spent much time at Norland since I was a boy. First I was at Eton, then Oxford, and now I prefer the entertainments of town to country living."

Unlike so many other women in the room, whose eyes roamed while in conversation with one partner to see whether anyone better happened nearby, Kitty bestowed her full attention on Mr. Dashwood—a fact not lost upon him. When the press of people attempting to squeeze through a too-narrow doorway required their party to pause, he observed that they stood mere feet from the Marquess of Avonbury, one of society's most eligible young gentlemen.

"Have you met the marquess?" Mr. Dashwood asked.

Kitty, who just hours earlier would have swooned at finding herself in such proximity to any unattached peer, barely spared him a glance. "No."

"Would you like me to introduce you?"

Mr. Dashwood extended his offer in a nonchalant manner, but Elizabeth sensed a larger question lay beneath the surface. His eye held a subtle look of appraisal.

"Perhaps later. You were speaking to me of Sussex," Kitty replied. "Is your mother still at Norland?"

His expression bespoke approval. The marquess was left behind as Mr. Dashwood guided them through the doorway. "She divides her time between Norland and London, though she's been in town since my father died."

"Is that when Norland fell to you?" Elizabeth asked.

"Yes, although it was entailed to me when I was a child by the will of a great-great-uncle I can't even remember."

"I'm sure it's a lovely house," Kitty said.

He shrugged. "As I said, I don't spend much time there." He led them around a cluster of ladies who eyed them with particular interest. He ignored their curiosity. "I understand Pemberley is quite grand?" he asked Kitty.

"It is! Lizzy calls it the most beautiful house in all England. I look forward to visiting there this summer."

He regarded her as if she'd said something odd. "You don't live there, then?"

"No. Why would I?"

He cast her another approving glance. "I see we are of like mind."

Kitty drew her brows together in puzzlement, not knowing how to interpret his reply. For that matter, neither did Elizabeth.

"In preferring town over the country," he clarified.

"Oh! Yes—town has so much more to offer, doesn't it?"

Mr. Dashwood acknowledged three more friends, one of whom bestowed a rakish grin on Kitty.

"You are keeping fine company tonight, Dashwood," he said.

"Save the charm for your wife, Cavanaugh." After they passed, he leaned toward Kitty and spoke in a conspiratorial voice Elizabeth heard only with difficulty. "Only one week wed, and already the baron is back on the prowl."

Kitty's jaw dropped. "Does his wife know?"

"I don't think so. She's been too busy this evening making eyes at his closest friend."

Mr. Dashwood delivered the gossip as dispassionately as if

reading a *Times* item about wholesale tea prices. The *beau monde,* with its endless intrigues and scandals, was a world away from the small Hertfordshire village where the Bennet sisters had grown up. It remained an utterly foreign culture to Kitty and a place Elizabeth would much rather visit than inhabit. But Mr. Dashwood was clearly in his element, moving through the intricacies of this society as easily as he navigated the busy rooms.

At last, they reached the tea table. Mr. Dashwood saw that they were served, but did not partake of anything himself.

"Are you not thirsty?" Kitty asked.

"Perhaps I'll want refreshment after dancing the next set."

Kitty's smile faded. "I didn't realize you had engaged a partner." She glanced round at several of the ladies nearest them and seemed disconcerted to discover many of them already regarding her.

"I haven't. I hope to dance with you."

Joy lit her face. "I would like that very much." She glanced again at a cluster of ladies nearby who spoke in whispers and avoided her gaze. "Mr. Dashwood, perhaps you can explain something to me?"

"I shall do my best."

"We seem to be drawing quite a bit of notice."

"Correction, my dear miss. You are the one drawing notice. I merit attention this evening only because I am talking to you."

Kitty shifted uncomfortably under the scrutiny. "Of what interest am I to any of these people?"

He paused, his gaze once more probing. "Do you play at modesty, or do you truly not know?"

She shook her head.

"You are a new face at the Middletons'. Everyone is assessing your prospects in the marriage market. Within three minutes of your arrival, there was a report in general circulation that Miss Darcy has thirty thousand pounds, and within four, rampant speculation about which gentlemen would be leaving their cards at your house tomorrow."

Kitty simply stared at him in confusion. "But what have those thirty thousand pounds to do with me?"

His eyes sparkled with amusement. "Of course, any lady wants to be courted for herself, not her dowry. But Miss Darcy, surely you realize how attractive your fortune makes you in the eyes of the *ton?*"

Kitty's whole posture deflated as she absorbed the import of his words. "I am not Miss Darcy," she said in a small voice.

Now it was Mr. Dashwood's turn to look confused. "But when Lady Middleton introduced us—"

"Nor do I have thirty thousand pounds."

Mr. Dashwood stared at Kitty. "Then who—"

Kitty swallowed hard and opened her mouth to speak, but no words came.

Elizabeth interceded. "It was not the clearest introduction. We were all distracted by Marguerite," she said. "Mr. Dashwood, may I present to you Miss Catherine Bennet? She is not Mr. Darcy's sister, but mine."

Mr. Dashwood continued to regard her in stupefaction. Kitty looked away, struggling to contain deep disappointment and retain her composure with so many eyes upon her.

Elizabeth's heart broke for her sister. To learn that the attention she'd been enjoying was intended for another! And to know that her own meager dowry was so paltry in comparison to Georgiana's that she couldn't possibly hold the fashionable Mr. Dashwood's interest. It was all so mortifying that Kitty would probably want to leave as soon as Mr. Dashwood stammered out whatever excuse he could quickly invent to flee her company.

In the ballroom, the music drew to a conclusion. Kitty met Mr. Dashwood's gaze once more. "Georgiana's set with Mr. Middleton is ended," she said. "I believe you wanted to dance the next with Miss Darcy."

Mr. Dashwood at last recovered himself. "No, I wanted to stand up with you."

"But I'm not the person you thought you were conversing with. Doesn't that change things?"

"It certainly does."

Kitty drew a shaky breath. Elizabeth could tell she fought back tears.

"I shall now enjoy the distinction of being the first gentleman here to dance with Miss Catherine Bennet." He held out his hand to her. "If she will so honor me."

Three

To wish was to hope, and to hope was to expect.
                    —Sense and Sensibility, *Chapter 4*

he expectation of one thousand pounds was all Elizabeth had brought to her marriage, all Jane had brought
to hers, and all Mr. Bennet could afford to dower upon each of
his remaining two unwed daughters. Elizabeth and Jane had
made such advantageous matches that they had been willing to
give up their shares to improve their sisters' chances, but their
father had checked their generosity. "You are marrying good
men whom I trust to take proper care of you," he had said. "But
I want you to have something of your own." Lydia's scandalous
elopement had required a larger settlement—to which Darcy
had contributed considerably—to buy back her respectability.
Fortunately, Kitty and Mary were not inclined to increase their
dowries at such cost to themselves. Unfortunately, that left
Kitty with a settlement one-thirtieth the size of Georgiana's.

As gentlemen's calling cards piled up in the silver tray on the
hall table the day after the Middletons' ball, Elizabeth couldn't
help but wish that at least one of them had been left for Kitty.

"There are some here for you," Elizabeth told Darcy as she

fanned the cards out to examine the names. "Including one from Lord Hartford."

Darcy grimaced. "An hour proved insufficient for him to complete his foxhunting saga. He promised to call upon me to share the remainder."

"What a pity you were out. Now you shall have to hear it during the shooting party."

"I have no doubt of the full version being repeated then, too."

Elizabeth set his cards aside and glanced at the others. The one she most sought was not among them.

Mr. Dashwood had promised to call that afternoon. After the revelation of Kitty's true identity, he had spent the remainder of the evening proving himself as attentive a gentleman as propriety allowed. He danced two sets with Kitty and had no other partners save his cousin Regina, with whom a promise to his aunt had obliged him to dance one set. Elizabeth had no idea what Kitty and Mr. Dashwood talked of while on the dance floor, but she could see that he drew many smiles and occasional laughter from her sister. When he was not dancing, his conduct toward both Kitty and Elizabeth had been utterly charming.

For her part, Kitty had spoken of nothing but Mr. Dashwood for the entire carriage ride home, and she seemed to have risen from her bed with his name on her lips. Breakfast had been spent recalling his every look and gesture. That Kitty had danced with two other gentlemen, she seemed to have forgotten, though she did pause often enough in her adulation of Mr. Dashwood to compliment Georgiana on the handsome looks and manners of Miss Darcy's many partners. Miss Darcy, however, had not been taken with any one of them to the extent that Mr. Dashwood had captivated Kitty.

Yet Georgiana's entourage had found their way to the townhouse this afternoon, while Mr. Dashwood had not. And Elizabeth could not help but reflect on why.

She sighed. "The rest of the cards are for Georgiana."

Darcy, who waited for a servant to bring his greatcoat, picked up the stack of cards left for Georgiana and shuffled through them.

"Do any of those names meet your approval?" Elizabeth asked.

He frowned at two cards. "Mr. Sutton and Sir Harvey are ridiculous coxcombs." He tossed their cards aside and looked at the next. "St. Germain is a hothead—he has been in two duels this year alone." The next card also fell to the pile. "Wybourn drinks too much."

Darcy's man appeared with his coat. She took the remaining cards from her husband while he slipped his arms into its sleeves. "Sir Reginald Perringdale. Who is he?"

"A widower with seven children looking for a third wife."

"So much for him." She moved to the next. "Lord Tyndale seemed nice."

"He is indeed quite pleasant. He is also up to his neckcloth in debt."

"Lord Highcroft?"

"A notorious rake."

"Lord Ashton?"

"A worse rake."

"What about Mr. Fillmore?"

"Too old."

"Mr. Sinclair?"

"Too young."

"The Marquess of Avonbury?"

"I am told he snores."

"Darcy! Can any gentleman who wants to court your sister possibly win your approbation?"

"No."

Although she detected a flash of humor in his eye as he made the declaration, she knew he only half jested. Any suitor of Georgiana's would have to prove himself a man of flawless character, spotless reputation, and substantial fortune just to win permission to cross their threshold.

Darcy took his hat from the valet, who then disappeared as discreetly as he'd arrived. She handed the cards back to her husband, who pocketed them.

"Are you even going to show those cards to Georgiana?" she asked.

"Yes. She will want something to read after I lock her in the tower you seem to think I am building."

"So that is why you agreed to a London season for Kitty—so that you could dispatch masons to Pemberley in our absence."

"You have found me out. They are constructing a turret with a winding, rickety stair as we speak."

The repartee softened her mood, and she allowed a smile to reach her lips. "Will the moat be finished by the time we return?"

"It is under way. I am having difficulty, however, locating a troll to guard the entrance."

"I thought you would entrust that duty to no one but yourself."

"They must pass by me to reach the troll."

"Then he will soon become a very lazy troll, for he shall have nothing to do."

The sound of a carriage pulling up indicated that Darcy's driver waited. Darcy bade her farewell and started to go, but turned round before he reached the door.

"Do you truly believe I am unreasonable concerning Georgiana?"

She paused a moment before replying. "I believe you will not allow her to settle for anything less than a man whose conduct and sense of honor equal your own, and I admire your determination to protect your sister from choosing poorly." She walked to him, to better hold his gaze. "I hope, however, that when the time comes, you will allow her to have a voice in the matter of her own marriage."

"Of course I shall."

She heard restless footsteps above—no doubt Kitty, crossing to the front window yet again only to discover that the carriage below belonged to the Darcys, not to Mr. Dashwood. In a way, Kitty kept watch from her own tower.

"Will you hold Kitty's suitors to the same standards?" she asked.

"Your father's authority supersedes mine in that matter, but I hope you know I will guard her interests as vigilantly as if she were my own sister."

"I do know." She looked toward the door, wishing a caller for Kitty would suddenly materialize on the opposite side of it. "I only hope she will have someone for you to be vigilant *about*."

"I thought you expected Mr. Dashwood to call?"

"Last night I was certain of it. He seemed so sincere in his attentions, even after he found out Kitty was not Georgiana. But each hour's delay makes me fear that either his intentions were never as serious as he led Kitty to hope, or—"

"Or that in the bright light of morning, he more fully considered the implications of marrying a young lady with no fortune."

"Any sensible man would. You did."

She knew Darcy had weighed his love for her against the financial and social benefits of marrying more advantageously. She had no fortune, no title, no connections; in fact, in wedding her he had allied himself with a family of compromised reputation following her sister's elopement. The very notion of an engagement between them had brought the wrath of his aunt, Lady Catherine de Bourgh, down upon them both.

"Yet despite worldly considerations, I chose you."

That he, whose every action was dictated by reason, had done so remained a source of wonder to Elizabeth. "Not every man has the ability or the willingness to disregard all that you did."

"If Mr. Dashwood cannot, then his absence today is for the

best. Better he lets reason cool his romantic impulses now than rue them later."

Had Darcy ever regretted his decision? She was not a vain, insecure girl, but neither was she insensible of the sacrifices he'd made on her behalf. She busied herself in straightening his lapels. "Marry in haste, repent in leisure?" She attempted to adopt a light tone, but her voice sounded unnaturally high to her ears.

"Mrs. Darcy, what I feel for you in my leisure hours strays far indeed from repentance."

After a parting kiss, Darcy left for his appointment. Elizabeth went to the drawing room, where she found Kitty hovering by the window. In constant anticipation of Mr. Dashwood's arrival, she had turned down the opportunity to join Georgiana shopping in Bond Street, or do anything else that would take her out of the house. She had instead spent the day fluttering aimlessly from one room to the next, unable to focus on a single occupation for more than a few minutes. If Mr. Dashwood did not call soon, she would surely drive Elizabeth to distraction.

"Kitty, do sit down. Watching the street will not make him come."

Kitty reluctantly perched on the edge of the sofa, where she twisted a button on her skirt until Elizabeth thought it would fall off. "He said he would call. What can be keeping him?"

The sound of a hackney coach pulling up signaled the arrival of a visitor. Kitty rushed to the window.

"Oh! It is only that odd scholar fellow you know."

"Professor Randolph?"

"Yes, him. I needn't stay, Lizzy, must I?"

Elizabeth dismissed her, as interested in a private conversation with Julian Randolph as Kitty was in granting one. She had not seen the archaeologist since just before Christmas, when he'd helped the Darcys rescue the Bingley family from a murderous houseguest. Randolph's professional knowledge of mysterious antiquities had proven critical in apprehending the villain, who had been using a centuries-old artifact with unusual properties to enact his scheme.

From the safety of Pemberley, and now their London townhouse, Elizabeth sometimes still could not quite believe that the eerie events they'd experienced at Netherfield had not been simply a midwinter night's dream brought on by reading too many gothic novels. But she had only to pull out the protective amulet Randolph had given her to remind herself that not everything in this world—or the next—could be rationally explained. Darcy, on the other hand, had gone back to dismissing the professor's supernatural studies as nonsense almost as soon as they'd been proven otherwise. There was little room in his world for things from beyond it. In logic he trusted.

She rose to greet her visitor. "Professor Randolph, what a lovely surprise!"

"I heard you and Mr. Darcy were in town." He looked the same as she remembered, from his slender build to the spectacles that had a habit of sliding down his nose. He wore a new suit, a consequence, she presumed, of the poor scholar having at last found steady employment. Like his other clothing, the suit exhibited an unusual number of pockets. She'd seen him pull everything from pocketknives to candles from his costume.

"How do you like your new post?" she asked. Under the patronage of Darcy's friend Lord Chatfield, Professor Randolph had recently secured a position as the British Museum's resident archaeologist.

"I could not be happier. I have just returned from examining a formation of standing stones in the North Country, and there is talk of sending me to the Continent as soon as the war is over. I would love the opportunity to return to Athens and Rome."

"Return? I know you came here from America, but I did not realize you were so well traveled." Upon reflection, there was much she didn't know about Professor Randolph.

"This would mark my third expedition to the sites of those ancient civilizations."

She rang for tea. As they waited for the refreshments, he enquired after her and Darcy. She reported that they'd enjoyed a quiet sojourn at Pemberley since the archaeologist had last seen them.

"You appear happy," he said, "which I am glad to witness after the troubling events that transpired right after your marriage. Do you still have the amulet?"

"Indeed, yes. I would not part with such a generous present." When she'd first met the professor, he'd carried a silver pocketwatch with ancient protective symbols he'd specially commissioned engraved upon it. Following their ordeal at Netherfield, he'd given it to her.

"Do you carry it on you?"

She felt a pang of conscience. "No," she confessed. "But please don't think it goes unvalued. I keep it safely in a drawer. I am afraid my husband does not care for the sight of it."

Randolph chuckled. "I am little surprised. He does not seem to be a man who possesses much tolerance for things he does not himself believe in."

"Either that, or he prefers gold timepieces to silver." They shared a smile. Then she added, "Mr. Darcy, like many people, trusts only what he can observe with his own five senses."

"And you?"

The arrival of tea prevented immediate reply. She was more willing than her husband to accept the inexplicable, to concede that science had limitations and that sometimes the ability to see a thing had nothing to do with eyesight. She had long relied on instinct in addition to reason when forming judgments and making decisions. In her experience, an impression unsupported by objective evidence could nevertheless be accurate. But she'd also seen some of her impressions proven false in the end, and so hesitated to place all her faith in them.

"I believe in intuition," she said when the servant withdrew, "but I know it is not infallible."

"Many people—women especially—are perceptive," the professor said. "But you seem unusually so. It may merely be that your acknowledgment of the unknown makes you more aware of subtleties that *can* be observed but that go unnoticed by those who do not look. In any event, don't be afraid to trust your intuition. Or to carry the amulet, if it won't cause trouble with Mr. Darcy. You never know when it might come in handy—if only to keep track of the hour."

The sound of another carriage pulling up brought the breathless entrance of Kitty a moment later.

"Lizzy, he is here!" Kitty stopped short upon realizing that the archaeologist was still in the room.

"Miss Bennet." Randolph rose and bowed.

She made a hurried curtsy. "Lizzy, Mr. Dashwood climbs the stairs even now!"

"Gracious, Kitty. With you to announce all our callers today, I should have given Mrs. Hale the day off."

The long-anticipated gentleman appeared at last in their drawing room. He greeted Elizabeth warmly, then had eyes only for Kitty. He took her offered hand. "It is a pleasure to see you again, Miss Bennet. I would have come sooner, but my mother summoned me to Harley Street this morning and has occupied me all afternoon. I hastened here directly I concluded with her."

Kitty's smile suggested that she would have forgiven Mr. Dashwood a detour to the moon, now that he was finally come. "Of course your mother has a superior claim on your time." She went to the sofa, where he sat down beside her. "I was so happily occupied in recalling our dances last evening, I hardly noticed the hour."

Elizabeth refrained from observing that Kitty's serene reflections on the previous evening's entertainment had nearly worn out the carpet. She instead introduced Mr. Dashwood to

Professor Randolph. "Mr. Randolph is an archaeologist with the British Museum," she said.

"Indeed?" With apparent reluctance, he withdrew his gaze from Kitty to afford the archaeologist something that passed for polite interest. "Do you dig up old bones? Mummies? That sort of thing?"

"I prefer to leave the dead at rest. My interest lies primarily in art and ritual objects."

"Why, then, I should have you out to Norland sometime to have a look through my attics. There are all sorts of musty old items gathering cobwebs up there."

"I think his studies tend toward more ancient artifacts," Elizabeth said. "Do they not, Professor?"

"Actually, some astonishing treasures turn up in the attics and cellars of old houses."

"I think an ancestor or two of ours did a good deal of collecting. Lots of sculptures and such. An old looking glass, some Chinese vases. Mother doesn't care for any of it, so it's never left the attics since we took possession of the house. Huh! I haven't thought about that stuff in years. I used to explore up there when I was a boy—it was a good place to hide from my nurse."

"I should very much enjoy the opportunity to see your collection," Randolph said.

"As would I," Kitty echoed.

Mr. Dashwood laughed. "You would like to traipse through my dusty attics, Miss Bennet?"

"I would love to see all of Norland."

Elizabeth winced at Kitty's boldness but, not wishing to correct her before the gentlemen, let it go unchecked.

Mr. Dashwood seemed surprised and flattered by her interest. "I confess, the house never held much appeal for me. I'm hardly ever there, and when I am I soon grow bored."

"The country *can* be tiresome," Kitty agreed, expressing an opinion Elizabeth had never before heard her utter. "But any place can be made more pleasant by pleasant company."

"Miss Bennet, I believe your company could make even a month in the country tolerable."

Kitty ducked her head, unused to receiving compliments from handsome gentlemen.

"Fortunately," Mr. Dashwood continued, "I shan't be gone that long this time."

His statement brought Kitty's head up sharply. "What did you say, Mr. Dashwood?"

"I'm afraid I must leave town tomorrow. My mother is of the opinion that I have delayed for too long some duties of estate since my father's death. That is what she wanted to speak to me about today. She insists I take care of matters at once."

Kitty's countenance held the look of a girl who'd been given a new ball gown, only to have it taken away before she could wear it. "How long will you be away?"

"I hope to conclude my business within a week."

"A whole *week?*" Kitty said the word as if it had been a twelvemonth.

"Sooner, if I can." He rose and held out his hand to draw her up. "Might I call upon you when I return?"

"Most certainly—the minute you arrive in town."

"Kitty," Elizabeth gently admonished.

"I shall. I promise." He seemed about to say more, but then became conscious that others observed them. And that he still held Kitty's hand. With obvious reluctance, he released it.

Professor Randolph stood. "I'll take my leave, as well. It was a pleasure to meet you, Mr. Dashwood."

"Likewise. While I'm at Norland, I shall have a look about the attics to see if I spot anything worth your notice."

"I'd be honored to examine whatever you find."

The ladies escorted their callers to the door, where they

collected their greatcoats and walking sticks. Kitty sighed heavily as the gentlemen departed.

"A whole week," she repeated. "How shall I ever survive?"

"Kitty, a se'nnight ago—no, a mere *two* nights ago—you did not even know Mr. Dashwood. I'm sure that in all of London you can find something to occupy yourself."

Four

"Nothing in the way of pleasure can ever be given up by the young men of this age."

—Mrs. Jennings to Elinor,
Sense and Sensibility, *Chapter 30*

G ood match."

The Earl of Chatfield removed his fencing mask to reveal damp, dark blond locks pressed against his forehead. He offered his hand, which Darcy grasped heartily.

"Indeed," Darcy agreed. Their bout had proven an intense contest. Both he and his friend Chatfield were men of varied interests who did few things by halves, and their mutual pursuit of perfection extended to their training at Angelo's fencing school. Several years ago they had established a standing weekly appointment to cross foils whenever both were in town, an engagement Darcy considered one of the highlights of any trip to London.

"When you left town with Mrs. Darcy in December, I did not expect to enjoy the challenge of your blade for some time," the young earl said. "I hope nothing urgent called you from Pemberley?"

Darcy laughed. "That is a matter of opinion. To my mother-in-law, chaperoning my wife's sister through her first London season is a matter of utmost urgency."

"Ah, the obligatory premarital promenade! You have my deepest sympathy. How many times have you endured Almack's thus far?"

"None."

"You truly lead a charmed life. You cannot avoid it all season, you know."

"I can if Miss Bennet meets an acceptable gentleman elsewhere."

"Any prospects yet?"

"Perhaps. A Mr. Harry Dashwood has come to call. Do you know him?"

"Dashwood," Chatfield repeated as he and Darcy removed their gloves. "I think he's a friend of my wife's youngest brother, Phillip. Bit of a wild bunch, their set. Most of them barely finished university—more interested in learning sixteen different ways to tie a cravat than in learning anything from a book. Tumbled out of Oxford and into town to pursue a full-time occupation of general carousing. Too much money and not enough responsibility. You know the type."

Unfortunately, Darcy did; it was all too common among his peers. Born into privilege and untempered by duty or conscience, many of his fellow "gentlemen" behaved like anything but. They lived lives of self-absorbed leisure, frittering away their time and fortunes on meaningless pursuits. The worst of them carried this extravagance to excess—slavish attention to clothes, overindulgence in drink, high-stakes games of chance, fast horses, faster women—and in many cases ultimately found themselves undone by it.

"I am sorry to hear this of Mr. Dashwood. For Miss Bennet's sake, I had wanted to like him."

"Those are just my general impressions of Phillip's crowd, Darcy. I've heard no genuine harm of Mr. Dashwood in particular," the earl said. "Say, he isn't related to old Sir Francis Dashwood, is he? Now *he* was a hell-raiser."

"Let us hope not." Sir Francis Dashwood, though dead more than thirty years, had been a libertine so notorious that schoolboys still talked of him in the dormitories of Eton and Westminster when they wanted to impress younger schoolmates with their worldly knowledge. Perhaps, Darcy mused, that is why Mr. Dashwood's name had sounded familiar.

"So, you are here long enough to find a husband for Mrs. Darcy's sister, and then it's back to Pemberley. Is that the scheme?"

"Essentially. I do hope to locate a good clergyman while in town. I recently received word that the vicar of Kympton is taken quite ill, so the living will likely become vacant by year's end."

"How much is it worth?"

"About four hundred a year."

"You have not already sold it? A living that valuable? I should think someone would have paid you handsomely to hold it for him."

Darcy had never much cared for the practice of accepting payment from a gentleman or his family in exchange for appointing him as a parish priest. Fortune and connections had their place in the worlds of business, law, politics, and the military, but not, he believed, in matters of the spirit. The men who guided their parishioners from baptism through death, who married and buried them, who counseled and consoled, should be selected for their office on the basis of merit alone.

"According to my father's will, it was to be held for an individual who has since elected not to take orders," Darcy said. "When the living became vacant about three years ago, I granted it to the best candidate I could find, despite his advanced age. Now that his health is in decline, I once again wish to select a clergyman based on aptitude alone. I would grant the benefice free and clear to the right person."

"Simply circulate that fact, and you'll have half the clerics in Christendom knocking on your door."

"I would settle for a single good one."

As they left the fencing club and entered the street, the earl invited Darcy to dinner. "Lady Chatfield wishes very much to see your wife again. Can you come round on Wednesday?"

"Only if you engage to be our guests the Wednesday next. I believe Mrs. Darcy and I are already one dinner in your debt."

"Agreed. Bring Miss Darcy and Miss Bennet, too. We'll invite some young gentlemen. Perhaps, Darcy, we can save you from Almack's this season after all."

Though the Chatfields' dinner party was a success by all other standards, it failed to interest Kitty in any gentleman lacking the name Dashwood. Even the attendance of Lady Chatfield's brother, Lord Phillip Beaumont, could not excite her beyond his status as a friend of Mr. Dashwood's. From this association, they all managed to learn that Mr. Dashwood preferred faro to hazard, surtouts to box coats, and curricles to gigs. He bought his boots at Hoby's, rode a thoroughbred stallion named Dionysus, and was among the thrusters in any foxhunt.

And so it was that Kitty left the earl's home satisfied that she knew all the essentials of Mr. Dashwood's character, and the Darcys, none of them—a deficiency they undertook to correct as expediently as possible.

"Your report first," Elizabeth said to Darcy. She sank into a chair before the fire in their bedchamber, looking exhausted by their seemingly endless social engagements. The week of Mr. Dashwood's absence had seen them attending soirées, assemblies, and dinner parties every night. The events had helped keep Kitty occupied and had also provided the Darcys with opportunities for discreet enquiries regarding Mr. Dashwood. Between evening events and daytime conversations—Darcy's at various clubs, Elizabeth's in social calls—they had learned all they could about the gentleman.

Darcy stirred the fire. He'd heard enough about Mr. Dashwood to form an opinion of him already, but he wanted to hear what Elizabeth had discovered. "I defer to the superior communication of women in matters of gossip. What have you learned?"

"Harry Dashwood is the son of Mr. and Mrs. John Dashwood of Norland Park in Sussex. He is twenty years old and will reach his majority next month. Upon his father's death last autumn, he came into possession of Norland, which provides him an income of four thousand a year. John Dashwood's remaining estate, a sizable fortune inherited from his mother, went to his widow, Fanny Ferrars Dashwood. As Harry is an only child, this fortune, along with Fanny Dashwood's own legacy of ten thousand pounds, presumably will pass to Harry upon her death, adding another two thousand a year to the income derived from Norland."

He took the other chair and sat facing her. "This confirms what I heard. What have you learned of his connections?"

"Mr. Dashwood's mother has two brothers. Edward Ferrars, a clergyman in Devonshire, is married to John Dashwood's half-sister, Elinor. They have two children, or perhaps three—the couple never come to town and Fanny Dashwood seldom talks about them. Her other brother, Robert, though the younger of the two, became the heir to the Ferrars estate following a breach between Edward and his mother. Apparently, the family row somehow involved Robert's wife, the former Miss Lucy Steele, but that story could fill a book by itself. Lucy Ferrars brought to their marriage no fortune or connections of her own. The couple have a house in Norfolk and one daughter. Regina Ferrars came out this season, and by all reports, her mother is promoting her prospects quite aggressively."

"My, you *have* been busy. Did you also learn the name of Mr. Dashwood's favorite hunting hound?"

"Rex."

He smiled at her thoroughness. When his wife undertook a mission, she saw it to completion.

"I also heard that he has a few more relations through his grandfather's second marriage, all quite respectable. One of them is married to a colonel," she said. "So much for his fortune and family. What have you ascertained about the man himself?"

Darcy leaned back in the chair. "Lord Phillip's intelligence, shallow though it was, unfortunately forms an accurate summary of Mr. Dashwood. Never serious in his studies, he attended Oxford only at the insistence of his parents. Now that his father's death has granted him complete independence, he spends all his time gadding about town with his friends. When not otherwise engaged, he can be found lounging on Bond Street from one to four o'clock, riding in Hyde Park at five, then off to some social affair or the theatre."

"So, he wants seriousness and meaningful occupation. But then, so do most of his peers. Dissipation is an epidemic among gentlemen in town. Have you heard any real ill of him? Is he a drunkard? Does he have debts? Does he treat ladies as a gentleman should?"

"By all reports, his reputation is sound in those respects."

She sighed and rose to prepare for bed. "Then I think we ought not interfere with any courtship between Mr. Dashwood and Kitty."

He caught her by the hand to stop her as she passed. "You would see her marry a man of so little substance?"

"I'd hardly consider six thousand a year 'little substance.'"

"His material circumstances are, of course, beyond objection. I was speaking of his character."

"He comes from a respectable family. He seems to have few

real vices and the ability to regulate them himself. More important, he has already engaged Kitty's affections, and I believe his regard for her is sincere. Add to that his generous income, and a young woman of Kitty's fortune cannot realistically hope to do better, nor, at this point, do I expect she wishes to."

"But his idleness! Could you be happy with a man whose idea of an afternoon well spent is selecting the perfect fob chain?"

"No. But I am not Kitty, and what makes me happy would not satisfy her." Still holding his hand, she came round to settle on his knee. "Indeed, that I found happiness with such a serious man continues to baffle most of my family."

"I promised you that I would protect Kitty's interests as if she were my own sister. Your father is relying on my judgment."

"Then let that judgment derive from a better observation of Mr. Dashwood himself. He returns to town tomorrow. Why don't you call upon him? Invite him to dine with us."

It was a sound idea. Darcy would not have wanted his future with Elizabeth decided upon the basis of public impressions and reports in general circulation about him when they had first met.

"I will," he agreed. "Perhaps I will also suggest that a young man wishing to pay addresses to Miss Bennet would do well to conduct himself in a more useful manner."

"Now Darcy, don't go scaring him."

Five

"My protégé, as you call him, is a sensible man; and sense will always have attractions for me."
—Elinor Dashwood to Mr. Willoughby,
Sense and Sensibility, *Chapter 10*

*H*arry Dashwood possessed an address as fashionable as the rest of his accoutrements. Upon coming into his inheritance, he had taken a townhouse in Pall Mall from which he could enjoy his new independence free from his mother's watchful eye. From what Darcy had heard of Mrs. John Dashwood, Harry need not have bothered. By all accounts, Fanny was an indulgent mother unlikely to curb any pleasure of her only son, so long as he did nothing to seriously jeopardize his own or the family's reputation.

Darcy handed his card to the servant and waited patiently at the door while it was determined whether the master was at home. Mr. Dashwood's voice emanating from the hall indicated that he had indeed completed his journey back to London, but that didn't necessarily mean he was receiving visitors. A few moments, however, brought the servant back with an invitation to step inside.

"Mr. Darcy!" Dashwood exclaimed upon sighting him. "You honor me with this visit." He paused to direct three footmen who carried a large looking glass. "Put it in my dressing room."

The servants ascended the stairs with the mirror. Darcy noticed a pair of trunks also awaiting relocation.

"Forgive me," Mr. Dashwood said, gesturing toward the baggage. "I've just arrived home."

"Perhaps I should return at a later time."

"No—do stay! You must, however, allow me to change my shirt. This one is travel-worn."

"Of course."

"Come along, then. This way."

Harry took the stairs two at a time, forcing Darcy to trot to keep up with him. At the landing Darcy paused, presuming he was to wait in the drawing room. Mr. Dashwood, however, urged him up the next set of stairs. "You *must* see the looking glass I brought home with me. Found it in Norland's attic."

Darcy followed Mr. Dashwood to his dressing room, where the servants were propping the mirror against the wall.

"Leave it for now," Harry instructed. "You can mount it when I've decided exactly where I want it." The servants departed.

The mirror was indeed a striking objet d'art. The glass itself was perhaps five feet long and two feet wide, with a heavy gold frame that added another six inches to the sides and bottom. Intricately carved images of nude athletes stood out in bas relief, laurel leaves entwining their muscular forms. At the top, a twelve-inch crown boasted a man's face at its center, his features perfectly capturing the classical ideal of male beauty.

"What do you think?" asked Mr. Dashwood. "It has to be centuries old, at least—a real antiquity. Looks to me like it could have come from ancient Greece."

Darcy paused before replying. Though he appreciated its artistry, he doubted the treasure could be as old as Mr. Dashwood believed. To his knowledge, the ancient Greeks had made only hand mirrors of polished metal; the techniques used to fashion a looking glass of this size and construction were much later developments. This mirror, therefore, must be a relatively modern creation, designed to appeal to the current vogue for classical art and architecture.

Yet the mirror seemed older. Despite the differences in construction, somehow it could stand among other ancient artifacts in the British Museum and not be out of place. He supposed Elizabeth would say it had the character of a genuine antique—an aura of history about it. "How long has the glass been in your family's possession?" he asked.

"I have no idea. My housekeeper thought it belonged to Sir Francis Dashwood, an ancestor, but where he got it from, I don't know."

"You are descended from Sir Francis Dashwood?"

Mr. Dashwood grinned. "Heard the shocking stories, have you? The Hell-Fire Club and all that? Yes, he occupies a branch somewhere in my family tree, but he died childless, so I'm uncertain exactly how he fits in. I also don't know how this mirror found its way to Norland, as his main estate was in Buckinghamshire. But when I saw it, I simply had to bring it back here with me."

His valet entered. The servant removed Mr. Dashwood's coat and started to unfasten his cuffs.

Darcy took this as his cue to leave. "Shall I await you in the drawing room?"

"No. Do stay! I've always aspired to be like Beau Brummell, entertaining visitors while completing my toilette." He shed his rumpled shirt for a clean one.

"Quite a lofty ambition," Darcy said dryly.

"I wish I had but half his skill with cravats." The valet offered a highly starched neckcloth. Harry stationed himself before the mirror. "What do you think, Mr. Darcy? Should I try the mathematical today? Or settle for the Napoleon? Which does Miss Bennet prefer?"

"I am not privy to Miss Bennet's opinions on the subject of gentlemen's neckwear." Darcy ardently wished for another topic of conversation altogether. To emulate the vain Brummell's practice of holding court in his dressing room seemed the most ridiculous form of idolatry. A rooster imitating a peacock.

Mr. Dashwood attempted the mathematical, fumbled its folds, and had to discard the cloth for a fresh one. "I'm told Brummell often goes through stacks of neckcloths before achieving perfection."

"Such a practice sounds like an incredible waste of his own and his servants' time."

Mr. Dashwood met Darcy's gaze in the mirror. His natural exuberance dimmed at the disapproval he detected in Darcy's eyes. "I suppose you are right in that." He began tying the next cravat in the simpler Napoleon style.

Darcy studied Mr. Dashwood's reflection. He was so very young—not only in age, but also in knowledge of the world. In many ways, Darcy had never been that young. But he also recalled his own sense of lost direction in the period following his father's death. Harry Dashwood was even younger than he had been, and Darcy suspected his own foundation was steadier than Dashwood's to begin with. Perhaps cravats and looking glasses claimed Harry's attention because he did not feel adequate to the responsibilities he had just inherited along with John Dashwood's estate.

Darcy regretted the mild criticism he'd tendered. "Forgive me. I meant only that an intelligent man benefits from devoting his resources to more worthwhile endeavors. And you strike me as a man possessing the potential to do much more with his life than Mr. Brummell ever will."

Mr. Dashwood turned from the mirror to face Darcy directly. "I do?"

"Did you not, I would never have come here today bearing an invitation. If you are not previously engaged, Mrs. Darcy would be pleased to have you at her table tonight for dinner."

"Tell her I am most gratified and look forward to her hospitality. Will Miss Bennet be among the party?"

"Assuredly."

"Then I can think of no pleasanter way to spend an evening."

Seven o'clock had been the appointed hour for Mr. Dashwood to present himself at the Darcys' townhouse. He arrived at half past six, bearing flowers for Kitty and a bouquet of apologies for his hostess.

"Pardon my untimely appearance," he said as Elizabeth received him in the drawing room, "but the anticipated delight of seeing Miss Bennet this evening caused the day to grow unbearably long. At last I found I could not wait thirty minutes longer."

"You may have to," Elizabeth replied, "as my sister is still readying for dinner. But I will tell her you are come."

In truth, the announcement was hardly necessary. Like a thunderclap proclaiming the arrival of a spring storm, Mr. Dashwood's presence reverberated throughout the house, sending Kitty into a flustered frenzy of preparations she'd thought she had more time to complete. Elizabeth had left her upstairs rushing to make up her toilette, torn between equally violent desires to perfect her appearance and have done with it.

Elizabeth believed, however, that she could forgive Mr. Dashwood nearly anything with an earnest devotion to Kitty as its motive. She gestured toward the flowers. "Shall I deliver those to Kitty now, or would you prefer to present them to her yourself?"

"Oh, please take them now, with my most sincere compliments."

"*Those* I will leave you to tender yourself, as I surely possess neither the inspiration nor the eloquence of their true author."

She was spared the trip by the immediate entrance of Kitty herself, wearing an entirely different gown than the one in which Elizabeth had seen her just minutes earlier. Her hair was attractively arranged, though swept into a much simpler style than the maid had been working on when Elizabeth left to greet their visitor.

Mr. Dashwood presented his flowers and compliments to the lady, who accepted both with equal delight.

"I adore daffodils! Are they from Norland's gardens?"

"Covent Garden, I'm afraid. My trip to Norland did, however, inspire the gift. The daffodils and crocuses were in bloom, and as I walked the grounds, I found myself thinking of you and wishing you could see them. I consulted my gardener about bringing some back for you, but we both doubted they would survive the journey from Sussex."

"If they arrived utterly wilted, I should have valued them. But I do appreciate these." She admired the bouquet again before relinquishing it to a servant for placement in a vase.

They were joined presently by Darcy and Georgiana, and soon went down to dinner. Mr. Dashwood enquired how Kitty had kept busy in his absence. She rattled off their list of entertainments.

"I declare, Miss Bennet," he said when she'd finished, "you have been more engaged in a single day than I was the entire se'nnight."

"Did you conclude your business at Norland?" Darcy asked.

"Yes and no. I handled the affairs that originally took me there, but it seemed that with every dispatch, another item of business arose to take its place."

Darcy nodded, his eyes reflecting perfect understanding. "As your father no doubt taught you, proper management of an estate requires constant vigilance. Even when in town, I maintain close communication with my steward. Rarely do more than two days pass without a letter between us."

"Indeed?" Mr. Dashwood appeared surprised by the revelation. He seemed about to say more, but Kitty spoke.

"I hope these new matters won't force you to leave again?"

"Actually, I intend to return to Norland three weeks hence."

Disappointment clouded Kitty's face. "So very soon?"

"Yes, but for another reason entirely. My twenty-first birthday approaches, and I've decided to celebrate with a country house party at Norland. It is my dearest hope, Miss Bennet, that you and your family will honor me with your company."

"Lizzy, may we go? Do say we might!"

Elizabeth cast Kitty a mild look that bade her show a little restraint.

"The grand fête will be Friday the thirtieth," Mr. Dashwood continued. "I am inviting most of the guests to arrive on Wednesday, but I would be delighted if you could come on Tuesday so that I might show Miss Bennet—show all four of you—Norland before the house becomes crowded."

Kitty held her tongue but now begged just as passionately with her eyes.

Of course they would attend. Elizabeth would hardly deny Kitty the opportunity to see the home of a man with whom she seemed to be forming an attachment. But, wanting to keep her younger sister in suspense a bit longer, she glanced to Darcy. "That is after Easter. Does not the London season pick up once Lent has passed?"

"It does. There will be balls, and masquerades, and many more routs."

She nodded gravely. "Perhaps we ought not leave town just as much of the *ton* is arriving."

Kitty appeared ready to burst. "Oh, forget the silly *ton!*"

Elizabeth raised her brows, her astonishment only half-exaggerated. That statement would never have issued from her sister's lips two weeks earlier. "Are you not afraid of missing something momentous in our absence?"

"For heaven's sake, Lizzy! What could be more exciting than visiting Norland and celebrating Mr. Dashwood's birthday?"

Mr. Dashwood, who had been following the exchange with amusement, seemed gratified by Kitty's eagerness.

"I cannot imagine." Elizabeth, unwilling to prolong Kitty's torment further, smiled. "We happily accept your invitation, Mr. Dashwood."

Harry's face broke into an expression of elation. "I hope Norland offers much to interest you all. And should its pleasures prove insufficient, Brighton is not far."

"Brighton? I have always longed to go to Brighton! Lizzy, might we—"

"Norland, yes. Brighton, no," Darcy declared.

Elizabeth concurred. As far as she was concerned, their family had experienced quite enough of Brighton, the scene of Lydia's disgrace. Though the Prince Regent's fondness for the seaside resort drew the fashionable to it in flocks, Elizabeth had no desire ever to lay eyes on the place.

Kitty released a sigh of resignation. "I suppose it is too cold yet for seabathing anyway."

"Perhaps on a future visit," said Mr. Dashwood.

The implication that Kitty would be spending more time in Sussex eradicated her remaining disappointment. Anticipation lit her features once more. "I should like that."

Mr. Dashwood, his attention now focused entirely on Kitty, failed to notice Darcy studying him. Darcy's countenance was open, yet assessing, and Elizabeth wondered how Mr. Dashwood was faring in the evaluation. She rather liked him herself, and wanted to distract Darcy before their guest sensed he was on trial.

Playfulness still dominating her mood, she turned to Harry. "Mr. Dashwood, my husband has developed quite an interest in hunting of late. Since meeting Lord Hartford, he simply cannot hear enough sporting talk. Does Norland offer good quarry?"

She felt Darcy's gaze shift to her. His expression thanked her profusely for reminding him of the longest social call he'd ever endured, and promised she'd pay for her raillery later. She responded with wide-eyed innocence.

"Yes, indeed! In fact, I plan numerous hunts and shooting outings during the week of the party. Are you partial to any particular game, Mr. Darcy?"

"No," he said, his eyes still on Elizabeth. The slightest smile played at the corners of his mouth. "But apparently my wife is."

Mr. Dashwood, mistaking Darcy's meaning of "game," regarded Elizabeth with surprise. "Do you hunt, Mrs. Darcy? We shall be too late for prime fox season, of course, but the pack will still give us a good run."

She laughed. "I find it difficult enough to maintain my balance in a sidesaddle on flat ground."

"You are a better rider than that," Georgiana asserted.

Elizabeth realized Darcy's sister had said little during the meal. Though handsome and accomplished by even the strictest standards, Miss Darcy disliked drawing notice and participated in many conversations primarily as an attentive listener. Some erroneously perceived her silence as arrogance, but Elizabeth recognized it as simple shyness.

"It is kind of you to say so," Elizabeth said. "Nevertheless, if I ever tried to hunt, I no doubt would fall off my mount while jumping the first ox fence. You, on the other hand, could probably manage fairly well. Better than I, at least."

Georgiana ducked her head at the praise of her equestrian skills. "I would have to stop before the fox was treed, for I do not think I could witness what follows."

"Neither could I!" Kitty exclaimed. "I couldn't bear to see the poor fox set upon by hounds and killed."

"That is precisely why foxhunting is an inappropriate pastime for ladies," Darcy said. "Blood sport runs counter to their gentle natures."

Elizabeth thought about many of the well-bred women who occupied society's highest ranks, and chuckled softly. "Ladies are quite capable of blood sport, darling. Their field is the drawing room."

After dinner, the gentlemen withdrew to the library. Darcy offered Mr. Dashwood a glass of port, then took his customary chair beside the fire. Though invited to avail himself of the seat opposite, Mr. Dashwood instead perused the titles lining the walls.

"Homer, Chaucer, Shakespeare, Milton, Johnson, Wordsworth . . . You have an impressive collection."

"I keep some favorite volumes here. Pemberley's library is far more extensive. Whenever I come to town for long periods of time, I bring additional books for study and pleasure—and visit booksellers to add to the shelves."

A row of novels caught Mr. Dashwood's eye. He traced their spines with his fingertip. "Mrs. Lennox, Mrs. Burney, Mrs. Radcliffe." He selected a volume and thumbed its pages.

"Those belong to Georgiana and my wife. Do you have a large library at Norland?"

Mr. Dashwood frowned. "I'm not sure, come to think on it. Oh, the room's big enough, but as for what occupies its shelves, I have little idea. I don't think I've been inside above half a dozen times."

"Six times in your whole life?" Darcy could scarcely comprehend such a thing. His own thirst for knowledge, the lessons of his private tutor, and hours spent at his father's elbow learning to administer their estate had seen him practically raised in Pemberley's library. Economics, business, law, literature, philosophy—only Cambridge had offered more wisdom than that room contained.

Mr. Dashwood shrugged. "When I was a child, my lessons were in the nursery, of course. Then it was off to Eton and Oxford. I was seldom home, and when I was, the library was the last place that held any interest for me."

"Your father conducted all his instruction in the field then? My own father did a good deal of that, too."

Darcy's father had been a strong advocate of direct experience, encouraging his son to talk with tenants and occasionally get his hands dirty as he prepared to one day assume the responsibilities of a landlord. He'd believed a man who has never seen a calf born or rubbed soil between his fingers cannot ever truly understand the principles of agriculture. One's status as a gentleman might free him from toiling to survive, but the best landlords were at least passingly familiar with the land and people in their care.

"Instruction? I don't understand you, sir."

"Training you to take over for him eventually."

Mr. Dashwood replaced the book on the shelf. "We seldom talked about Norland. Or much else."

"You were not close?"

"Not especially." He moved toward the fire. "As soon as I could read, my parents sent me off to obtain a gentleman's education. Each month, I received a parcel containing an allowance and a letter from my mother expressing her hope that I was cultivating the right sort of acquaintances and conducting myself in a manner that promoted our family's reputation. So long as I met their expectations, they left me to myself. I suppose my father would have explained a few matters about estate management to me had I ever asked—it seemed at times that money was all he ever talked about—but I never asked. I was content to simply enjoy the privileges of wealth without any responsibilities."

"And now?"

Mr. Dashwood studied Darcy, seeming to weigh how much more he cared to reveal about himself to the sponsor of a woman he hoped to court. "Now I find myself in possession of an estate I know little about," he said finally.

"You certainly are not the first gentleman to discover himself ill prepared to govern his affairs." Darcy could think of many estates that had fallen into mismanagement by heirs who lacked the interest or aptitude to properly administer them. It reflected well on Mr. Dashwood that he had recognized this failing in himself, particularly at such a young age. As Harry had owned Norland for only a few months, Darcy hoped his indifference had been of a duration too short to cause damage. "The question is, how do you intend to correct that deficiency?"

"I hadn't planned to do anything about it. None of my friends seem to pay the least attention to such matters—if they own land at all, they just leave everything in the hands of their solicitors and stewards. And I don't know that I really have the temperament to supervise so many little details."

He took a chair, perching on the edge of the seat and leaning toward Darcy. "But this past week, I roamed all over Norland, from its attics to its parkland. I thought about what it would be like to show it to Miss Bennet, to see it through the eyes of someone beholding it for the first time. I wanted it to be a place that would impress her. And then I realized that in wanting her approval of Norland, what I really sought was her approval of me. That when I inherited Norland, it became as much a part of me as any other possession, a representation to the world of who I am. And just as I would never neglect my appearance or my manners, neither can I afford to neglect my estate."

Darcy would hardly have equated the importance of overseeing Pemberley with that of selecting a waistcoat, but if that mode of thinking had led Mr. Dashwood to a fuller cognizance of his responsibilities as a landholder, he could not criticize the comparison.

"In my experience, a good steward is invaluable," he suggested. "Though your father is gone, perhaps your steward can educate you. He will likely be gratified by your interest in Norland."

"Or threatened by it."

"An honest man would not be so."

"Unfortunately, I'm not entirely confident that I'm dealing with an honest man." He took a swallow of port. "I spent some time this week reviewing Norland's accounts for the period since my father's death. I'd never looked at the record books before, so I had trouble making sense of them. When I went to our steward with questions, he became defensive."

Darcy frowned. "Do you believe he cheats you?"

"I don't know what to believe. He has been at Norland since I was a boy. I never had cause to deal with him while my father was alive. I doubt, however, that my father would have retained a steward he didn't trust."

"He might simply resent a young, inexperienced new master questioning his work. Though I had assisted my father for years, I encountered that prejudice among some of my older tenants when he passed away."

"Truly? You, Mr. Darcy?"

"Why should that surprise you?"

"You are a man born to run an estate."

"If you have inherited one, then so are you."

He smiled ruefully. "I suppose I am. You, however, know what you are doing, while I do not."

"Then you must change that."

Dashwood swirled the port around in his glass, his face pensive. "Mr. Darcy, I wonder if I might impose upon you to—that is, when you come to Norland, if you would take a look at the accounts and advise me as to whether everything appears in order?"

"Certainly. Not being familiar with Norland will limit my ability to detect inconsistencies, but I will determine what I can."

"I am most grateful for your help, sir."

Darcy hesitated, not wanting to insinuate himself further into Harry's affairs than he'd been invited. But he was pleased to see the younger man taking an interest in his new responsibilities and wanted to encourage him. "If you like, Mr. Dashwood, I would be happy to explain the records to you so that in the future you can make you own determinations."

"I would appreciate that very much."

He finished his port but declined Darcy's offer of more. He appeared to have something further he wished to say. Darcy waited patiently, letting him seek his words.

"I am most desirous of your good opinion, Mr. Darcy, and that of your family," he finally said. "For as long as I can remember, my mother has held great ambitions for me. She longs to see me distinguished in the world somehow, or at the very least to gain entrée into the drawing rooms of every great family in England. I've never had any interest in politics or Parliament or any of the other schemes she's set before me, nor in the debutantes she perpetually throws in my way as candidates for an advantageous alliance. The young ladies she presents harbor even more ambition than she does. They would not be satisfied as Mrs. Harry Dashwood until I made a great name for myself.

"Miss Bennet, however, is different. I think that if Norland meets with her approval—if I meet with her approval, as I am, today—that will be enough. She won't spend the rest of my life trying to mold me into someone I don't want to be."

Darcy was inclined to agree. Kitty might not possess the accomplishments and polish of most young ladies of the *ton*, but neither did she suffer from their social-climbing pretensions. Yes, she chattered about the possibility of meeting a young duke or earl, but, as Elizabeth said, her hopes were no more than the idyllic dreams of any girl. Realistically, she knew her slight dowry made a modest marriage probable, and she was prepared to accept that.

Too, there had been no talk of dukes since Kitty had met Mr. Dashwood. In her eyes, he wanted no improvement.

"I believe you already possess Miss Bennet's good opinion," Darcy said. "And today's demonstration of a more serious approach to your affairs puts you well in the way of securing mine."

"My interest in Norland is genuine. I appreciate your guidance, Mr. Darcy." He rose and set his empty glass beside the port decanter. "Do you suppose the ladies look for our return, or have they forgotten us altogether?"

They passed the remainder of the evening in pleasant conversation with the ladies. Mr. Dashwood enquired whether Kitty had yet enjoyed many of London's amusements. At her negative response, he insisted she allow him to escort her to the Vauxhall Gardens, drive her through Hyde Park, and visit Madame Tussaud's. Before he left, he'd invited them all to accompany him to a concert the following night.

"Mr. Dashwood seems to have risen in your esteem tonight," Elizabeth observed as they prepared for bed. She had changed into a white lace nightgown and sat brushing her hair at the dressing table. "Of what did you speak in the library for so long?"

Darcy loosened his cravat. "He is developing a greater interest in his property at Norland."

A sly smile played across her lips. "Does he think of settling down?"

Recalling her earlier badinage about his love of sport, he deliberately withheld the information she sought, teasing her in turn. "A man requests bookkeeping advice and you are ready to order Kitty's wedding clothes. That is a leap of logic I would expect from your mother."

"You accuse me unfairly. Besides"—she turned back to the mirror and continued brushing her hair—"I notice you did not answer no."

"If a lady has indeed inspired this newfound regard for Norland, I would not betray a gentleman's confidence by revealing that fact to her sister. One might as well just tell the lady herself and spare the intermediary."

"You know me to be a better keeper of secrets than that."

"Who said I referred to you and Kitty? Perhaps I spoke only hypothetically."

"Oh—hypothetically." She set down the brush. "In that case, you need say nothing more." Mischief danced in her brown eyes, but he could not make out her meaning.

She worked her hair into a braid, then walked to the bed, slid beneath the covers, and opened a novel while she waited for him. He thought no more of Mr. Dashwood, or Kitty, or anyone save his wife. Anxious to join her, he finished changing into his nightclothes and went to extinguish the candle at the bedside.

She looked up from her novel. "What are you doing?"

He took the book from her hands and set it atop the night table. "You suggested we retire early tonight."

She picked the book back up. "Didn't you realize, darling?" She cast him an innocent look and reopened the volume. "I was speaking hypothetically."

Six

Mrs. John Dashwood had never been a favourite with any of her husband's family; but she had had no opportunity, till the present, of shewing them with how little attention to the comfort of other people she could act when occasion required it.
—Sense and Sensibility, *Chapter 1*

*U*pon learning that her son planned to hold his birthday fête at Norland, and that a certain Miss Catherine Bennet topped the guest list, Mrs. John Dashwood paid a call upon the Darcy family.

The announcement of her arrival sent Kitty into a state of shock followed immediately by a flurry of nervous agitation. She cast aside her needlework frame and raised her hands to her face. "Mr. Dashwood's mother! Lizzy, whatever shall I say to her?"

Elizabeth set down her own stitchery and rose in preparation for their visitor's entrance. "'How do you do?' might form a good beginning."

Georgiana, who had been practicing her harp in the corner, abandoned the instrument to join Kitty's side in support. "I am sure she is as kind as her son," she said.

"Oh, gracious!" Kitty exclaimed. "Please tell me my hair looks tolerable!"

No one had opportunity to offer Kitty reassurance on issues

of grooming or any other, as the lady in question just then appeared in the drawing room. Fanny Dashwood was a thin, proud-looking woman, with sharp cheekbones and a tilt to her chin that threatened an unrestricted view of her nostrils to those of shorter stature. Her sharp eyes assessed the three ladies to determine which was her hostess. Elizabeth greeted her and performed the necessary introductions.

"It is a pleasure to make your acquaintance," Mrs. Dashwood said to a Chinese vase as her appraising gaze drifted about the room. She took in the draperies, artwork, and furniture, then studied Elizabeth, Georgiana, and Kitty with the same calculating interest, her attention lingering longest on Miss Bennet. Elizabeth wondered if Kitty had been judged more or less valuable than the chesterfield.

Kitty, already flustered, struggled to maintain her composure under the intense inspection. Elizabeth attempted to divert Mrs. Dashwood's attention.

"We had the pleasure of dining with your son last night," she said.

"Yes, I know." She held Kitty in her unyielding gaze a full minute longer before finally turning it on Elizabeth. "He told me at breakfast this morning. I summoned him as soon as I rose, and my Harry always accords me the utmost respect and deference. He came directly he received my note."

"He seems a fine gentleman."

"He is. And a good son. Not like some of these wild young men who run about making their own decisions regardless of the consequences. Harry knows his responsibilities to his family." She studied the room's appointments once more. "That is a lovely harp. Was it you whom I heard playing as I came up, Miss Bennet?"

"No, the harp belongs to Miss Darcy."

"Harry adores music. Has he heard you play the pianoforte yet?"

"That is also Miss Darcy's. I don't play any instrument."

Mrs. Dashwood's face registered mild disapproval. "You sing, then?"

"No."

"Oh." Mrs. Dashwood blinked. "Well, perhaps if he calls here again, Harry will have an opportunity to enjoy Miss Darcy's talent." Fanny cast a warm smile at Georgiana. At least, it would have been a warm smile if Fanny Dashwood possessed any warmth.

As it was, Harry's mother shuddered and shifted closer to the fire screen. "It is a blustery day for April."

"I hope you did not catch a chill coming here," Kitty offered.

"I possess a hearty constitution," Mrs. Dashwood declared, "and little patience for those who do not." She looked more closely at the fire screen. "This is covered very prettily. Is it your handiwork, Miss Bennet?"

"No, Georgiana's."

"This is Miss Bennet's first visit here as our guest, so our house does not yet enjoy her influence," Georgiana said in defense of her friend. "Perhaps she will grace it with a gift, but until then, I am afraid my things clutter it, as I have spent most of my time here these past five years."

"You speak too modestly, Miss Darcy. I would hardly call 'clutter' something as beautiful as this screen, or that watercolor on the wall. Do I assume aright that it is yours, as well?"

Georgiana confessed that it was.

Kitty fidgeted and took up her embroidery. Elizabeth, desirous of something to do with her hands, picked up her own hoop but left the needle secured in the muslin.

"Are you skilled with a needle, Miss Bennet? What do you work on?"

"An infant's cap—a gift for our sister Jane."

"Has she recently delivered?"

"She expects her first child in autumn."

"How delightful. I see you also work on infant clothes, Mrs. Darcy. I wish I'd had sisters to help with Harry's layette when he was born."

Elizabeth indeed had a sleeve for a tiny frock stretched in her frame, though it was for her friend Charlotte Collins, due to be brought to bed any day. After completing the frock, she would finish the quilt she'd started for Jane. Elizabeth had never been fond of needlework but took pleasure in creating these gifts. The more she worked on them, however, the more she found herself wishing, in the secret recesses of her heart, that they were for a child of her own.

She would contemplate those feelings in a more private time and place. For now, she merely smiled politely as Mrs. Dashwood asked to see Kitty's work.

"Your backstitch is a trifle uneven there. But otherwise it is a competent effort, Miss Bennet. I'm sure your sister will appreciate it." She handed the bonnet back to Kitty. "My niece Regina does excellent needlework. Why, even Harry complimented her on a sash she made, and you know gentlemen seldom notice those things. Have you met Miss Ferrars? This is her first London season."

Kitty was too rattled by Mrs. Dashwood's lukewarm praise to answer. Elizabeth replied that while they had seen Miss Ferrars at the Middletons' house, they had not been introduced.

"You shall certainly meet her at Norland. Harry tells me you are all to be our guests for his birthday fête?"

"Oh, yes!" Kitty said. "We look forward to it."

"So do I. After losing my husband last fall, it will be nice to celebrate something, and I cannot think of a finer event than my darling Harry reaching his majority. My little boy, all grown up! Before I know it, he will be married with a son of his own. I think that is every mother's wish, to see her child well married."

At this, a hint of color crept into Kitty's cheeks.

"I hope, Miss Darcy," Mrs. Dashwood continued, "that you will also be of the Norland party?"

Georgiana replied in the affirmative.

"Excellent. The inclusion of another accomplished young lady will add to everyone's pleasure. Miss Ferrars is quite accomplished, too. If I had a daughter, I would want her to be just like Regina. Or you, Miss Darcy." She added lamely, "Miss Bennet, with your sisters wed, it must be a comfort to your mother to have you at home."

"I think my mother shall be most comfortable when all five of her daughters are married," Kitty replied. "Meanwhile, my sister Mary also remains at Longbourn."

"Your mother is wise to want you settled. Five daughters would tax any family's fortune. When my husband passed away, our having just one child made everything tidy—Harry had no unmarried sisters to worry about providing for. The terms of his great-great-uncle's will ensured that the Norland estate would pass through successive generations whole, but you know how gentlemen sometimes feel a sense of obligation toward siblings for whom no other provision was made. Now, since I understand you have no brothers, to whom will Longbourn pass?"

"To none of us. It is entailed on a male cousin."

"I see. How very unfortunate."

Mrs. Dashwood stayed only a short while longer, just time enough to invite them all—Georgiana especially—to call upon her in Harley Street. "I do so enjoy conversing with Harry's friends."

Kitty trembled with humiliation the moment Harry's mother walked out the door. Georgiana, embarrassed by the whole visit, quickly excused herself to perform some imaginary errand.

"She hates me, Lizzy! Mr. Dashwood's mother hates me."

"She does not hate you, Kitty."

"She likes Georgiana."

"She likes Georgiana's thirty thousand pounds."

"It is the same thing."

Elizabeth came to Kitty's side. "Perhaps to someone as disagreeable as Mrs. Dashwood. But not to Georgiana. Do you think she wants to be admired only for her fortune?"

"Her fortune, her music, her painting—" She tossed her embroidery onto the sofa. "I can't even trim a cap properly. Who wouldn't choose Georgiana over me?"

"Mr. Dashwood."

Elizabeth retrieved the hoop from the floor and handed it back to Kitty. "Mr. Dashwood came here last night with flowers for *you.* He spent most of the evening talking to *you.* And when he left here, he lingered the longest over his farewell to *you.*"

"That doesn't mean he will want to marry me."

"No, it does not. But should he offer, you will know without question that he wants to marry *you,* not your thirty thousand pounds. That is a fortune Georgiana will never have."

Kitty turned the hoop around in her hands. "*If* he offers. And what are the chances of his ever doing so with his mother wishing him to tender his addresses elsewhere?"

"Let his mother court whomever she wants. He can afford to marry where he chooses."

Elizabeth said the words in a confident tone, attempting to console Kitty, but she could not help recalling Mrs. Dashwood's assertion about her son's sense of family duty. To what extent would he allow filial obedience to dictate his future happiness? Harry was young; his mother's will, strong. A word from her might be all it took to redirect him.

Mr. Dashwood already possessed Kitty's heart. She prayed he would not break it.

She placated Kitty with additional assurances, then suggested they take a walk. Fresh air and fresh sights, she hoped, would divert her sister's thoughts from this unfortunate first meeting with Mr. Dashwood's mother. Kitty yielded to Elizabeth's persuasion and the two parted to retrieve their bonnets.

After donning both her hat and a light wrap, Elizabeth found herself descending the stairs to the accompaniment of Mozart. Georgiana had returned to the drawing room, where her fingers now flew through the opening movement of a sonata. Elizabeth approached the pianoforte and located Georgiana's place in the music, turning the page when Georgiana reached its end. Further observation of the performer, however, revealed that Elizabeth need not have troubled herself. Georgiana played from memory.

When the movement concluded, Elizabeth invited her to join the walk. Georgiana declined, stating a desire to continue at the piano.

"I have been thinking," she said, starting the adagio section, "that perhaps I ought not go to Norland."

"Of course you should go. Mr. Dashwood's invitation included everybody."

"His mother's invitation very nearly excluded Kitty. I do not wish my presence to cause your sister any unhappiness. If I stay behind, Mrs. Dashwood might treat Kitty with more civility."

"Mrs. Dashwood's behavior toward Kitty has far more to do with Mrs. Dashwood than with either you or Kitty."

"Nevertheless, Kitty will enjoy the party more without me."

"Kitty would feel horrid if she knew you missed the fête on her account."

She paused on a minor chord. "Then do not tell her."

Elizabeth studied Georgiana. Her head was bowed over the keyboard, her expression guarded. Did she truly wish to remain behind, or was she declining the invitation because she thought she should? Elizabeth did not want her new sister-in-law to feel excluded from this or any other family happenings. Nor to believe that anyone considered her own happiness secondary to Kitty's or anybody else's.

"Georgiana, do reconsider. This season in London was to have been a pleasurable time for you, as well, yet it seems you have not met any gentleman worthy of your esteem." That Darcy protected his sister so closely had not helped, but Elizabeth refrained from voicing that thought. "Perhaps someone at the fête will earn your regard."

Georgiana completed an intricate passage before responding. "I did not realize you hoped to bring about a match for me this season," she finally said. "But of course you and my brother must feel my continuing at Pemberley an intrusion on your privacy now that you are married."

"Oh, Georgiana! How ever could you think that? Pemberley is your home—for the rest of your life, if you wish. I do not scheme to have its empty rooms to myself. I thought only of you—that perhaps you yourself had begun to long for another home, and a husband to share it."

"I cannot deny imagining such scenes from time to time, but I am in no hurry to realize them. I—" She stumbled over a simple grace note and corrected herself. "I know my brother surely must have told you of my imprudence two summers ago involving Mr. Wickham. Since that time, I do not trust my own judgment in matters of the heart."

This marked the first time she had spoken of the incident, or how it had affected her. "It is Mr. Wickham who cannot be trusted," Elizabeth declared.

"Nevertheless, I am not yet ready to form an attachment with anybody."

"Your own judgment seems very sound on that point. You are absolutely correct. There is no reason for haste."

Her fingers slowed as she approached the end of the adagio. "When I am prepared to accept a suitor's attention, the right gentleman will reveal himself. Meanwhile, let this be Kitty's season. Allow me to excuse myself from the Norland party."

Elizabeth regarded Georgiana doubtfully. "You are certain?"

"Quite. In fact, my friend Miss Sedgewick has invited me to a concert on the thirtieth and I had hoped to attend." She struck the final chords of the movement and met Elizabeth's gaze. "Please indulge me?" Her expression was earnest.

"As you wish."

"Thank you."

She started on the allegro assai. Elizabeth listened to Georgiana's perfect execution, repeating their conversation in her mind. Anyone could appreciate her sister-in-law's accomplishments and gentle spirit. But she was discovering in Georgiana a young woman of greater depth and intelligence than was evident upon first acquaintance, and felt privileged to be developing a more intimate understanding of her.

"Can I persuade you, at least, to join us for our walk?" Elizabeth asked.

Georgiana started to shake her head, but then abruptly halted the music. "Actually," she said, rising from her instrument, "I think I shall."

Seven

*"To say that he is unlike Fanny is enough. It implies every
thing amiable."*

—Mrs. Henry Dashwood to Elinor,
Sense and Sensibility, *Chapter 3*

Whatever pressure Fanny Dashwood may have exerted on her son to bestow his addresses on a wealthier woman, Harry Dashwood remained steadfast in his attention to Kitty. He visited the townhouse daily, securing Kitty's affections even more firmly and rising in Elizabeth's esteem if only for possessing the good taste to adore her sister. Georgiana made herself scarce during his visits, not because anyone suspected Mr. Dashwood vulnerable to fickleness, but to spare Kitty any pain from recollecting his mother's incivility. An obligatory return call in Harley Street had proven as enchanting as their first visit with Mrs. John Dashwood, and everyone seemed much happier forgetting the existence of Harry's mother altogether.

Darcy's opinion of Mr. Dashwood rose, as well, particularly when he encountered the younger man at Angelo's fencing school and heard of his application for membership in one of the more intellectual gentlemen's clubs.

"Mr. Dashwood seems to be genuinely striving to improve himself and find more worthwhile ways to spend his time,"

Darcy remarked to Elizabeth one rainy afternoon. She had wandered into the library in search of a novel, but, upon finding him there, had abandoned her errand for the superior diversion of conversation with her husband.

"You sound surprised."

"I did not anticipate such a rapid transformation, nor one so sincere."

"Mr. Dashwood is apparently capable of great change when he sets his mind to something," she said. "His regard for Kitty may be his primary inspiration, but I think your encouragement has also contributed. He respects you."

"Perhaps he will make a suitable husband for Kitty, after all."

"Why, Darcy! I believe you are starting to like him."

He shrugged. "Perhaps I feel a sort of kinship with him. It does not seem like very long ago that my own father died."

"You both lost your fathers at a relatively young age. He, even earlier than you."

"Though his father's death was recent, the more I talk with Mr. Dashwood, the more I form the impression that he has lacked paternal guidance for a long time. John Dashwood seems to have acquiesced to his wife in most matters, and she seems to have expended more effort in trying to dominate her son than teach him. It is small wonder he spent so little time at Norland."

"So now you have taken the fatherless young man under your wing, offering the direction that John Dashwood did not."

"You are too generous. I am not yet thirty myself; I have not the wisdom to be a surrogate father to him."

"And you are too modest—a trait of which I cannot often accuse you. Very well, then. You can be an elder brother to Mr. Dashwood. Georgiana can vouch for your qualifications in that role."

Darcy contemplated that for a moment. "I should like to regard Mr. Dashwood as my brother."

"I am glad to hear it," she said. "For if he marries my sister, you will have no choice in the connection."

It was with light hearts that they all set out for Sussex—all except Georgiana, who remained in London to attend the performance of a noted Italian harpist with her friend Miss Sedgewick. She would stay with Miss Sedgewick's family while Elizabeth and Darcy were away, an arrangement that provided both a proper chaperone for Georgiana in her brother's absence and an opportunity for her to spend more time with her friend.

When Kitty and the Darcys arrived at Norland, the young master himself met their carriage. Mr. Dashwood helped Kitty alight, studying her face the whole while for her first impressions of his home.

"It is beautiful, Mr. Dashwood!" she exclaimed. "The most perfect house I ever saw."

Her delight clearly pleased him. He regarded the house with quiet pride. "I am glad you think so, Miss Bennet," he said softly. "Most glad."

Though Pemberley would always remain foremost in Elizabeth's affections, Norland was indeed a magnificent house. It was prettily situated in a wooded parkland, surrounded by seas of daffodils still in bloom. As they neared, she saw that equally abundant waves of tulips prepared to overtake the daffodils when their reign was exhausted.

Their party was the first to arrive; Fanny Dashwood and other relations were expected later that day and the majority of guests on the morrow. Mr. Dashwood proposed taking a walk about the grounds once they'd refreshed themselves, to which they readily assented. While they changed out of their traveling clothes, however, the sky darkened, and by the time they regrouped in the drawing room, a steady rain fell.

The shower failed to dampen Kitty's pleasure at being in

Mr. Dashwood's home, or his eagerness to show it to her. He suggested instead a tour of the house and led them through its rooms. He soon discovered that he made a poor docent, as his years of absence and lack of interest had left him unfamiliar with many of the house's characteristics. He also possessed but few memories to share with them.

The housekeeper, however, was pressed into service as a guide. She had been at Norland since the days of Harry's great-great-uncle and knew each panel and newel post as if she had fashioned them herself. As she led them through the great hall, music room, morning room, dining room, drawing rooms, and so on, her narrative formed at once a history of the house and a history of the Dashwood family. The original house, they learned, had been built during the reign of Henry the Fifth, and had been altered and expanded several times. Most of the present house had been built during the Tudor monarchy, with another wing added during George the First's time. Care had been taken, however, to blend the different architectural styles as well as possible, so that the variations added interest without detracting from the structure's overall grandeur.

Under John Dashwood's tenure, the house had seen modifications both inside and out. He had annexed surrounding land and enclosed the common; to please Fanny, a grove of old walnut trees had given way to a greenhouse and flower garden. Fanny, too, had selected all the china, plate, and linen in use.

As they moved through the dining room, Kitty, in a whisper, asked Elizabeth her opinion of the place settings.

"Rather too pretentious for my own taste," she whispered back.

"I thought so, too."

Noting a small alcove on one end of the dining room, Elizabeth enquired as to its purpose.

"The dining room used to be a bedchamber in the original house, and a servant slept in that alcove," the housekeeper replied. "When the chamber was converted into the dining room, a table was put in the center of the alcove. At one time, breakfast was set out there instead of on the sideboard during large parties. But the present Mrs. Dashwood prefers the sideboard, so the nook generally goes unused now, except as a place to set flowers to help ornament the dining room."

They moved on to other rooms, where they learned that the settle had been a wedding gift to Sir Stephen and Lady Dashwood in the sixteenth century, that the tapestries in the blue bedchamber had come with another long-ago bride, and that the pianoforte had last been played regularly by Harry's aunt Marianne Dashwood, now Mrs. Brandon, when she lived in the house as a girl. The genealogy lessons continued in the long gallery, where generations of Dashwoods lined the walls.

"That's Sir Stephen, there," said the housekeeper, gesturing toward a full-length portrait of a man in a ruff collar, "the last knight in the family. His lady wife is beside him. They say the two of them were inseparable. Over there is Mr. Albert Dashwood, my first master at Norland. A fine-looking man in his youth, though I don't remember him that way, as he was old when I came here. At least, he seemed old to me as a girl. Perhaps Mr. Dashwood remembers him?"

Harry shook his head. "I couldn't have been more than five when he died."

"Four, I believe, sir. But you certainly made an impression on him when you visited with your parents." She smiled in recollection. "You near about talked his ears off with your little voice, telling him about your latest discoveries and using only half the right words. That's when he decided to entail the estate to you."

"Instead of leaving it to his own children?" Elizabeth asked. The anxiety such an arrangement had caused her own family through the years left her perpetually puzzled by the logic of men who settled their affairs so unjustly.

"He never married," the housekeeper said. "His nephew, Henry Dashwood—grandfather of young Mr. Dashwood here— lived with Albert in his later days. By then Henry's son, John, was grown. Henry lived here with his second wife and their daughters, Elinor, Marianne, and Margaret. That was a happy time. The girls adored their uncle Albert, and I do believe he lived longer for the pleasure of their companionship."

"Where are they now?" Kitty asked.

"Henry died just one year after Albert. According to the terms of Albert's will, Henry could not divide Norland among multiple heirs. Upon Henry's death, therefore, everything went entirely to John, so that the estate could eventually pass whole to his son, Harry. When Mr. and Mrs. John Dashwood took possession of the house, Mrs. Henry Dashwood and the girls moved to a cottage in Devonshire owned by a cousin of hers."

"Sir John Middleton," Harry said. "You have met him."

It did not surprise Elizabeth that the widowed Mrs. Henry Dashwood had chosen to live near the genial Sir John rather than continue at Norland with Fanny Dashwood as its new mistress. She somehow suspected that Fanny, having just come into own- ership of the great house, had not been a particularly gracious hostess toward her predecessor.

"The girls are all grown now, correct?" Elizabeth asked.

"Yes, and comfortably settled with husbands of their own," the housekeeper replied.

"I invited them all to Norland this week," said Harry. "But I believe only my aunt Elinor and uncle Edward Ferrars will join us. Margaret is in confinement, with Marianne and their mother attending her and the infant."

Another new baby. It seemed all the world had entered an uncommon state of fecundity.

Kitty strolled farther along the gallery, studying various portraits in their turn. She stopped before a full-length paint- ing of a young, dark-haired man with an almost tangible air of self-possession. "Is this a likeness of your father, Mr. Dashwood? His resemblance to you is striking."

In that, Elizabeth concurred. The subject had been captured at about the same age as Harry Dashwood and bore many of the same physical characteristics. But for the clothing that clearly marked him as an inhabitant of the previous century, he and Harry could pass for twins. His eyes, however, seemed to mock the viewer with secret knowledge, and Elizabeth found his sardonic smile unsettling.

"No, my father's portrait hangs over there. This is Sir Francis Dashwood, probably our most notorious ancestor."

"What is he notorious for?" Kitty asked.

Darcy cleared his throat. "If Sir Francis had an estate in Buckinghamshire, as you told me, how did his portrait come to be here?"

"Perhaps it arrived on the same coach as did the looking glass I showed you." Harry shrugged. "I discovered the two items together in the attic when I was last here, and thought it highly amusing that Sir Francis and I looked so much alike. So I had the portrait brought down and hung. As for why it may have been brought here, your conjecture is as good as my own. I understand there are numerous paintings of Sir Francis at West Wycombe—perhaps his heirs didn't think they needed quite so many remembrances of the fellow. If I remember aright, the estate went to a half brother. Maybe the new owner wanted to clean house and live down the old chap's reputation."

"What reputation?" Kitty asked again. "What did he do?"

"Where did you say your father's portrait is?" Darcy attempted to usher them farther along the gallery.

Elizabeth resisted his shepherding and instead regarded her husband closely. Had his color risen?

"Darcy, that marks the second time you have diverted attention from Kitty's question. What, exactly, is Sir Francis notorious for?"

He hesitated. "Ungentlemanlike conduct."

"A great many men are guilty of that."

"Not to this degree."

"Which degree?"

"Suffice it to say that he engaged in behavior unbecoming to himself and his associates."

The vexing man spoke in circles. "What does history accuse him of?"

"Things unfit for a lady's ears."

Darcy's prevarication only fueled her curiosity, but his tone brooked no appeal. She resolved to renew the subject later. Perhaps he would reveal more about the mysterious Sir Francis Dashwood when they were alone.

She looked to Mr. Dashwood. "Well, then. Let us see the portrait of your father."

John Dashwood's likeness hung very nearly in the center of the gallery, flanked on one side by a painting of Fanny in her youth and on the other by a pair of portraits depicting young boys of about six and twelve. The children's portraits reminded Elizabeth of several others she had seen in the house.

"Who are the boys?" Kitty asked.

"Me. Both of them." Mr. Dashwood looked sheepish. "My mother has a fixation with having my likeness drawn. She insisted I sit for another last month. I have not yet seen the final painting, though the artist seemed pleased as he worked."

"Your mother is clearly very fond of you." Elizabeth spoke in what she hoped was a convincing tone, though in truth she suspected Fanny of being more interested in the image of her son than in the person himself. Mrs. John Dashwood had packed her boy off to boarding school the moment he was old enough to go, apparently preferring still pictures of him to the boisterous company of a real child. Though children of the gentry commonly attended public school, Harry's parents, like Darcy's, could have afforded a private tutor if they had wanted one.

Now that Harry had reached adulthood, his mother's behavior toward Kitty, the chosen object of his affections, indicated that she still valued his appearance—his advancement in society—more than his happiness. Fanny Dashwood was at once indulgent and indifferent, showering her son with all the accoutrements of his class without troubling herself to actually become acquainted with him.

As they left the gallery and returned downstairs, Fanny Dashwood's carriage pulled up to the door. They met her in the foyer, where her rain-soaked afternoon of travel and the news of Georgiana's absence combined to render her mood as black as the sky.

"Harry, I thought all our guests were arriving tomorrow," she said through a frozen smile that did not reach her eyes. She reminded Elizabeth of a ventriloquist, but Harry resisted being manipulated like a doll.

"Because Miss Bennet and the Darcys come as my special guests, I invited them to arrive a day early."

She drew him aside. "But this evening was to be reserved for family," she whispered harshly, continuing to display her forced smile for the Darcys' benefit.

"Yes, it is." Harry removed her hand from his arm and stepped away. Mrs. Dashwood glared after him as he addressed Kitty and the Darcys. "My mother has just reminded me that my aunt and uncle, Mr. and Mrs. Robert Ferrars, will be joining us for dinner with their daughter."

"Will we also have the pleasure of meeting Mr. and Mrs. Edward Ferrars tonight?" Kitty asked.

"They are expected," Fanny Dashwood responded. The ice in her voice made Kitty look to Elizabeth with trepidation.

"Dinner is at half past five." Without another word to her son or anyone else, Mrs. Dashwood turned and rigidly climbed the stairs. Harry offered Kitty his arm and suggested that a pot of tea might warm the damp reception Norland had given them thus far.

Elizabeth and Darcy stayed behind a moment as the younger couple walked away. "Mr. Dashwood *does* refer to the weather?" she asked.

"I believe so. One would use other words to describe the atmosphere indoors."

"And we are to stay in Sussex for a full week." She released a sigh. "Happy thought, indeed."

"The weather might clear." A mighty thunderclap shook the house, and rain pelted furiously against the windows. "Eventually."

"Let us hope so." She took Darcy's arm and they followed their host. "For if the air within the house remains this chilly, we might be forced to flee to Brighton after all."

Elizabeth chose her dinner attire carefully, though not, she guessed, with as much nervous deliberation as her sister. She ultimately selected an olive-green sarsenet gown with a short train and instructed her maid to dress her hair simply in order to spend more time on Kitty's. As she finished her preparations alone, Darcy entered.

"You are already dressed," she noted. He wore his dark blue coat, a favorite of hers.

He watched her clasp her necklace, his gaze lingering on her neck long after her hands had dropped to her sides. "I want only your company to complete my ensemble," he said.

"So that I can deflect Mrs. Dashwood's aura of ill will? You would do better to don the suit of armor in the library."

"Too heavy. Though I do regret having left my fencing mask in London."

She retrieved her slippers and sat near the fireplace to put them on. "One wonders how Mr. Dashwood turned out as amiable as he has, with such a parent to influence him."

"From the sound of it, she did not maintain enough proximity during his youth to influence his disposition much at all." He took the slippers from her hands and knelt to slide them on her feet himself.

"Fanny Dashwood does represent a good argument for the benefits of boarding school." She studied her husband's face as he grasped her left ankle and slid on one shoe. "Would you have wanted to attend one at such a tender age, though?"

He stopped what he was doing to consider a moment. "No. I believe the early education I received from my tutor and father superior to any I could have obtained at a public school, and had I gone away at five or six, I would hardly have known my mother at all before her death. Besides, the older boys at school are often very cruel to the younger ones, and it is hard enough for a lad twice that age to defend himself."

"How awful! I had no idea."

"You have no brothers." He slipped her other shoe over her heel but remained kneeling at her feet. "I do not want to send our sons away so early."

"Nor do I," she said.

His words tugged at her heart. They had not spoken much about children. Though they had a tacit understanding that children were desired, she did not know whether he wished for a large family or small, whether he harbored partiality for boys or girls, how soon he hoped they would come. That he already had given thought to how they should be raised occasioned only mild surprise. Of course Darcy would afford something so important as the upbringing of their children the same careful deliberation he gave all decisions.

That he believed children a certainty touched a different response within her. They were over four months into their marriage, with no sign of increasing their family any time soon. Four months, she knew, was not cause for alarm, not long enough to fear that they might remain childless forever. Truth be told, she was rather enjoying the extended honeymoon. She and Darcy were still getting used to each other. But with reports of babies circulating on all fronts, the tiniest seed of doubt had entered her mind. It had not yet germinated, but it was there, buried in the back of her thoughts. She wondered if he felt it, too.

"Darcy, do you ever worry that—" She stopped. He waited patiently as she chose her words. "We have not talked a great deal about children," she began again.

He smiled. "I am in favor of them."

"I—well, I am, too, of course. But we have not yet—that is, it seems like everyone else we know has very quickly—" She let out her breath. "Four months is not such a very long time, is it?"

His gaze met hers in understanding. He leaned forward and took both her hands in his. "No, Elizabeth. Four months is not very long at all."

"I did not think so."

He smoothed the crease from her brow. "Then why the concern?"

"It is not concern, so much. Just something that has been on my mind since Jane wrote with her news."

"I did not realize we were in a race."

"We are not. Not at all! But it is not only Jane who influences my thoughts. When even Charlotte and Mr. Collins have a child so early in their marriage—"

"I hope you do not compare me to Mr. Collins?" It was not a serious question, but one delivered with a conspiratorial smile meant to lighten her mood. "Or, at least, I hope I do not suffer by the comparison?"

"Though the bliss of producing a miniature Mr. Collins could have been mine, I shall never regret turning down his proposal," she said. Indeed, the thought of marriage to the obsequious clergyman still made her cringe. "And I compare you to no one, for in my eyes you have no equal."

He yet held her hands, and leaned forward to meet her lips.

They lingered over the kiss, wishing they were anywhere but at Norland, expected down to dinner momentarily. But obligation parted them. As he released her, she cast him a saucy look.

"If four months stretch to forty, however, perhaps you should seek Mr. Collins's advice on the matter."

An assortment of new persons awaited Elizabeth's observation when she and Darcy joined the party gathered in the drawing room before dinner. Mr. and Mrs. Edward Ferrars had just arrived, their journey having been slowed by the rain, and had scarcely had time to change out of their traveling clothes. They seemed in good humor, though, despite the damp ride.

Edward expressed genuine pleasure at meeting Kitty and the Darcys. He greeted them warmly upon Harry's introduction. His wife, Elinor, said she was also very pleased to make their acquaintance, and the kindness of her manner lent the words the sincerity they all too commonly lacked when uttered in polite society.

"When did you arrive at Norland?" she asked. "Have you had an opportunity to see much of it?"

"Mr. Dashwood and his housekeeper showed us the house this afternoon," Elizabeth said. "It is lovely."

"Indeed, it is. I have many happy memories of this place." Elinor glanced about the drawing room, her expression growing wistful.

"I understand you grew up at Norland?"

"Yes, from eight to nineteen. My mother, sisters, and I moved to Barton after my father died. This is the first time I've returned."

The admission startled Elizabeth. "You never visited your brother here?" she blurted out before considering a less bald way to couch the query.

Elinor met her gaze, and each woman quickly assessed the

other. Though Elinor was a good fifteen years older than she, Elizabeth read in her a common understanding and intelligence that instantly identified her as a kindred spirit. Elinor seemed to sense the same.

"We occasionally saw my brother and his wife in London." What she left unsaid, but that Elizabeth heard perfectly, was that the brief London visits had constituted enough family togetherness for all parties.

"Does Norland remain as you remember it?" Elizabeth asked.

Elinor studied a large portrait of Fanny hanging above the mantel. "In many ways, yes," she said. "But in others, it almost feels as if I never lived here at all."

Elizabeth suspected that was Fanny's entire object.

Fanny Dashwood's other brother was also present with his family. Robert, with his bold striped waistcoat and elaborate silver snuffbox, she soon dismissed as an aging fop. Elizabeth had seen Lucy and Regina Ferrars at the Middletons' soirée, but had not gotten close enough to form an impression beyond noting a strong resemblance between mother and daughter. Both enjoyed passable looks, Lucy's a somewhat faded version of Regina's full bloom. They shared narrow eyes and dark, arched brows. Lucy reminded one of a cat, her bearing exhibiting a decidedly predatory aspect. Regina, in contrast, carried herself with bovine grace. She was considerably plumper than her mother, with a figure that even her high-waisted gown could not flatter. Lucy's thin frame looked almost skeletal in contrast, as if since Regina's birth it had been daughter, not mother, eating for them both.

An evening of Lucy and Regina's company proved that in postponing the opportunity to become acquainted with them, Elizabeth had not deferred any pleasure. Lucy was agreeable enough, far more so than her sister-in-law Fanny, and Elizabeth had initially struggled to pinpoint exactly what she disliked about the woman. But as the night wore on, she realized that it was precisely Lucy's ingratiating manner—echoed to mind-numbing effect by Regina—that made her almost nostalgic for the company of Darcy's domineering aunt, Lady Catherine. Lucy complimented Elizabeth's dress, Kitty's hair, the cut of Darcy's coat. The flowers in the small alcove were lovely—were they from Norland's greenhouse? Indeed, everything about Norland was splendid, and their host was up to the nines.

"Harry, I declare this is the best rabbit I've ever tasted."

Elizabeth wondered that Lucy had much basis for comment on the rabbit or any other dish, as her steady stream of flattery prevented her from actually bringing much of the food to her mouth. Regina, in contrast, had managed to clear her plate between accolades.

When Harry denied any right to the praise, Lucy offered it instead to the superior environment of Norland Park. "Truly, nothing in London can compare, and even Norfolk don't have rabbit this plump. Isn't that right, Robert?"

Her husband, whom Elizabeth could have sworn was admiring his reflection in the bowl of his spoon, admitted uncertainty as to the relative plumpness of the rabbits raised on their estate.

Once the subject of rabbits had been discussed beyond endurance, conversation turned to the china. Regina pronounced the dense floral motif exquisite as she obscured it from view with a second helping of duck. "Where did you find it, Aunt Dashwood? I want the same pattern for my own hope chest."

Fanny roused herself from the sullen silence into which she'd sunk. "It's a Royal Worcester service. I don't know if the company still produces it." She cast a pointed glance at Kitty, then pulled back her lips to form what might have been a sweet smile on another person. On Fanny, it was intimidating. "Perhaps, my dear niece, this very set will find its way into your possession."

Elizabeth didn't know how to interpret the comment. Did Harry's mother mean to give away the set before a new mistress arrived at Norland? Or, relinquishing her aspirations of an alliance with Georgiana's thirty thousand pounds, did she now harbor a wish that Regina might secure Harry's hand? Nothing in Harry's manner indicated that the latter possibility had ever entered his own head.

By the time dessert concluded, Fanny had managed to subtly insult Kitty three more times, Lucy had performed an aria on the smoothness of the syllabub, and Regina had consumed as many maids of honor as had waited upon Henry the Eighth's six queens together. Miss Ferrars's conversation between mouthfuls demonstrated a simplicity of both manner and mind.

After dinner, the ladies withdrew to continue the torment.

"I suppose it would be improper for me to remain here with the gentlemen?" Elizabeth whispered to Darcy on her way out.

"You wish to smoke and drink port?"

"I wish to engage in conversation more stimulating than what Lucy and Regina Ferrars are likely to provide."

A flash of something metallic catching the candlelight drew their attention. Robert Ferrars was gazing at himself in the lid of his toothpick case.

"I do not think you will find it here," Darcy told her.

The women settled into the drawing room. Elinor, suffering from a lingering chill following her damp ride, sat down near the fire. Lucy took the seat opposite and immediately commenced an ode to the perfection of the fire screen. It was exquisite. Had Fanny embroidered it? She had such talent. Had she embroidered the one in Lucy's room, as well? How could one possibly choose which to admire more?

Lucy's attentions to her other sister-in-law were less inspired and even more transparent. "Elinor, I understand your sister Margaret was safely delivered of a boy this month," she said.

"A girl," Elinor corrected.

"Her first, yes?"

"Her third."

"How redundant," Fanny declared. "One daughter is a gift to her mother." She cast her gaze toward Regina, who, now that the meal was ended, appeared to be chewing her cud. "A second is a comfort—she might care for her mother in old age. But more than that merely taxes a family's ability to provide for them all, especially if they become spinsters."

"It is fortunate, then, that you weren't so burdened," said Elinor.

"No, but I also was not blessed," said Fanny. "I look forward, therefore, to gaining a daughter when Harry weds. A genteel, accomplished young lady will make a wonderful addition to our family. Perhaps someone like Miss Everett. Do you know of her, Elinor? She and her brother are among the guests arriving tomorrow."

Elinor confessed a lack of familiarity with either Miss Everett or her superior accomplishments.

Lucy, however, trumpeted her knowledge. "Miss Everett? Surely you don't mean Miss Maria Everett?"

"Why, yes." Fanny said.

"Gracious, Fanny! Have you not heard? But no—you mustn't have. I'm so sorry to be the one to tell you this, but I believe she is engaged to Mr. Montrose. Or nearly so. Almost officially. Anyway, she could not possibly accept Harry's addresses."

Or his mother's.

"Well!" Fanny's disappointment was evident, but fleeting. "That is no matter. I invited several other accomplished young ladies. Lady Harriet Stenbridge, for instance."

Lucy shook her head sadly.

"What?" asked Fanny. "What do you know of her?"

Lucy leaned forward. "It's only a rumor, mind you—" She spoke in a conspiratorial tone. "So I oughtn't repeat it at all. But I understand she was found in a compromising situation with a certain heir to a dukedom who's managed to hush it up."

"If he hushed it up," Elizabeth said, "how do you know of it?"

She shrugged her shoulders. "People just tell me things, I suppose."

Elizabeth resolved not to be among them.

Kitty attempted to initiate a discussion with Regina about favorite shops in London. They discovered a common partiality for Layton and Shears before Regina became nearly paralyzed with indecision over whether she preferred the ices or cakes at Gunter's. She ended the crisis by resolving to visit Number 7 Berkeley Square directly she returned to London so as to test each again. She did not invite Kitty to join her in this excursion, nor, Elizabeth mused, could the shop likely produce enough sweets to serve another customer in addition to Regina.

Tea arrived, and soon after it, the gentlemen. Harry headed toward Kitty but was ambushed by Fanny and Lucy en route, and so wound up sitting beside Regina instead. Or rather, he perched on the small bit of sofa that remained beside Regina. Edward Ferrars seemed to be trying to continue a discussion with his brother as they entered, but Robert was examining the room through his quizzing glass as if he had not just been in it a couple of hours ago.

Darcy trailed in last. His gaze immediately sought out Elizabeth and warmed at the sight of her.

"I missed you," he said softly.

She handed him a cup of tea. "Was your gentlemen's time as bad as all that?"

"Actually, no. Robert Ferrars so occupied himself with the mechanics of opening his new snuffbox one-handed that the rest of us were able to talk intelligently."

"I envy you. Our discourse in here was not intelligent, merely educational."

She sipped tea from her own cup and surveyed the room. Harry had risen from the sofa and was subtly backing toward

Kitty under the assault of Lucy's chatter. Fanny had commandeered Edward's and Elinor's attention and presently expressed outrage on some matter. Robert now used his quizzing glass to study the tea service pattern, an inspection Regina aided by clearing a plate of tea cakes three at a time.

"How long will it be," Elizabeth asked, "before everybody decides that we have endured enough of one another's society for the evening?"

"I suspect that once one person makes good his escape, the rest will soon scatter."

"We all spent a good part of the day traveling. Do you suppose you and I could leave now with propriety?"

He consulted his watch. "Unfortunately, it is early yet."

"But I am ready to retire."

He regarded her with concern. "Are you fatigued from the journey?"

"I believe I am." She coyly broke their gaze and scanned the room once more. "At least . . . hypothetically."

Eight

"Nothing should prevail on him to give up his engagement. He would stand to it, cost him what it might."
—John Dashwood to Elinor and Marianne,
Sense and Sensibility, *Chapter 37*

*B*y the night of Harry's grand birthday fête, the rain had cleared, and Norland reverberated with the sounds of youthful merriment. Harry, it seemed, had left no acquaintance uninvited, and as the house and grounds filled with school chums and club friends, frivolity ruled. The billiards room never emptied, the air echoed with shots at game birds, and the hunt was pursued with a wildness and intensity that rivaled any fey legend.

Fanny accepted the invasion with surprising graciousness. Though by law the house officially belonged to Harry since his father's death, it remained very much hers in essence. Elizabeth suspected Fanny's indulgence of Harry's rambunctious friends stemmed from a hope that their antics would distract him from Kitty.

If that were indeed her design, however, Harry himself thwarted it. When a young man's vision is filled by only one lady, all the entertainment in the world cannot divert his attention from her. Though he played the generous host and partook of the fun, he distanced himself from its more frenetic activities. Despite his mother's none-too-subtle encouragement to spend as much time as possible with his gentlemen friends—in lieu of the young ladies of fortune who one by one had been discounted by Lucy Ferrars—Harry eschewed their companionship for that of Miss Bennet. Not that the besotted Kitty was herself anything approaching staid, but Elizabeth observed in them a growing seriousness that met her approbation.

Darcy noted it, too. "I think Mr. Dashwood is even more of a changed man since our arrival at Norland," he said as they watched Harry lead Kitty to the center of the ballroom for the first dance. Elizabeth stole a glance at Fanny, who appeared about to choke on her own bile at the sight of Kitty being accorded the honor of opening the ball.

"Yes. He seems very much to desire not only Kitty's approval of himself and his estate, but ours, as well. I never would have thought of Kitty as a settling influence, but I am glad for it."

"You do approve of him, then? We have spoken of my thinking of him as a brother, but would you also welcome him as such?" He offered Elizabeth his hand, and they joined the couples forming a line on the floor.

"I would. But it is premature for either of us to speak openly of Mr. Dashwood that way when the gentleman himself has not yet declared that intention." The opening strains of the music sounded. She bent in a curtsy.

"Not yet declared it to whom?"

She jerked to a stand, rapidly assessing him in the few moments the dance's first figure would allow her to face him. His face was completely impassive, but his eyes held amusement.

"Darcy! Has Mr. Dashwood—"

The steps of the dance forced them apart. She stumbled through the figure, distracted by his cryptic question. Had Mr. Dashwood sought Darcy's permission to marry Kitty? Had he already proposed to Kitty herself?

Elizabeth nearly bumped into one of her fellow dancers as her gaze ricocheted from Darcy to Harry to Kitty. The dance had brought the latter two back together, but as they faced each other, Elizabeth could detect in their manner no secret understanding.

Darcy at last stood opposite her once more. "Will you now explain yourself?" she asked.

"Explain what?"

"Are you in Mr. Dashwood's confidence?"

"I believe so. Why, today he entrusted to me a review of Norland's accounts."

"Darcy! You are being deliberately obtuse. Are you in his confidence on more personal subjects?"

The dance parted them again, and Elizabeth was forced to endure shuttered expressions from Darcy as his only response. With growing impatience, she walked through the succeeding figures until they were reunited.

"Do not keep me any longer in suspense," she said.

Before he could speak, the figure brought Regina Ferrars and her partner directly next to them. "Mrs. Darcy! Are you enjoying the dance?" Regina puffed with exertion. "I think there are twenty couple! We'll be half an hour in this set, at least. Isn't it splendid?"

Elizabeth met Darcy's gaze. He crooked his lips in a maddening smile and said not a word.

"Yes—splendid," she replied.

This was going to be the longest half hour of her life.

When the set at last ended, Harry immediately led Kitty off the floor, through the throng, and out of the ballroom. Elizabeth caught Darcy's arm and drew him to a quiet corner. "Tell me," she demanded.

"I have nothing to tell."

"Your expression suggests otherwise."

"Does it? I shall have to work on that."

"Has Mr. Dashwood spoken to you? Has he proposed?"

"Why would he propose to me? I am a married man."

"With a more patient wife than you deserve." She released an exasperated breath. "Has he proposed to Kitty?"

"I do not know." He smiled—a real smile this time, not the taunting one he'd borne until now. "The night is still young."

She seized upon the intimation. "He plans to offer tonight?"

"He asked me this afternoon whether I thought your father would approve a match between them. I told him that I believed so, and that he could rely upon my endorsement should Mr. Bennet solicit my opinion. Beyond that, I am not privy to Mr. Dashwood's intentions." Something past Elizabeth's shoulder caught his attention. "But I suspect your sister is. Here she comes."

Kitty didn't walk across the room—she floated, oblivious to the sea of people as she made her way straight for Elizabeth. Mr. Dashwood followed in her wake but became sidetracked by William Middleton. Kitty did not wait for him but pressed on until she reached her sister's side.

"Lizzy! I have the most wonderful news!" She lowered her voice so that no one but Elizabeth could hear, but she needn't have spoken at all—her face revealed everything. "Mr. Dashwood just proposed, and I have accepted him."

Elizabeth hugged her with genuine joy. "You will be very happy together, I am certain."

"He means to go to Longbourn directly he leaves here to ask Papa's permission in person. I would like to go with him. Will you and Mr. Darcy take me?"

"Of course."

The evening slipped by in a blur from that moment until supper. The sisters could not talk openly of wedding plans or trousseaus, but they did determine that the distance between Norland and Pemberley was not so very great if one traveled with four horses and fair weather. Mr. Dashwood joined them long enough to receive quiet congratulations from Elizabeth and Darcy, but his duties as a host prevented him from spending as much time in Kitty's company as he obviously wished.

About an hour before supper, Elizabeth and Darcy left the noisy ballroom in search of a spot where they could indulge in a few minutes' quiet conversation without fear of being overheard. They wandered into the dining room, where servants were coming in and out as they prepared to serve the meal. The small alcove stood empty except for a large arrangement of spring flowers that emitted a fragrance too lovely to leave.

Elizabeth inhaled deeply. "Mmm. Do let us linger here a moment."

They slipped into the alcove and around one side of the table. The nook was unlit, but the dining room's many candles provided sufficient indirect illumination that they could talk without standing in the dark.

"You are happy," Darcy said. It was a statement, not a question, for her delight in the betrothal was so evident that she feared her expression would announce the engagement before Mr. Dashwood and Kitty could.

She nodded, grateful for the opportunity to speak freely of her joy for at least a few minutes before returning to the party. "This is a good match for Kitty."

"I would not in general consider you a woman prone to matchmaking."

"Neither would I," she said. "I certainly do not share my mother's belief that any husband is better than no husband. But I truly cannot imagine a superior partner for my sister than Mr. Dashwood."

"Nor can I."

"Now you admire your own handiwork. You have helped him become a steadier man, one worthy of my sister."

"I did no more than offer direction," he said. "Mr. Dashwood is his own man. He himself made the transformation, and he could not have done so if he did not wish to. The change would not last."

"Nevertheless, I thank you for extending him your friendship."

"You need not. Though you encouraged my initial overtures toward him, it was not long before genuine amity motivated me. Why, I think I now like him quite as well as I do Bingley."

"We are fortunate in having two such gentlemen as my sisters' husbands." Of her third brother-in-law, Mr. Wickham, she omitted mention altogether. Darcy could scarcely tolerate the utterance of his name, and she did not want to allow Lydia's scapegrace spouse to spoil such a perfect evening.

"Does Kitty's betrothal mean we can leave London without finishing the season? Or do you wish to stay until the bitter end?"

Elizabeth recalled her conversation with Georgiana at the pianoforte. One engagement was enough for their family this season. "I believe once Kitty's wedding clothes are ordered, our business in town is finished. I imagine, however, that Kitty might wish to remain in London longer so as to see Mr. Dashwood regularly."

"I thought you might say that. Very well. Though I had hoped to take you back to Pemberley soon."

"Pemberley?" she asked in a light tone. "Why ever would I want to return to Pemberley now that you have immersed me in the glittering society of the *beau monde?*"

Darcy lowered his voice. "I am a selfish man, remember? I do not want to share you with the *beau monde.*"

She glanced quickly toward the arched entrance to the alcove, suddenly quite conscious that no one could see them where they stood. Meeting Darcy's gaze again, she saw that he— her utterly straitlaced, ever-proper husband—was also very aware of the unexpected privacy of the moment.

"Mr. Darcy," she whispered, "I hope you are not contemplating something shocking, like kissing your wife in the middle of Mr. Dashwood's birthday fête?"

"Never." He took one of her gloved hands in his and slowly interlaced their fingers. "But I confess," he whispered back, "that I *was* contemplating kissing her here. Only contemplating, mind you." He leaned toward her.

"*What* are you *doing?*" came a haughty, all-too-familiar voice from the dining room.

Elizabeth and Darcy jumped apart, dropping each other's hands as if burned.

"I had those place cards carefully arranged!" Fanny Dashwood's voice bounced harshly off the china and crystal settings in the dining room. Elizabeth, still startled, required a moment more to finally realize Harry's mother was speaking not to her and Darcy, but to someone else entirely. They, thankfully, remained unseen in the alcove.

"You have titled guests," Fanny hissed. "You are defying the proper order of precedence."

"They are my friends," said Mr. Dashwood. "They will not mind."

"*I* mind. Will you let the news circulate throughout the *ton* that at a fête I hosted—"

"Norland is my house now. I will accept the earth-shattering repercussions of sitting beside the woman I love at my own birthday celebration."

Elizabeth met Darcy's gaze. He, too, clearly wished they could escape the alcove, but they remained trapped until Mr. Dashwood and his mother left. As much as they regretted overhearing the private conversation between mother and son, revealing themselves now would only make the situation worse—they would embarrass Mr. Dashwood and make themselves look ridiculous in the process. Feeling acutely the awkwardness of their position, they backed farther into the shadows.

"Do not talk so foolishly. This interest you have in Miss Bennet is mere infatuation. I will find you a wife more worthy of you, one who can bring something to your marriage."

"Miss Bennet has consented to bring herself. That is enough for me."

A long silence followed. Elizabeth forced herself to take slow, shallow breaths so that the Dashwoods would not become aware of their accidental audience. She also prayed she would not be seized by the sudden need to sneeze.

"You have made her an offer of marriage?" Fanny finally said, her voice strangled.

"Yes. And she has accepted me."

"Of course she has. What other gentleman of your consequence could she hope to snare?"

"I will not hear you speak about my future wife in this manner."

"Harry, you are still young. You don't know what you are about. Marriage is too important to your future to enter into unadvisedly. Let me guide you."

"My heart has guided me."

"Your heart should have nothing to do with it. You owe it to yourself and your family to make a materially advantageous alliance. If you must have Miss Bennet, indulge in a liaison with her after you have married someone else and produced a proper heir."

Elizabeth stifled a gasp. Harry's was more audible. A look of disdain crossed Darcy's face.

"Don't be so naïve, son. It happens all the time."

"I have heard enough of this."

"In time, you will understand that I am right," Fanny said. "I only hope it happens before you commit the greatest folly of your life."

Harry made no answer.

"Harry? Are you listening? Harry!"

To Elizabeth's intense relief, sounds of movement suggested that Mrs. Dashwood followed her son out of the dining room. Darcy put a finger to his lips and moved to the alcove entrance.

"They have gone."

Elizabeth at last released her breath. "What do you make of that?" she asked as she reached his side.

"I think your sister has a difficult road ahead of her, but that Mr. Dashwood will do all in his power to smooth it." He took her hand, but this time with a different purpose than when he'd last held it. "I also think," he said, pulling her behind him as he crossed the dining room with rapid strides, "that we should make good our exit before Mrs. Dashwood returns to rearrange those cards."

Somehow, Harry managed to shake off the exchange with his mother well enough to seem his usual good-natured self at supper, though Elizabeth perceived the effort his show required. It probably helped that Fanny was seated across the room, presiding over a second table. Mother and son had no occasion to exchange words or even glances until the meal neared conclusion. Just before dessert was served, Mrs. Dashwood stood up and called for the attention of all assembled.

"I wish to thank you for joining us to mark my son's twenty-first birthday." She nodded to a servant, who threw open the dining room doors. Two more footmen entered, carrying a large rectangular object covered with silk. They brought it to the front of the room and rested it on a stand that apparently had been placed there for this purpose.

"Harry, I can scarcely believe twenty-one years have passed since you let out your first cry. And I know that in another twenty-one years, I shall wonder how the time since tonight's celebration passed so quickly." Fanny's chin was tilted higher than usual, her voice more steely.

Elizabeth sensed the anger suppressed beneath the maternal words, though Fanny, like Harry, was delivering a stageworthy performance for the benefit of their guests. Whatever lessons and values Fanny had or had not managed to impart to her son growing up, both shared the ability to present a convincing façade when required.

"Your years of young adulthood will someday be only a memory for you, too," Fanny continued. "I wanted, therefore, to fix this moment in time. And so, my darling son, I present my birthday gift to you."

The footman lifted the fabric to reveal a full-length portrait of Harry. It was an amazing likeness, the artist having perfectly captured not only Harry's physical characteristics but his essence, as well. The image seemed ready to spring from the canvas to seize the pleasures of life with all the zeal of the original.

"Thank you, Mother." Harry rose and stiffly crossed the room to kiss the air above his mother's cheek. "You are generosity itself."

The following morning, Elizabeth walked through a quiet house down to breakfast, where she found Elinor Ferrars alone.

"Is no one else about yet?" she asked.

Elinor smiled. "'Tis only ten o'clock. Do you truly imagine we'll see many of the other guests before one?"

"Yet you are awake."

"I have three children. I haven't slept past dawn in years."

Elizabeth welcomed the chance to converse more with Elinor. She found Harry's aunt kind and forthright, with a directness that was refreshing after so many weeks among London's *ton*. They talked at first about the previous night's festivities, then drifted to other subjects. Elizabeth kept the news of Kitty and Harry's engagement to herself, as the couple would not announce it until her father had sanctioned the match. But she wanted to learn more about the family Kitty would marry into, and trusted Elinor to provide an honest, if tactfully delivered, view.

Elinor and Edward, she came to understand, had married for love and had never known a moment's regret since. Elizabeth believed the same would prove true for her and Darcy, and fervently hoped Kitty and Harry would be so blessed.

"What of your nephew?" Elizabeth asked. "Do you think Mr. Dashwood could ever be satisfied with an alliance of affection that did not also bring wealth?"

"To be honest, I'm not sure," Elinor said. "We have not had many opportunities to spend time with him and form an opinion of his character."

Before Elizabeth could learn any more, Regina Ferrars entered the breakfast parlor.

"Lord, but I'm starving! I never danced so much in my life as I did last night. Is the chocolate still hot?"

She headed straight to the buffet, where she piled a plate high with ham, cheese, eggs, plum cake, and one roll for each variety of jam offered. "What a splendid party! Didn't Harry look handsome? Mama says she hopes our children inherit his profile."

Elizabeth choked on her toast. "Your children?" she asked when she recovered herself.

Elinor appeared equally surprised. "I was unaware that you and Harry had an understanding."

"Oh, we don't. Not yet, anyway. But Mama thinks he should keep all his lovely money in the family, and says it shouldn't be hard for a girl with a figure like mine to catch his eye."

No doubt because there was so much of her figure to behold.

"And last night, I heard my aunt Dashwood tell Mama that she'd rather see Harry wed me than some penniless girl. So it's only a matter of time."

Not if Elizabeth had anything to do with it. With his whole

family conspiring to oppose a marriage to Kitty, she would offer Harry a bit of reinforcement until they were able to depart for Longbourn.

Regina's mouth was soon too full of plum cake to provide any additional news. Elizabeth excused herself and headed back to her chamber to see whether Darcy had yet risen. On the way she passed Elinor and Edward's room. The door stood slightly ajar, and Fanny's voice carried from within.

"If you would only speak to him. Please, Edward. You're my brother, and his father is no longer here to guide him."

"Fanny, I simply cannot comprehend your objection. She comes from a respectable family, and her elder sisters' marriages offer good connections. With Harry's income, he doesn't need a bride with a large dowry."

"Hmph. You would think that a man of Mr. Darcy's fortune would settle something on his wife's sisters to improve their marriageability."

"As you and John took care of his sisters?"

Silence.

Elizabeth reached her chamber, only to find it vacant. Darcy had apparently risen and embarked on some other occupation before breakfast. She returned to the hallway just as Fanny emerged from Edward's room. Harry's mother acknowledged her with minimal civility, then turned on her heel and retreated down the stairs. Having no desire to follow her, Elizabeth instead wandered into the long gallery.

Harry Dashwood stood inside. He had been studying the portrait of his father, but her entrance diverted his attention.

"Forgive me," she said. "I did not intend to disturb you."

"Nonsense, Mrs. Darcy. Your company is always a pleasure." He gestured toward the painting. "I was just contemplating what my father would think of my engagement to Miss Bennet."

"And what did you conclude?"

He shrugged. "He would have wanted to see me happy, but I

suspect he might have shared my mother's . . . reservations." He gazed at her directly. "It could not have escaped your notice that my mother would prefer I marry a woman of large fortune."

"I confess it has not."

"I apologize."

"Why? You are not responsible for your mother's opinions."

"No, but I am now responsible for Miss Bennet's happiness. I think it best to remove Kitty from my mother's proximity at present, to spare her any further unpleasantness. I also wish to secure your father's permission and announce the engagement as soon as possible. To that end, I plan to leave for Longbourn immediately—this very day. Can the three of you be ready by this afternoon? If not, I will go on ahead."

"We can depart within the hour if necessary. But how will you explain the abrupt departure to your other guests?"

"I will tell them the truth—that I must attend to an important matter requiring immediate action."

"And what will you tell your mother?"

"Nothing whatever. I am done with her. At least for this visit." He issued a disgusted sigh. "She has harped on me about family duty and reputation as long as I can remember, but you have only to look around this room to see people who did far more to compromise the Dashwoods' standing than what she accuses me of. Sir Stephen might have been a knight, but his youngest son was a pirate. And Sir Francis here—" He gesticulated forcefully. "If the Dashwood family honor can survive *his* infamous conduct, it certainly won't be tarnished by my marriage to a gentle, well-bred young lady."

Mr. Dashwood's manservant entered. "Your trunks are packed and await only your order to load them, sir. Will you also be taking the portrait?"

"The one from my mother?"

"Yes, sir."

"Absolutely not."

"Yes, sir. What would you like done with it?"

"My mother can do whatever she likes with it. I don't need it with me as a reminder of her manip—" He cut himself short as his gaze fell once more upon the portrait of Sir Francis.

"Come to think on it, pack this one instead." He laughed bitterly. "Sir Francis and I can keep our disgraceful selves company."

Nine

"I am convinced that there is a vast deal of inconsistency in almost every human character."

—John Dashwood to Elinor,
Sense and Sensibility, *Chapter 41*

M r. Dashwood easily won the approval of both Kitty's parents. A half hour's observation of Harry's earnest devotion to Kitty, paired with the testimonials of his most sensible daughter and son-in-law, proved sufficient recommendation for Mr. Bennet to grant his consent to the marriage without reservation. Mrs. Bennet's admiration was secured still more quickly, with the mere utterance of the words "six thousand a year." The couple fixed upon a date three months hence and returned to London with the Darcys.

While Elizabeth and Georgiana made the rounds of warehouses with Kitty to order the bride's trousseau, Darcy returned to his own affairs. The soon-to-be-vacant living at Kympton still needed filling, and a rare opportunity had arisen to discuss land enclosure—a practice Darcy contemplated implementing at Pemberley—with the country's foremost expert. The Earl of Chatfield had invited a small group of friends to meet Arthur Young, former secretary of the Board of Agriculture. Hoping to encourage Mr. Dashwood's newfound interest in estate management, Darcy had secured an invitation for Harry, as well.

As arranged, Darcy met Mr. Dashwood at the younger man's townhouse before proceeding to the earl's. He arrived promptly at the appointed time, Darcy considering tardiness the eighth deadly sin. Harry, however, kept him waiting in the drawing room a full quarter hour. Darcy paced impatiently, thankful that at least upon this visit he hadn't been invited to attend Harry in his dressing room. Despite his growing kinship with Mr. Dashwood, he preferred to maintain more formality in his relationships. He did have to admit, however, that the previous opportunity to see Mr. Dashwood's newly discovered looking glass had proven an unexpected pleasure. He wondered if the portrait of Sir Francis had also found its way to Harry's suite, as he had not seen it more publicly displayed when he'd been ushered to the drawing room.

When Mr. Dashwood at last joined Darcy, he appeared to have rushed his toilette. His cravat slanted asymmetrically, and his hair looked even more unruly than was the current fashion. 'Twas a far cry from the style-conscious buck who had held court before his looking glass, or even the elegant host who had so recently entertained them at Norland.

"Mr. Darcy, do forgive me." Harry immediately sent for his hat and greatcoat. "But one minute more, and we can be off."

"I hope nothing is amiss?"

Harry shrugged into the overcoat. "Pray remind me, who are we meeting?"

"Mr. Arthur Young."

Harry stared at him blankly.

"One of the greatest English writers on agriculture?" Darcy prompted.

"Oh, yes—yes, of course. And we will be discussing what, exactly?"

"Land enclosure." Darcy suppressed his growing annoyance.

When he'd tendered the earl's invitation a se'nnight ago, Mr. Dashwood had accepted enthusiastically. Darcy's review of Norland's records had revealed that, far from cheating Harry, Norland's steward had seized upon the lack of direct supervision following John Dashwood's death as an opportunity to implement practices the estate should have adopted years earlier. Harry's father had enclosed the land but not altered its tillage methods to take advantage of the larger holdings; as a result, crop production fell far short of its potential. Darcy had suggested that Harry study Jethro Tull's agricultural theories to better understand the changes his steward now sought to make, and Young was a strong advocate of Tull's methods.

Darcy remained undecided about whether to enclose Pemberley's lands. Though there was no doubt that the practice vastly improved productivity, it turned small farmers into landless laborers with no stake in the earth they worked so hard to cultivate. Darcy disliked the thought of robbing his tenants of their independence. Yet he had to consider the greater good of the people in his care, and with England at war, growing enough food to feed its families was the duty of every landowner. In Harry's circumstances, since Norland was already enclosed, the fields ought to be cultivated to their full potential. Mr. Dashwood had agreed, and welcomed the invitation to learn more. Now, however, Harry seemed completely uninterested.

"Do you still wish to accompany me, Mr. Dashwood?"

"What? Oh—yes. Certainly! I remember our conversation now. I'm sorry—I just forgot for a moment there. I'm sure this afternoon will prove most instructional."

They stepped into the street, where Darcy's carriage waited. A light mist enveloped the city, casting everything in greyness. In the dreary light, Darcy noted circles under Harry's eyes. Had he been out all night? If he had risen late, that might explain his careless appearance and distracted demeanor.

"Mr. Dashwood, are you quite well?"

"Hmm? Oh, fine—fine. I didn't sleep well last night, that's all. But I assure you, Mr. Young shall have my full attention."

Mr. Dashwood remained true to his word and managed to attend to Arthur Young's discourse well enough so as not to embarrass Darcy, who'd gone to some trouble on his behalf to obtain a coveted invitation to the private party. His distraction, however, returned at dinner the following evening. Harry was their guest for a family supper, but poor Kitty had all she could do to carry on a conversation with her fiancé. Were it not for Elizabeth, Georgiana, and Darcy, the confused bride-to-be would have spent most of the meal in soliloquy.

"I cannot account for Mr. Dashwood's conduct this evening," Elizabeth remarked later, when they had retired for the night.

Darcy could not explain it, either. "He behaved similarly on our way to Chatfield's yesterday. When I enquired whether he was all right, he said he had not slept well."

"He did look tired."

In fact, the circles under Mr. Dashwood's eyes had darkened in the four-and-twenty hours since Darcy had last seen him. "I wonder what disturbs his rest."

"I hear his mother has returned to town. Perhaps she provokes him."

"From the exchange we overheard at Norland, it does not sound as if her disapprobation is likely to cost him any sleep."

"He did seem quite confident in his decision, and equal to the challenge of opposing her."

Darcy hoped nothing too grave caused Mr. Dashwood's sleeplessness. He indeed now regarded Harry as a brother. Independent of Mr. Dashwood's relationship with Kitty, they'd struck a rapport in which they both seemed to take pleasure. Harry was eager to benefit from Darcy's greater experience of the world, and Darcy found that he enjoyed lending his guidance. He looked forward to their friendship soon being reinforced by a true family connection.

As Darcy's reflections strayed to the approaching wedding, a troubling thought entered his head. One that would explain an apparent lack of sleep.

Elizabeth noted his frown. "What is it?" she asked.

"Nothing. Idle musings." He reached for the candle snuffer, but she stayed his hand.

"Darcy?"

He sighed. "Many an engaged young man has spent his last precious days of bachelorhood sowing wild oats."

Her brows rose. "And you think Mr. Dashwood—"

"Not necessarily. Mr. Dashwood seems to have settled down since meeting Kitty."

"But now that he has secured her hand, perhaps he indulges his more carefree impulses?"

"London offers plenty of temptation to a young man about to lose his freedom." The clubs abounded with tales of prewedding excess on the part of prospective bridegrooms. Were dissipated nights of drinking, gaming, or worse to blame for Harry's recent fatigue?

"We shall give Mr. Dashwood the benefit of the doubt," Elizabeth declared. She released his hand, freeing him to extinguish the candles. She watched as he snuffed out all but the one beside their bed.

"So, how did you spend them?" she asked.

"Spend what?"

"Your *last precious days of bachelorhood*—before you *lost your freedom?*" She gave him an insouciant look. "Another wife might take language like that amiss, you know."

"Then thank heaven I have only one." He blew out the last candle. "For if I had two with tongues as saucy as yours, I should never be able to keep up."

Ten

The imaginations of other people will carry them away to form wrong judgments of our conduct, and to decide on it by slight appearances.

—Sense and Sensibility, *Chapter 36*

"Now Kitty—I may call you Kitty, mayn't I, since we are to be family soon? Kitty, dear, I wouldn't bring this up to save my life if I didn't think it was something you ought to know. But people are *talking*."

Lucy Ferrars, her daughter in tow, had called upon Kitty and Elizabeth early. This was their second visit to the Darcys' townhouse, the first, motivated far more by duty than delight, having taken place the day Kitty and Harry's engagement announcement appeared in the papers. It had been returned with equal brevity and palpable lack of interest. Today, however, Lucy had made a dramatic entrance, announcing that she had desperately important news about Harry to impart.

Kitty held her breath, unable to utter a syllable as she sat beside Lucy on the sofa. Elizabeth had ordered tea, but no one save Regina partook of it. Kitty simply regarded Lucy in bewilderment as Harry's aunt completed her oratorical warm-up exercises, priming her audience with avowals of her reluctance to speak. As Miss Ferrars helped herself to a third jam tart, Elizabeth poured the last of the tea into Regina's cup and motioned the maid to bring more refreshments. She could only hope Lucy's gossip would run out before their provisions did.

Finally, Lucy got to the substance of her report. "At Almack's yestereve, Lady Pendleton told me that she saw Harry in Bond Street one night earlier this week, wearing the most peculiar clothing. A long coat with a full skirt and huge, embroidered cuffs—a ruffled shirt—high heels. The fashionable Harry Dashwood, in a suit so out of style it could have belonged to his great-grandfather! She could only surmise that he wore a costume. What else *could* she think? But when she encountered him in Hyde Park the next day and asked if he'd participated in a theatrical, or attended a masquerade, he claimed to have no idea what she was talking about."

This was Lucy's momentous news? "How well does Lady Pendleton know Mr. Dashwood?" Elizabeth countered. "She spied the costumed gentleman on a dark street. Can she be certain that it was he?"

"Quite certain."

"Lady Pendleton's youngest daughter's brother-in-law went to Eton with Harry," Regina declared with the air of one revealing profound truths. Unfortunately, the effect was marred by her need to dab jam from the corners of her mouth.

Elizabeth slept with Darcy, and she wasn't confident she could with certitude identify *him* so attired in a casual sighting on a dark street. She sensed, however, that any further attempts on her part to add intelligence to Lucy's "intelligence" would prove equally ineffectual.

"Well, then," Elizabeth conceded, "there is no denying her authority."

"None." Lucy shook her head sadly at Kitty. "I wouldn't trouble you with the incident, curious though it may be, for all the world. But it happened a second time. Mr. Sutton saw Harry the following night, dressed the same way. And in the morning, he denied it again!"

Elizabeth emitted an exaggerated gasp. "No!"

"Yes! And I'm afraid there's more." Lucy leaned toward Kitty, her voice dropping to a conspiratorial tone. "I do so hate to be the bearer of ill tidings, my dear Kitty. It pains me beyond anything. But it is best you hear of this from someone who loves him." She took a deep breath and touched her hand to Kitty's. "William Middleton encountered Harry on Wednesday evening outside Boodle's Club, and Harry gave him the cut direct—walked right past him without acknowledgment!"

"Not the cut direct!" Elizabeth said, her sarcastic tone completely lost upon Lucy.

"Indeed!" Lucy pressed a hand to her chest. "Can you believe it? Our Harry!"

Regina started on a fourth tart.

Kitty looked to Elizabeth, at last finding her voice. "William Middleton is one of Mr. Dashwood's particular friends. Neither could have mistaken the other."

"I am certain some explanation exists," she assured her sister. Elizabeth had her own theory about the events—if "events" they could be called without investing them with more significance than they deserved. She suspected Lucy still harbored ambitions of a union between her simpleminded daughter and the very eligible Mr. Dashwood. With Harry's mother now united in purpose, she had called this morning to launch a campaign against Mr. Dashwood's character in hopes that Kitty would cry off. Every charge Lucy had brought forth would be forgotten by the *ton* in less than a fortnight, but if in the meantime she could convince the inexperienced Kitty that his offenses held greater import, the way might be cleared for Regina to ease the sting of a broken engagement.

Elizabeth could see that tiny seeds of doubt had already taken root in Kitty's mind. It was time to end this interview.

"Mrs. Ferrars, we are most grateful for your kindness in coming to us with these reports. Is there anything further we must hear?"

"Gracious me, I hope not. You don't know how I pray that these are Harry's only transgressions."

Lucy looked as if she wished she had more bad news to spread so reluctantly, but having run out, she had little excuse to prolong her call. She soon rose and pressed Kitty's hand as she took her leave. "Do not let this morning's communication lead you to doubt Harry. What are a few barefaced denials and the mistreatment of a childhood friend? Try to disregard these incidents as you prepare for the wedding."

Regina cast a look of sympathy at Kitty, and one of regret at the remaining tart, before following her mother out the door.

Kitty sank back onto the sofa. "Lizzy, whatever can this mean?" Her voice trembled.

"It means nothing," Elizabeth responded vehemently.

"But Mr. Dashwood's behavior—"

"We have no assurance that these tales even involve Mr. Dashwood. We have never seen him in anything but up-to-the-minute attire. Whatever would he be doing going about dressed that way? More likely, Lady Pendleton and Mr. Sutton saw an actor who bears resemblance to Mr. Dashwood. And even if the gentleman in question were he, the only crime he stands accused of is going out in public unfashionably dressed. Howsoever that may constitute a hanging offense among the *beau monde*, within our own circle, I think we can forgive it."

"But what of his rudeness to Mr. Middleton?"

"All London has been cloaked in fog for the better part of this week. Perhaps Mr. Dashwood simply did not see his friend. Regardless, you should ask Mr. Dashwood himself about these incidents the next time he calls. He will soon be your husband—you owe him the opportunity to explain himself, and he may reveal information to you that he would not share with others."

She sagged in relief. "Of course you are right. Either his friends are mistaken, or there is some reasonable explanation for his conduct that will make perfect sense once we hear it. I only needed you to say aloud what I secretly hoped."

"Mr. Dashwood is a good man, Kitty. You could not have fallen in love with him otherwise."

Darcy, having left the townhouse before Lucy's arrival, missed the performance she gave the ladies, but he, too, heard news of Mr. Dashwood that day. He arrived early at the fencing club for his standing appointment with Lord Chatfield. While Darcy waited for the earl, an older gentleman enquired whether anyone in the room knew the present whereabouts of Mr. Dashwood. Darcy said he did not, but that he anticipated dining with him that evening and would be pleased to convey a message.

"Tell Dashwood that Felix Longcliffe doesn't appreciate being stood up. We were to match swords today."

"Perhaps there has been some confusion about the designated time," Darcy suggested by way of apology.

"He seemed perfectly clear about it at the Pigeon Hole last night."

Darcy hoped he misunderstood Longcliffe. "The Pigeon Hole?" He had heard of the notorious hell in St. James's Square. In addition to being a seedy gaming house that catered to a low clientele, it was said that one of the owners also operated a house of ill repute.

"Tumbled in with a bunch of rowdies, after they got tossed from one of the clubs," Longcliffe said. "A pretty high-flying crowd. Most of them were too foxed to hold on to their money long."

"How did Mr. Dashwood do?"

Longcliffe's brow creased. "I don't think I saw him actually play. Perhaps he was already cleaned out when he arrived.

Anyway, he and his friends were obnoxious, even by the standards of that establishment. When I suggested their conduct interfered with the pleasure of other patrons, he informed me in most impolite terms that none but his own pleasure was of consequence to him. I thought he was going to challenge me to an affair of honor, but then he looked at me closely and said, 'I know you—Felix Longcliffe.'

"How he knew my name, I cannot fathom, as I knew his only from hearing his companions bandy it about. It caught my ear because I knew another Dashwood years ago. Well, he stood there staring at me until he finally says, 'You've grown old.' 'I'm two-and-sixty,' says I. 'And still agile enough to cross swords with a young whelp who needs to learn a thing or two.' He said he wouldn't engage in an affair of honor with a man my age, but he would meet me for a sporting match if I named the place. So here I am, and he is nowhere to be seen!"

So troubled was Darcy by Longcliffe's account that he could not concentrate on his own match with Chatfield. The earl easily bested him in half the time of their typical contests.

"Care to try again?" Chatfield offered.

Darcy shook his head. "I have a dinner guest coming this evening for whom I need to prepare."

The earl regarded him quizzically. "Are not such matters Mrs. Darcy's province?"

"Not tonight."

"How intriguing. Perhaps I should drop by to see how things turn out. What is on the menu?"

"One young buck."

Eleven

M r. Dashwood did not come to dinner that night.
Or the following.

Or any night that week.

He sent his regrets, explaining only that urgent business
would prevent him from enjoying the pleasure of Miss Bennet's
company for at least a se'nnight, perhaps longer.

Elizabeth often caught her sister looking out the window down
to the street, as if willing Harry's carriage to appear. Kitty maintained her belief in Mr. Dashwood's character, but with each
passing day, uncertainty pressed more heavily upon her. Her
confidence, which had blossomed in the warmth of his regard,
now withered in his absence. Determined not to doubt him until
he could defend himself, she began to doubt her own ability to
hold his interest.

It did not help that each day brought more accounts of inexplicable conduct on his part. Whatever "urgent business" kept
Mr. Dashwood from Kitty apparently did not prevent him from
being sighted by everyone else all over town. Lucy's reports

126

were echoed by others of a similar nature, and while none of them accused Harry of any real harm, they combined to create an increasingly unbecoming portrait and a most perplexing puzzle. Lucy herself figured in some of the tales, apparently having been observed in deep conversation with Harry on several occasions after her call at the Darcys'. News of the tête-à-têtes confirmed Elizabeth's conviction that Mrs. Robert Ferrars schemed to alter Mr. Dashwood's marriage plans in her daughter's favor.

The story Darcy had heard at the fencing club constituted more worrisome intelligence. Not only did it reflect poorly on Mr. Dashwood's integrity, but as the week wore on it also seemed that Longcliffe's encounter had not been an isolated incident. Rumor said that Harry visited different clubs and gaming hells each night, and had begun to amass an odd assortment of new companions. Some were young men like himself, some were old, and a few bordered on ancient. But all of them were rakehells with devil-may-care attitudes and reputations Darcy only delicately hinted at to Elizabeth. She suspected that much of what he heard, he left unsaid to her, and to Kitty he said nothing at all.

Though Kitty's faith in Mr. Dashwood remained steadfast, Elizabeth's and Darcy's began to falter. Their greater knowledge of his alleged activities rendered them even more impatient than his fiancée for him to explain himself, and his reluctance to face them—for what else could be keeping him away?—only added to their misgivings.

"I declare, Kitty spent the better part of the day at that window," Elizabeth said. She and Darcy were alone in the drawing room, she halfheartedly working a satin stitch upon a handkerchief, he writing a letter at the corner secretary. Kitty had retired to her chamber immediately after dinner, and Georgiana had gone to a concert with the Gardiners.

"It is a shame you could not persuade her to join Georgiana and your aunt and uncle."

"She did not want to leave the house. It seems to me, however, that she stands a better chance of seeing Mr. Dashwood about town than by staying at home waiting for him to arrive at our door."

"If he does not present himself here on the morrow, I am going to call upon him again," Darcy said. He had gone to Harry's townhouse on Tuesday but had been forced to settle for leaving his card when Dashwood's butler told him the master was not at home. As Darcy retreated from the door, he'd spotted Mr. Dashwood in an upstairs window. While he understood the servant's statement had meant Dashwood was not receiving visitors—the *ton* drew a distinction between being physically at home and being socially "at home"—Dashwood's avoidance had not raised him in Darcy's esteem. Nor had the fact that four days later, Dashwood still had not returned the call. "Perhaps this time he will receive me."

Elizabeth struggled to loosen a knot in her thread. "I simply cannot reconcile these unfavorable accounts of Mr. Dashwood with the man we know. But the longer he stays away, the more I wonder if we ever really knew him at all." The whole matter had created dissonance within her. She had liked Harry, trusted him, but the facts surrounding his recent conduct cast him in an increasingly unflattering light. Had her instincts been that far off the mark?

The knot refused to unravel, and she set aside the needlework in frustration. She hadn't really felt like working on it; she'd taken it up this evening just to have some occupation beyond contemplating Mr. Dashwood's movements. As the handkerchief, however, was intended for Kitty to carry on her wedding day, the project only vexed her by reminding her of the doubts plaguing them all.

The sound of a visitor at the door drew curiosity from them both. "Who calls at this hour?" she asked.

Before Darcy could reply, Kitty rushed into the room. "Mr. Dashwood is here! I saw his carriage arrive."

Harry entered a moment later. The housekeeper trailed behind, belatedly announcing him. He immediately fixed his attention on Kitty.

"Miss Bennet." An air of weariness enveloped him. His eyes were red, with puffy circles beneath them that made them appear smaller. Faint stubble lined his cheek. His posture, though not stooped, failed to exhibit its usual erectness. As he beheld Kitty, however, his shoulders lost their slump.

"Mr. Dashwood." Darcy greeted him stiffly. "How good of you to call."

Harry wrested his gaze from Kitty to acknowledge Darcy and Elizabeth. "Forgive the lateness of my visit. I have been out of town and just now returned. I could not wait until morning to see Miss Bennet again."

"You are indeed tardy in presenting yourself here."

Mr. Dashwood glanced nervously from Darcy to Elizabeth. Darcy was using his most formidable tone, one that had intimidated older and more worldly individuals than Harry. When Darcy adopted that demeanor, even Elizabeth hesitated to cross him. She almost felt sorry for Mr. Dashwood. Almost. He still owed Kitty—owed them all—an explanation.

"I have missed you, Harry," Kitty said. "Where have you been?"

"In Devonshire. I visited my Dashwood relations."

"Mr. and Mrs. Edward Ferrars?"

"Yes. Also my aunt Marianne Brandon, and their mother."

Elizabeth regarded him skeptically, disliking the mistrust growing within her. "Mrs. Edward Ferrars told me she lives three days' journey from London. When did you leave for Delaford?"

"Friday last."

"And you returned today?"

"This moment," Harry said. "I did not even stop at my own residence, but came here straightaway."

The cool cast of Darcy's countenance revealed his displeasure. "We are to understand that you have not been in town these past nine days?"

"Just so."

The room fell silent. But in three minds at least, the falsehood echoed. Too many people, including Darcy himself, had seen Harry in the past nine days. He could not possibly be telling the truth.

Disappointment—in Harry, for Kitty—settled in Elizabeth's heart.

Harry regarded them all in confusion. "Miss Bennet, if I—" He broke off as if suddenly understanding. "I should have told you in my letter where I went. Forgive me. I did not mean to keep you in suspense for so long. My plan to travel to Devonshire was formed very quickly. I departed in haste, at too early an hour to take proper leave of you. When I wrote, I thought only to get a letter to you as soon as it could be delivered. I should have considered better what it contained."

"It's not that, Mr. Dashwood," Kitty said.

"Then what?"

Kitty looked deflated. A glance at Elizabeth implored her older sister to continue.

"A great many people have seen you in London during the time you claim to have been gone from town," Elizabeth said.

Mr. Dashwood shook his head. "I assure you, I have been in Devonshire. Or on the road in between. These people, whoever they are, must be mistaken."

"I am one of them," said Darcy.

Harry stepped toward him. "Upon my soul, Mr. Darcy, you must have seen someone else."

"In your own house?"

Harry opened his mouth, but no words came out. He stared at Darcy as if trying to comprehend him. "You saw me in my townhouse?"

"On Tuesday."

He pondered that a moment. "What was I doing?"

"Observing me from your window as I returned to my carriage. After you refused to receive me."

"I would never ref—" He stopped, seeming to remember something. "Which window?"

"The one in your bedchamber, I believe. Two stories up, overlooking the street."

Mr. Dashwood's bluff had been called. He looked bewildered at first, as if he couldn't believe his deceit had been discovered. Then agitation seized him.

"Forgive me, Miss Bennet," he said, putting on his hat. "I will call again in the morning, if I may. I—I have to go."

Darcy followed Mr. Dashwood down the stairs. He had words for Kitty's fiancé that ought not be spoken in the ladies' hearing. He stopped Harry in the front hall before he reached the door.

"Mr. Dashwood, have you anything further to say for yourself?"

"Upon my honor, Mr. Darcy, you quite mistake me."

"Your honor is in serious question at present. Perhaps you ought to swear on something more dependable."

"You doubt my honor because you think you saw me at a window?"

"No—because of some of the other places you have been sighted of late. Mr. Dashwood, do you honestly believe I would allow my wife's sister to marry a man who frequents gaming hells? Who surrounds himself with drunkards and rakehells?" He dropped his voice. "A man who visits nunneries?"

Harry turned white. "You accuse me of spending my time with prostitutes?" He looked as appalled by the idea as Darcy.

"I do not. But hearsay does." He glanced up to the drawing room, relieved to see that the door remained closed. "Mr. Dashwood, I do not, as a rule, give credence to public gossip. I have witnessed too many reputations unfairly destroyed by rumormongers to believe every *on-dit* that circulates. But when my own firsthand knowledge catches a gentleman in one lie, I find it hard to trust his word on other matters, or the principles by which he governs himself. I want to believe that the tales reaching my ears are not true, because I want to believe you are a better man than the one they describe. But you cannot restore my faith in your character without first revealing what you have actually been doing this week."

"I have been in Devonshire."

Darcy turned away in disgust.

"Mr. Darcy—" Harry moved round until he stood before him. He looked weary, and nervous, and more than a little desperate. He ran a hand through his hair, gripping the roots before letting go. "Something has happened—rather, may have happened— may be *happening*—" He broke off, distraught. "I cannot explain it just now."

Darcy studied Harry. He was obviously in some sort of distress. "Mr. Dashwood, are you in trouble?"

He shrugged vaguely. "No." He stared at some distant point. "Perhaps. I do not know."

What kind of mess had he gotten himself into? Was he in debt? Had he compromised a young lady? Darcy's mind raced with all the possible fixes in which an imprudent young gentleman could find himself. Despite recent events, Darcy still felt a strong interest in Mr. Dashwood's welfare. He wanted to assist Harry if he could.

"Mr. Dashwood, if you would but confide in me, perhaps I can help you out of this scrape."

Harry sighed and shook his head. "No. I— It may all prove to be naught."

"I wish you would reconsider."

"There is nothing to tell. At least, not presently." He crossed to the door. "Please excuse me, sir. I have to go home. There's something to which I must attend without delay."

Twelve

"Suspicion of something unpleasant is the inevitable conse-
quence of such an alteration as we have just witnessed in him."
—Elinor Dashwood to her mother,
Sense and Sensibility, *Chapter 15*

*D*arcy stood still for only a moment after the door closed
behind Mr. Dashwood.

"Mrs. Hale?" he called. "I require my greatcoat. I am going out."

The housekeeper hurried into the hall, followed closely by
Darcy's valet bearing his cloak. "Shall I have the carriage brought
round, sir?"

"No." If he was going to follow Mr. Dashwood, he did not
have time to order his own carriage. Besides, the family crest
on its door would give him away. "Summon a hackney."

Mrs. Hale's face betrayed a flash of puzzlement before returning to the standard-issue whatever-you-say-sir expression
of all well-trained English servants.

He jammed his arms into the coat sleeves. "Tell Mrs. Darcy
that I left with Mr. Dashwood and may be quite late."

"Tell her yourself," Elizabeth said as she reached the bottom
step. "But if you are leaving with Mr. Dashwood, where is he?"

The sound of Harry's carriage departing answered that query.
She raised a brow.

"Perhaps not so much *with* Mr. Dashwood, as behind him," Darcy clarified.

Her eyes widened. "You are following him? I shall need my mantle."

"You cannot come with me."

"Darling, Mr. Dashwood has already left. We haven't time to argue."

"How disappointing. He actually went home." Elizabeth leaned back in the hackney and pulled her cape about her more tightly. The warm spring day had given way to a cool night, and she wished she'd thought to bring her muff. She'd have to remember it the next time she flew out of the house on a whim to spy all night on a future brother-in-law. "But will he stay?"

"That is precisely what I intend to learn."

Darcy instructed their driver to remain at their present position, about thirty yards down the street from Mr. Dashwood's townhouse. The location offered a clear view of Harry's front door, a sight enhanced by the light of the full moon. Mr. Dashwood had just entered the house; his driver had then taken his carriage away. Fortunately, steady traffic in Pall Mall had helped prevent either man from noticing the Darcys' surveillance.

Candlelight brightened an upstairs window a few minutes after Mr. Dashwood's entry. "That is Dashwood's suite," Darcy said.

"If he simply goes to sleep, we are in for a dull night," she replied. Mr. Dashwood had looked so tired that he might just do that.

The window remained lit for some time, prompting in Elizabeth a desire to consult the hour. After her conversation with Professor Randolph some weeks back, she'd begun occasionally carrying the watch she'd received from him. She now withdrew it from her pocket and tilted it to catch the moonlight.

Darcy frowned. "What are you doing with that?"

"Determining how long we have been sitting here."

"No, I mean, why are you carrying that thing around with you?"

"Why not?"

"I dislike the idea of its being so close to your person."

"Now, Darcy, *you* are the one who keeps saying it is nothing more than a watch. If that is true, then what harm lies in carrying it?"

His silence transmitted his displeasure. He turned his attention back to the townhouse. A hackney stopped two doors down from Harry's, releasing a pair of older gentlemen who stood talking on the street long after the carriage departed.

"An hour, by the way," she said. "We have been sitting in Pall Mall over an hour. It is nearly half-past ten. How much longer ought we—"

"The light just went out."

Both of them now peered toward the darkened residence. It appeared as if Mr. Dashwood may have indeed retired for the day. No other signs indicated movement elsewhere in the house.

"Well, this was scarcely the night of debauchery we had been led to expect." Elizabeth slipped the watch back into her pocket. "I'm ready to return to a warm fire and— Oh! Now there is light one story down."

"That is the drawing room."

She burrowed farther into her mantle. "I suppose this means we shall be stopped here a little longer."

"It was you who insisted on accompanying me."

"I did not realize it would be so cold. Next time I shall dress more warmly."

"Next time I shall come alone."

The gentlemen who had arrived by hackney now walked to Mr. Dashwood's house and mounted the steps. "Darcy, look! Someone approaches the door."

"Sit back," Darcy instructed. "I do not want them to notice us. One of them is Felix Longcliffe."

"The man from the fencing club? Who is the other?"

"I do not recognize him."

Mr. Dashwood's servant answered the door and granted the gentlemen admission. No sooner had the door shut behind them, than another visitor arrived by private conveyance. This gentleman had to be at least eighty; he stooped heavily over his walking stick as he shuffled up the steps.

"Do you know him?"

"I believe that coach bears the Flaxbury coat of arms," Darcy said.

Two more carriages pulled up. Darcy didn't recognize the occupants or their liveries. "Miss Bingley once said that a thorough knowledge of drawing was essential in any truly accomplished young woman. Have I married one?"

Elizabeth almost laughed aloud. She labored to produce identifiable stick figures. "Would you *want* to have married someone admired by Miss Bingley?"

He withdrew a small notebook and pencil from his breast pocket. "Sketch the family crests on the sides of those two carriages as best you can."

Her artistic skills, aided by the lighting and angle by which she viewed the originals, rendered illustrations that any five-year-old would be proud to display. Her lines of partition were tidily executed, but her white horse rampant looked more like a small rodent, and the lion couchant resembled a rabbit suffering ear amputation.

"A new barouche just pulled up. How do the first two drawings come along?"

"My finest ever."

Darcy glanced at her efforts. "Perhaps we should simply write down descriptions."

In the course of an hour, twelve visitors entered the town-house. Darcy recognized one more on sight, and all but two of the others arrived in carriages marked by family crests. Most were far older than Harry; the gathering included at least three octogenarians.

The last man to arrive brought with him a trunk. The large ebony box was inlaid with gold images that caught the moonlight as the servants carried it inside.

"A most curious assembly," Elizabeth declared. From the look of the carriages, Mr. Dashwood had some very wealthy and influential friends. "And at an equally curious hour. If only we could see inside the drawing room." Given that the draperies were drawn and the room sat one story up, the possibility seemed unlikely.

The driver, who had done a fine job up until this point of minding his own business while indulging his eccentric but well-paying customers, now shifted in his seat. "Uh, sir? Any idea how long ye might be wantin' to stay?"

Elizabeth consulted her watch again. "It is nearly midnight," she told Darcy.

Candlelight appeared in Mr. Dashwood's suite once more. Its draperies opened.

"Driver, how would you like to earn an extra crown?" Darcy asked.

Thirteen

"How you will explain away any part of your guilt in that dreadful business, I confess is beyond my comprehension."
—Elinor to Mr. Willoughby,
Sense and Sensibility, *Chapter 44*

Lord Chatfield frowned as he scanned Darcy's list. "You wish to know what all these gentlemen have in common? Is this some sort of riddle, Darcy?"

"I am afraid not." Darcy paced the earl's library, hoping Chatfield could provide insight into the gathering he and Elizabeth had witnessed—or tried to witness—the night before. Their hackney driver had scaled a tree to peer inside Harry's window but had attained his perch only in time to see a white-robed figure draw the draperies once more. No other clue as to the activities within had presented itself until Dashwood's visitors had tumbled out—many of them deep in their cups—just before dawn.

Elizabeth still slept, but Darcy had risen after only a few hours. Eager to identify the men who had called upon Dashwood, he'd consulted his peerage books to match their coats of arms with family names, then had come to his friend. Lord Chatfield knew absolutely everybody worth knowing in London—from peers and politicians to poets, scientists, and scholars. The earl's own gatherings were legendary for drawing together seemingly disparate individuals for evenings of stimulating conversation. If any common interest linked the names Darcy had written down, Chatfield would know.

"Steepledown . . . Flaxbury . . . Westinghurst . . . Many of these men enjoyed considerable political influence years ago, but one hears little about them now." The earl leaned back in his chair and studied the list more closely. "Parkington is well known as an art collector. He owns an extensive collection of sculpture. I've never seen it, but I understand much of it is of a, shall we say, suggestive nature—definitely not something for public display. He was a notorious libertine in his day."

"So was Longcliffe." After encountering him at the fencing club, Darcy had made some enquiries about him. He was also a heavy gambler.

"Bellingford . . . Bellingford . . . Why is that name familiar?" Chatfield absently tapped his finger against the paper. "I seem to recall a scandal several years back. Something about a mistress. Whatever it was, it ended badly." He regarded Darcy apologetically. "I am sorry—I wish I could be more helpful. Might I ask where this list came from?"

"I would rather not say. At least presently."

"That's quite all right. I just thought the context might shed enlightenment." He scanned the names once more. "Darcy, may I keep this list for a day or two? I know someone who might be able to help us. I assure you, I will be most discreet."

"By all means."

Chatfield called upon Darcy the very next afternoon. The normally genial man appeared more serious than was his custom.

"Are Mrs. Darcy or your sisters at home?"

"No, they are gone out shopping."

"Good. I have news on the matter we discussed yesterday that I would not wish a lady to accidentally overhear."

Darcy ushered his friend into the library and closed the door. The earl declined Darcy's offer of refreshment, or even a seat.

"I hardly know where to begin."

"No one will interrupt us. Start wherever seems best."

Chatfield paused. "Perhaps I'll take that wine, after all."

Darcy pulled the stopper from a crystal decanter on the side table. The interview was not off to a favorable start for Mr. Dashwood. Chatfield was one of the most forthright men Darcy knew; his present hesitation presaged ill tidings.

"I shared your list with an acquaintance of mine," the earl continued, "a fellow highly placed in the Home Office. I kept your name in confidence, of course, though he was very curious about the source of the list—for reasons I shall soon relate."

"I thank you for your discretion." Darcy handed him the glass and poured one for himself.

Chatfield took a fortifying draught. "You have, I presume, heard of the Hell-Fire Club? Sir Francis Dashwood and his so-called Monks of Medmenham?"

"I know of it generally—what any young man hears from his schoolmates. But no real particulars."

"No one knows all the particulars, save those who participated in its activities, and most of them are long dead. The 'monks' kept the details of their rituals secret. Given what is known of their exploits, I cannot imagine what they considered too terrible to reveal. It was a most shocking organization."

"Most of the tales I have heard are too outrageous to be believed. Schoolboy exaggerations of sexual exploits and Black Masses."

"They are not exaggerations. The Friars of Saint Francis conducted obscene mockeries of Christianity. According to accounts, the rituals involved Satan worship, fornicating on altars, drunken orgies, black magic, and other wickedness I cannot even bring myself to say aloud. Its motto was *Fay ce que voudras.*"

"'Do what thou wilt,'" Darcy translated.

"And apparently, they did. Horrible, horrible business! Yet many of the club's suspected members were intelligent men who wielded considerable political power, especially during the years just before England's loss of the American colonies. Their influence secretly extended into the highest reaches of the government."

"But the Hell-Fire Club, so far as I understand, died with Sir Francis more than three decades ago. How does it relate to my present enquiry?"

"Darcy, all of the names on that list are men believed to have been members of the Hell-Fire Club. Not Sir Francis's inner circle, the superior members known as his 'Twelve Apostles,' but inferior—junior—members."

And Harry Dashwood was associating with them. Worse— had hosted a gathering of them at his home. To what purpose? A lark? A means of rebelling against his mother? A darker motive? Darcy could only begin to speculate.

"Is the organization still active?"

Chatfield shook his head. "Not to anyone's knowledge. But it is a secret society, after all, so who would know with certainty? I can tell you this—my source indicated that the government does not want to see the Hell-Fire Club rekindled. Given the current state of war with France, England cannot risk a group of depraved geniuses exerting the kind of political influence they enjoyed before the War of American Independence. Which is why your list generated no small amount of interest—one wonders how those names came to be collected, and why."

Though Darcy considered Chatfield a good friend and trusted him implicitly, he thought it best not to reveal Mr. Dashwood's involvement with the men in question. At least, not at the moment. Until he had a chance to confront Harry himself, he would not jeopardize Mr. Dashwood's reputation, or Harry's friendship with Lady Chatfield's brother, by informing the earl or anyone else of the gathering he'd observed.

And question Mr. Dashwood he would—this very day, if possible. If Harry indeed played with hell-fire, he dabbled in more danger than he realized. Someone needed to intervene before he got burned.

"I am in your debt," Darcy said. "I am afraid, however, that at present I cannot divulge the list's origin without betraying a trust."

"I understand."

"I hope my silence on the subject will not create difficulties between you and your acquaintance at the Home Office?

"Nothing too unpleasant. Though should you come into possession of evidence that the Hell-Fire Club is re-forming, he would be very interested in that intelligence."

"Of course."

He was not the only one.

Fourteen

"*O*h, why did we not come here earlier?" Kitty sighed bitterly. "Grafton House is always busy this time of day. We
never should have stopped at Layton and Shear's first."

"It is the sign of a successful season," Elizabeth responded.
"Do you think yourself the only girl in London preparing her
trousseau? We were fortunate to secure an appointment with
the mantuamaker before next week."

Elizabeth refrained from reminding her sister that the detour
to Layton and Shear's had been entirely Kitty's idea. She had
seen and passed on a lilac sarsenet during a previous visit to
the Henrietta Street silk mercer, and this morning, having
awakened with renewed interest in her trousseau after finally
seeing Harry again, she repented the decision. She had insisted
on returning to the shop directly they began the day's errands,
anxious lest some other young lady purchase the last yards
minutes before them.

Layton and Shear's had been crowded, forcing them to wait at
the counter nearly half an hour before anyone could attend to

them. When their turn did come, the shopkeeper immediately set their fears to rest by assuring them the desired sarsenet was still in plentiful supply. Kitty nonetheless bought a full ten yards, just to be safe. Georgiana, who had entered the shop with no personal errand, rewarded her own patience with a new pair of stockings.

From Covent Garden, they had proceeded immediately to Grafton House, only to find their favorite linendrapery teeming with even more customers. As they sized up the queue, they overheard one woman grumble that she had already waited a full three-quarters of an hour.

"Did you hear that, Lizzy?" Kitty moaned. "I had wanted to return to the house by now, in case Harry calls." Despite his promise to call the day before, Mr. Dashwood had not appeared, an omission which doubled Kitty's anticipation of seeing him today.

"We could come back here on the morrow," Elizabeth offered.

"Tomorrow?" Kitty's whole being reflected horror at the suggestion. "There won't be a yard of fabric left here tomorrow!"

Thirty minutes' time brought little change in their circumstance. Apparently, someone had neglected to inform them that this day had been designated specially for the indecisive to shop. Those waited upon ahead of them were thrown into acute distress by the choice between lawn or cambric, calico or muslin, patterned dimity or striped. One young lady, after examining every bolt of poplin in the shop, asked to see all of them a second time, then a third, before deciding upon a sprigged muslin instead. Her friend ordered gauze in silk, cotton, and linen rather than settle upon one. Elizabeth prayed neither would also ask to inspect lace or handkerchiefs.

Kitty occupied herself chiefly by fidgeting, to the point where Elizabeth was required to twice reach out to restrain the swing of her reticule. She then set about an intense scrutiny of every patron remaining between them and the counter, as if assessing how many minutes each might dally over her purchases. When that diversion ceased to amuse, as it did very quickly, her gaze drifted to the window.

"Lizzy! It is Mr. Dashwood—outside, looking through the glass!" She waved. "Do you think he sees me?"

She begged Georgiana to hold their place so that she might go speak with her fiancé, apparently willing to forsake all others on his behalf, but not her position in Grafton's queue. Georgiana readily consented, and Kitty and Elizabeth stepped out of the claustrophobic shop and into the street.

Mr. Dashwood continued to peer through the window.

"Harry, this is such a pleasant surprise!"

Mr. Dashwood glanced at her with mild curiosity, then wordlessly continued his examination of the linendraper's display.

Kitty's face flushed with mortification. Her gaze darted round to see whether anyone else had witnessed the deliberate slight. Unfortunately, two young ladies—they of the sprigged muslin and triple order of gauze—had emerged from the shop just in time to observe the insult. With titters of "cut direct," they scampered off to circulate the latest *on-dit*.

Kitty next looked to Elizabeth. Her eyes beseeched her older sister for guidance. Elizabeth took matters into her own hands.

"Mr. Dashwood, I should think you could spare your fiancée a moment's attention."

Harry stared at Elizabeth seemingly without recognition. "My—" His gaze ricocheted between Elizabeth and Kitty, before at last coming to rest on the latter. "Why, of course. Do pardon me, Miss—my dear. I was deliberating so deeply whether I liked those gloves in the window that I was quite insensible to all else."

His excuse did not fully satisfy Kitty but appeared to mollify her for the present. Elizabeth was rather less disposed toward forgiveness. His weeklong avoidance of Kitty, his manner during his most recent call, this latest rudeness—since securing Kitty's hand, Mr. Dashwood's conduct toward her sister had altered in a manner that did not bode well for Kitty's future happiness.

"Are not your present pair serviceable?" Elizabeth said frostily.

Mr. Dashwood looked less tired than when she last saw him—seemed, in fact, full of youthful *joie de vivre* straining to burst forth. A fresh haircut showed his eyes to advantage, and they reflected an intensity she'd not observed in him before. He must have caught up on his sleep since the midnight gathering she and Darcy had spied upon. She, on the other hand, was still dragging herself through the day. Given that he was the cause of her present lethargy, she resented him his liveliness.

"I find them a bit tight," he said. "Besides, I have just ordered two new coats and half a dozen pairs of pantaloons, and thought new gloves would complement them well."

"Why stop there? Add shirts and cravats to your order and you will have a trousseau to rival Kitty's."

"I have—a dozen of the former, and twice that number of neckcloths."

Elizabeth wondered at Mr. Dashwood's sudden wardrobe overhaul but simply added it to the rest of his recent inexplicable behavior. "We were disappointed by your failure to call yesterday. My sister, especially."

Kitty finally found her voice. "Yes, Harry. You had promised."

"I did? I—well, I suppose it just slipped my mind. I am terribly sorry to have kept such a pretty girl waiting." He cast her a rakish look. "If you will favor me with some attention tonight, I'll make it up to you."

Elizabeth blinked, taken aback by the suggestive undertone of his statement. Had it been deliberate? Given the accompanying look, she suspected it had. Fortunately, Kitty had not caught it, though Harry continued to regard her with an expression that threatened to make Elizabeth blush.

"You may join us for dinner tonight, Mr. Dashwood," Elizabeth said quickly, emphasizing the word "dinner" more heavily than she intended. "If you are not otherwise engaged."

"I shall, thank you." His countenance took on a more appropriate mien. "Will anyone else be of the party?"

"Only Mr. Darcy and his sister."

"I look forward to it."

"Splendid. Come round at the usual time."

Mr. Dashwood arrived an hour later than anticipated. He acknowledged his host and hostess with an odd blend of unnecessary formality for one who enjoyed such intimate acquaintance with them, and excessive familiarity for a gentleman who had not yet officially joined the family. He offered no excuse for his tardiness, but his jovial mood suggested that a previous engagement with a bottle of spirits might have contributed to the delay.

He greeted Kitty warmly—a little too warmly, in Darcy's opinion, even for a man affianced. There were limits to what a gentleman ought to say to a lady who was not yet his wife, especially in the hearing of others, and declaring that the sight of her caused him to look forward to their upcoming nuptials with "rising expectation" was beyond the bounds of decency. The comment, fortunately, escaped the understanding of both Kitty and Georgiana—so far as he could tell—but Elizabeth had immediately changed the subject.

Georgiana then, through no effort of her own, captured his attention. Mr. Dashwood expressed delight at dining with two such beautiful ladies, and enquired why no gentleman attended her this evening.

"I have no particular gentleman I cared to invite," Georgiana said.

"I'm sure many gentlemen would care for your particulars."

"Mr. Dashwood!" Darcy's shock was so great, it almost rendered him speechless. "I must have misheard what you just said to my sister."

Kitty looked bewildered by her fiancé's audacity. Georgiana grew flustered and ducked her head to avoid both Mr. Dashwood's and Darcy's gazes.

"Pardon me, Miss Darcy," Mr. Dashwood said, his expression anything but contrite. "I am afraid I forgot myself."

"I trust it will not happen again." Darcy let the matter drop for now so as not to embarrass the ladies further. But he intended to have a word with Mr. Dashwood in private later in the evening.

Once at the table, Mr. Dashwood entertained them with an anecdote peppered with so much vulgar cant that the ladies could hardly follow it—for which Darcy was grateful, because its subject was as inappropriate as the language in which it was expressed. The more he talked, the quieter everyone else grew.

When a servant approached to refill Harry's wineglass, Darcy discreetly motioned him away. Elizabeth caught the gesture and met his eyes across the table.

Is he drunk? she mouthed.

Darcy nodded. Inebriation was the only explanation he could conjure for Mr. Dashwood's extraordinary behavior. Either Harry did not hold his liquor well, or he had consumed a great deal more of it before his arrival than Darcy had originally suspected. Regardless, Darcy now intended to draw the evening to an early close, but tactfully enough to spare Kitty the humiliation of seeing her fiancé bounced from the house. As soon as the ladies withdrew, he would pour Harry into his carriage and send him home.

And call upon him bright and early tomorrow morning.

The meal, however, continued longer than Darcy anticipated. Somehow, between all the slang words and mild oaths to which Harry introduced his stunned audience, he also managed to eat more than Darcy had ever before witnessed him consume. Excessive drink evidently made Harry ravenous, as Darcy had sometimes observed in others. Mr. Dashwood partook of every dish, indulged in second helpings of most, and polished off three lemon ices at the end of the meal.

"You seem very fond of ices, Mr. Dashwood," Elizabeth observed.

"Exceedingly fond. A shame that they're so hard to keep in the summer, just when one wants them most. At Wes—my country home, I have a first-rate icehouse that supplies enough ice year-round to keep the cook's larder as cold as a witch's tit—"

Or as cold as Elizabeth's frozen expression.

"—so I can enjoy ices, or just about anything else, whenever I like. But this townhouse I'm saddled with has the most inadequate larder. The ice melts so fast that flavored ices won't keep at all." He broke off, suddenly pondering an idea. "Say, I bet a larder built deeper into the ground—well below the house—would hold the cold better. Ha! I'm going to make arrangements tomorrow to have one dug immediately! Then I can enjoy ices at midnight, if I wish."

Darcy had long observed the ability of excess liquor to inspire new levels of genius in its imbibers. Brilliant schemes seemed to proliferate in proportion to bottles emptied. "I expect your landlord might object to your excavating his house."

"Bah! He should thank me. And if he complains too much, I'll just buy the house."

Darcy knew full well that trying to reason with a drunk was a waste of breath. Yet he could not help himself. "Is this not a rather expensive undertaking, simply to satisfy impulsive cravings?"

"Perhaps, Mr. Darcy," he said with a devilish grin, "if you satisfied your own deeper desires occasionally, you wouldn't be so stiff." He chuckled. "As for me, I intend to buy many pleasures with my fortune."

Before Darcy could take issue with Mr. Dashwood's vulgarity, Elizabeth rose to her feet. "Kitty, Georgiana—I think it's time to leave the gentlemen and adjourn to the drawing room."

Past time. Long past time. As the ladies withdrew, Darcy regarded Mr. Dashwood with disgust. He'd hoped to question Harry this evening about the gathering at his townhouse, but Mr. Dashwood's present condition precluded an intelligible interview. The interrogation would have to wait for a more sober occasion. In the meantime, now that Darcy was at liberty to address Mr. Dashwood man to man, he intended to subject Harry's performance to a scathing review.

Mr. Dashwood slouched against his seat back and propped his legs on the chair next to him. He picked up his empty wineglass. "Have you any port about?"

"No."

"What? You're not all out?"

"I am out of a great many things at the moment, Mr. Dashwood. Patience is chief among them."

He laughed. "This is where you upbraid me for my sins against decorum."

"Correct."

"A flea bite. But do go on, if it will make you feel better." The younger man's cockiness provoked Darcy as much as anything had all evening.

"Mr. Dashwood," he said slowly, "you have insulted me directly. You have insulted my wife by arriving at her home intoxicated and conducting yourself in an appalling manner at her table. You have insulted your fiancée and my sister with ungentlemanly allusions. Because you are drunk, and out of a desire not to cause Miss Bennet any more upset than she has already experienced tonight, I have made allowances for your manners beyond anything I would tolerate from anybody else.

But I am done. I suggest you go home, sleep off your liquor, and endeavor to devise some way of atoning for the enormous affront you have visited upon this entire household tonight."

He rose and pushed in his chair. "Because, Mr. Dashwood, if this utter disregard for propriety continues, I may advise Miss Bennet and her father to rethink your engagement."

As far as Darcy was concerned, he was finished conversing with Harry for the evening. He turned to go.

"Do what thou wilt."

Darcy jerked round, stunned by the utterance. He blinked at Mr. Dashwood. "What did you say?"

Harry sprawled in his seat as if he hadn't a care in the world. He rolled the stem of his empty glass between his fingers, watching the last few drops of wine swirl in response. "Do what thou wilt."

Their gazes locked. Darcy read in Mr. Dashwood's eyes a hardness that hadn't been there before. At least, not before the gathering in Pall Mall. There was no mistaking him now, no need to give him any benefit of the doubt concerning his recent activities because he himself had just removed all doubt. Harry had indeed hosted a meeting of the old Hell-Fire Club. The only question that remained was why.

"Did you learn that motto from your new friends? The ones who called upon you the night before last?"

He laughed hollowly. "I would call them old friends."

"Yes, very old," Darcy agreed. "Old enough to have been Sir Francis's cohorts—members of his Hell-Fire Club."

"You mean the Monks of Medmenham." A sardonic smile twisted Mr. Dashwood's lips. "You surprise me, Mr. Darcy. I did not credit you with such penetration. But what does an upstanding gentleman like you know about the Friars of Saint Francis?"

"Enough to know that you flirt with danger if you seek to rekindle those fires." Darcy leaned toward him, resting his hands on the table. "What are you about, Mr. Dashwood? What attraction could that immoral organization hold for you, that you would jeopardize your reputation and honor to experiment with it? Those men you welcomed into your home are honorless scoundrels."

"They are men who know how to live. Not stiff-rumped pansies afraid of their own desires, who never act or speak but in deference to what might cause offense to their equally prudish acquaintances. Cowards who let 'I dare not' wait upon 'I would.'"

Such as himself? The insinuation was obvious.

Recognizing Dashwood's final words as an allusion to *Macbeth,* Darcy responded in kind. "'I dare do all that may become a man; who dares do more is none.'"

He was not about to sit in his dining room engaging in literary ripostes with an intoxicated fool. But he also was not yet prepared to abandon his attempt to redirect Harry's misguided steps—if not for Mr. Dashwood's sake, for Kitty's. With effort, he reined in his growing anger.

"Mr. Dashwood—Harry—trust me. You do not understand what you are getting yourself into by associating with—"

"Mr. Darcy, it is you who do not understand. You think yourself so wise in the ways of the world. But I have done more and seen more than you ever will; I have tried things you haven't the courage to imagine. I have not solicited your advice, nor do I need it."

Darcy clenched his fists in frustration. The confidence of one-and-twenty! Would that every young man entering his majority truly possessed the wisdom he thought he did. Unfortunately, it was apparent that only hard experience could teach Harry what he needed to learn. The best Darcy could hope for was to save Kitty from the carriage wreck Mr. Dashwood seemed intent on making of his life.

"I thought you a better man than this, Mr. Dashwood. I thought you a gentleman. But if you persist in clandestine proceedings and unpardonable public behavior, I shall have no choice but to dissuade Miss Bennet from allying her future with yours."

"As I said, do what thou wilt." He set his wineglass on the table upside down. Bloodred droplets rolled down to stain the white linen. "I intend to."

Fifteen

"His character is now before you; expensive, dissipated, and worse than both."

—Colonel Brandon to Elinor,
Sense and Sensibility, *Chapter 21*

*E*lizabeth waited in the drawing room with Kitty and Georgiana for the gentlemen to rejoin them. She expected Darcy and Harry would be closeted either a very short time or a very long time, depending on Mr. Dashwood's degree of inebriation. If their guest was too drunk for questioning, she doubted Darcy would have much else to say to him tonight.

"Lizzy, Mr. Dashwood seems so altered this evening. I feel as if I hardly know him."

Kitty's words echoed Elizabeth's thoughts. She wanted to reassure her sister, but hardly knew herself how to explain Harry's conduct. Drunkenness was no excuse—he should not have so compromised himself in the first place, let alone called upon his fiancée in such a state. But beyond that, the changes in his manner seemed to exceed the effects of liquor. Elizabeth had not been exposed to many men that far gone into their cups, but even so, she sensed something different in Mr. Dashwood, a more fundamental alteration that had taken hold before the alcohol and that would remain after his head ceased to ache in the morning. She'd perceived it earlier today at Grafton House, and could not yet define it, but it was there.

To Kitty, she merely said, "I am sure his devotion to you is constant. Rest easy in that." But the statement rang hollow in her ears, echoing her own uneasiness.

Mr. Dashwood and Darcy soon entered. One look at Darcy revealed to her that they had argued—she could read it in the tense line of his jaw. What an unpleasant evening this was turning into all around.

"Miss Bennet, I'm afraid I must take my leave."

Mr. Dashwood's announcement disconcerted Kitty, who glanced uncertainly from him to Darcy and back.

"So soon?"

"Unfortunately so." Harry raised Kitty's hand to his lips. He then turned it over and kissed the inside of her wrist, lingering over it long enough to make everyone in the room fidget. "Bonsoir, ma chérie."

Kitty turned deep scarlet. "Good—good night, Mr. Dashwood."

Harry next turned to Elizabeth. "Mrs. Darcy, I thank you for your hospitality." He reached for her hand.

Elizabeth hesitated, sincerely hoping her wrist wouldn't follow the same path as Kitty's, but Mr. Dashwood merely grasped her fingers in his palm. Nevertheless, she experienced a sense of revulsion at his touch—a reaction, she presumed, to his unconscionable conduct all evening.

She masked her discomfort, but he regarded her curiously. There passed between them something unspoken. Again, she had the sense that a shift had taken place within him. He was at once more and less the Mr. Dashwood who had entertained them at Norland—more intense in his address, more bold in his actions, more hungry in his pursuit of desires. Yet less disarming, less moderate, less kind. Where before his manner put one at ease, it now set one on edge. It was as if he'd lost his balance, and those around him shared that endless moment of anxiety before it is known whether one will fall.

"Take care of yourself, Mr. Dashwood," she said.

He stepped back, and the moment was broken. His expression became brash once more. "I always do."

Her husband's displeasure at the exchange was evident, and lingered longer than Mr. Dashwood. After their guest departed, Darcy's continued glower induced Kitty and Georgiana to seek the refuge of their own chambers for the night.

"You have been in ill temper since your private conversation with Mr. Dashwood," Elizabeth observed when they were alone. "What took place?"

"More of what you witnessed at dinner."

"Mr. Dashwood attempted to seduce you, too? I hope you told him I would object."

His scowl indicated that he was in no humor for humor. "I informed him that there were numerous elements of his behavior to which *I* object."

"And he said . . . ?"

"Essentially, that the devil may care, but he does not."

"Well!" She sank against the sofa, taken aback by this latest evolution—or, more accurately, devolution—in Mr. Dashwood's character. "Was it the wine talking?"

"I wish it were. Then we could hope he would awaken tomorrow embarrassed by this whole evening. But no, I think he knew exactly what he was saying to me, and the effect it would have. He knows everything, you see. At least, more than I do, or so he told me. He *is* one-and-twenty, after all—practically a sage."

"Careful—*I* am one-and-twenty."

"*You* possess common sense. I am in serious doubt as to whether Mr. Dashwood does."

"He had sense enough to fall in love with Kitty."

"And that is the last sensible act he performed. Since we left Norland, he has demonstrated nothing but poor judgment, self-absorption, and flagrant disrespect for the rules and conventions of society. He has brazenly told falsehoods right here in this house. He displays an irresponsible attitude toward money, a childish indulgence in the pursuit of pleasure, and an adolescent obsession with lewd innuendo. He has discarded his friends for the company of aging roués and blackguards—and all of this, on the eve of his marriage to a young woman of good family who cannot possibly countenance his conduct."

Elizabeth could not argue. Darcy had, in fact, articulated many of her own thoughts. "He was so affable when we first met him," she said. "Yet in the span of a fortnight, he has managed to offend nearly all his acquaintance—from his own family to William Middleton to us. At his current pace, the only persons still speaking to him by week's end will be the elderly gentlemen who gathered at his townhouse, and they, only because they cannot hear half of what he says and fall asleep through the rest." She shivered and crossed her arms in front of her. It had grown chilly in the room. "Did you learn yet who those men were?"

Darcy lifted the fire poker from its stand. "I learned more than I wanted to know."

"Well—who were they?"

"They were—are—former associates of Sir Francis Dashwood."

"That distant relation of Harry's? The man in the painting from Norland?"

"The same."

"You never told me what he was so infamous for—I assumed it was because Kitty was with us in the gallery that day. But we are alone now."

He turned his back to her while he stirred the embers. He took an overly long time about it; she'd never seen someone lavish half so much attention on a blaze.

"Darcy?"

He returned the poker to its place but continued to avoid her gaze as he crossed to the sherry decanter and busied himself in pouring a glass. "Sir Francis Dashwood founded a secret society that came to be known as the Hell-Fire Club."

"If it was a secret, how do people know about it?"

"Many of its suspected members were men of significant political and social standing. You have been in London long enough to know that nothing can remain a secret among the *ton* forever. Eventually, tales of the organization and its activities created an enormous scandal."

"Of what were the club's members accused?"

"Shocking acts of blasphemy and debauchery."

"Such as?"

"Deeds, Elizabeth, that a gentleman does not speak of to a lady." He replaced the stopper, but his hand remained atop the decanter.

"Not even to his wife?"

"*Especially* his wife."

He finally met her gaze. She'd expected his expression to be shuttered, for him to withhold himself from her along with the information he so obviously wished to keep back. But she instead found in his eyes a certain sadness that comes from knowing more than one wishes about the depths of human wickedness, and a desire to protect her from that. She let the matter drop.

"So, Mr. Dashwood brought the portrait of Sir Francis back to London with him, and now he's behaving like a rakehell himself and entertaining the old fellow's friends," she said. "One wonders what prompted this sudden interest in his family tree."

"It defies reason. Of all his ancestors, Sir Francis is the one Mr. Dashwood should least admire—especially now that he is engaged to a respectable young lady."

"Maybe that is his motive. By demonstrating to his mother what a truly wayward son he could be, he hopes to reconcile her to a marriage with Kitty as the lesser of two evils."

"If so, his method is shortsighted. He risks ruining himself in the process, and his behavior jeopardizes the likelihood of the marriage ever taking place."

"True. And were his plan indeed that of extorting his mother's approval, one might expect him to take Kitty into his confidence, which he has not. Instead, he left her bewildered by avoiding her for over a se'nnight."

Darcy studied his sherry glass, then set it down untouched. "Perhaps rather than bringing his mother around to his way of thinking, he has come round to hers."

"He regrets the proposal?" She contemplated that scenario. "His ardor has cooled, and now he wishes himself free to follow his mother's advice and marry more advantageously. So he conducts himself like a cad in hopes Kitty will cry off the engagement." She shook her head. "That might work if he confined his misconduct to Kitty alone. But his public behavior has left him ill qualified to recommend himself to another young lady, particularly one considered a better catch in the marriage market."

"I disagree. His misdemeanors among the *beau monde* amount to little of long-term consequence. So far as the Polite World is concerned, he has cut a few acquaintances on the street, been seen dressed out of fashion, and haunted some seedier gaming hells—nothing of which half the youngbloods in London cannot also stand accused. Even if the manners Mr. Dashwood exhibited here tonight find display in more public venues, his fortune can more than make up for that in the eyes of the right young lady's family, particularly if he eventually corrects himself. A month or year from now, when the *ton*'s interest has fixed upon someone else, his performance will be forgotten altogether or, at worst, remembered as an eccentric phase."

"But what about the gathering he hosted, this 'Hell-Fire Club'? Cannot his new associates damage his reputation?"

"At present, only you and I know about that meeting. Those who attended are unlikely to speak of it."

"Have you any idea what went on there? Do you think they have renewed their former activities? I cannot imagine Mr. Dashwood participating in acts so dreadful that you refuse to describe them to me." At least, not the Mr. Dashwood she thought she knew. But his conduct tonight left her doubting both his character and her own ability to judge it.

"I am afraid that I now believe him capable of anything."

"Can he not be saved?"

"I tried to prevail upon him, or at least gain his confidence, but he is past the point of listening to me." With an air of resignation, he sank into the chair opposite her. "I think we need to advise your father of the situation."

Had it gone that far, that fast? "We must be quite sure. One word from us, and the engagement will be broken." Along with Kitty's heart. "Perhaps if I talked to Mr. Dashwood myself—"

"Alone?" Darcy's expression made it clear what he thought of that idea.

"Do you not trust my ability to handle Mr. Dashwood?"

"It is Mr. Dashwood whom I no longer trust."

A Dashwood indeed called at the Darcys' townhouse the following day, but not Harry. Mrs. John Dashwood arrived as early as was socially acceptable, demanding to see Kitty. Elizabeth, who had been completing needlework in the parlor with Kitty, remained with her sister for moral support despite

Fanny's request for a private interview. Fanny's displeasure, obvious upon her arrival, was compounded by Elizabeth's polite unwillingness to abandon Kitty to a cozy tête-à-tête with her future mother-in-law.

Mrs. Dashwood accepted Elizabeth's invitation to sit, but perched so far on the edge of her seat that Elizabeth mused whether enough chair supported Harry's mother to keep her from sliding to the floor. Fanny managed, however, to maintain her balance, aided, no doubt, by the ramrod reinforcing her back.

"I have just left Harry in Pall Mall." Apparently, this declaration ought to have furnished the sisters with sufficient explanation for Mrs. Dashwood's present visit. They, however, required more clarification.

"I hope you left him well?" Kitty asked.

"I should say not!" Fanny scowled at Kitty as if she'd had something to do with it. Kitty melted into the sofa, holding her embroidery frame before her like a shield. Unfortunately, it lacked the power to deflect self-righteous indignation. "Oh, he was in high spirits, to be sure. But not well. Not behaving well at all!"

After the performance they'd witnessed the night before, Elizabeth could only imagine how Harry had treated the mother with whom he was already at odds. *That* was an exchange she wished she could have overheard.

"Since I returned to town, I have heard nothing but what a scapegrace my son is making of himself. I will not have him dragging the Dashwood name through the gutters of St. James's, to become the latest *on-dit* at Almack's. And I told him so. His aunt Lucy was there when I arrived, telling him the same thing."

How delighted Mr. Dashwood must have been, to have two harridans descend upon him in the early hours to continue Darcy's conduct lecture where it had left off the night before.

That Lucy had taken it upon herself to correct Harry surprised Elizabeth, as she presumed Mrs. Ferrars was still trying to maneuver her daughter into his affections, but perhaps hope that Regina would one day share the Dashwood name had motivated her desire to preserve it.

"The whole house was at sixes and sevens!" Fanny continued, apparently neither requiring nor desiring another participant in the conversation. "Workmen coming in to dig some sort of larder under the cellar! They continually interrupted us. You would think, from the amount of instruction Harry was obliged to offer, that he had just hired them this morning to start the project! Then two footmen brought a portrait of that dreadful Sir Francis down from Harry's chamber and on his orders started hanging it immediately—while we were sitting there conversing. The place was such a jumble I could scarcely hold his attention!"

"Mr. Dashwood has hung the portrait in his drawing room?" Elizabeth asked. She was starting to think Harry obsessed with his ancestor.

"Right above the fireplace! I didn't even know he'd removed it from Norland. I took one look at the thing and asked why he wanted that portrait displayed instead of the one I'd given him, and do you know what he said to me? 'Madam, five minutes in your presence have convinced me that Sir Francis is better company than any you can provide.' He said that! To his own mother!" She launched a piercing look at Kitty. "He never would have said such a dreadful thing to me before he met you, Miss Bennet."

At last, they had come to the purpose of Fanny's call. Harry's mother blamed Kitty for her son's recent alteration. Poor, bewildered Kitty, who was as helpless to account for it as anybody.

"Mrs. Dashwood—" Kitty began.

Fanny rose to her feet. "You have been a ruinous influence

on my son. He was never careless with his person, his fortune, or his reputation until he became engaged to you. Why you have molded him into a lesser man than he was, I cannot speculate, but I will tell you what I just told him: I will not countenance it. He may possess Norland, but I still have my own fortune to bequeath, and if he persists in this behavior I'll spin in my grave before it will be settled upon him. My mother divested her eldest son of his anticipated inheritance, and I can do the same. So in your own self-interest, Miss Bennet, I advise *you* to advise *him* to reform."

Kitty's trembling hand gripped the embroidery frame tightly. Her makeshift aegis having failed in its office, she absorbed the full force of Fanny's assault. "I shall do my best."

"I should hope so, Miss Bennet. Thus far, you hardly can have done worse."

Elizabeth could not bear to see Kitty so undeservedly abused. "Mrs. Dashwood, you cannot in fairness hold my sister responsible for your son's recent conduct. In fact, we are all as distressed by it as you are."

"Then why have you done nothing about it?"

"We have tried. But Mr. Dashwood, as you know, has his own mind, and at present seems disinclined to take direction from others."

Fanny regarded Kitty with disdain. "I should think a man's fiancée would possess *some* ability to influence him."

A few minutes ago, Kitty had exerted so much power over Harry that she was entirely answerable for his behavior; now she was condemned for not wielding enough.

"I should think his mother would, as well," Elizabeth said.

Fanny sputtered. "I cannot believe you would show me such disrespect as to—"

"It is no more than you yourself have demonstrated." Elizabeth had heard more than enough. While she did not want to damage Kitty's bond with her future mother-in-law, Fanny was already so decided against her sister that Elizabeth doubted any incivility on her own part could further fracture their relationship. She crossed to the drawing room door and opened it wide. "Come, Kitty. Mrs. Dashwood is leaving now."

Sixteen

"This seems to have been a day of general elucidation."
—*Elinor Dashwood to Colonel Brandon,*
Sense and Sensibility, *Chapter 30*

The whispers began in the theatre lobby.

The sounds of conversation and gossip always filled London's theatres before, after, and even during productions. Rumor and repartee supplied lines that rivaled those of the playwrights, while their speakers paraded in finery as elaborate as any costume. The audience itself—who was there, with whom, speaking to whom—formed as much of the spectacle as props and scenery, and often as much drama took place in the boxes, galleries, and pits as on the stages themselves.

This evening marked the first time, however, that Elizabeth sensed her own party was the subject of the *ouï-dire* that burbled through the theatre. She, Kitty, and Georgiana had taken a private box, and all hoped Miss Bennet would find some distraction from the fact that for three consecutive days, notes of regret instead of Mr. Dashwood himself had arrived at their door. He pleaded indisposition, claiming a disinclination to leave his bed. Elizabeth hoped the malady that kept him away might derive in part from embarrassment over his conduct the last time they had seen him, but she somehow doubted his ability to feel that much shame. Whatever the origin of his present excuse, she wished it swiftly dispatched, as she had seldom known the principals of a love match to spend so comparatively little time together during their engagement as Kitty and Mr. Dashwood had.

They'd arrived at the theatre to find it crowded. Tonight's comedy had opened the previous week to excellent reviews, so now it was a point of status among the *ton* to be able to boast of having seen the play before the rest of one's acquaintance. Elizabeth saw many faces she recognized, and many more she did not. She and her companions greeted those they knew and submitted to the usual small talk about the weather and Beau Brummell's latest *bon mot*.

As Elizabeth chatted with Mrs. Farringdale, a neighbor from Longbourn, she experienced an increasing sense of being watched. Surreptitious glances to the side and over Mrs. Farringdale's shoulder revealed that she was not imagining the attention. There were indeed gazes upon her—many gazes that darted away when challenged by her own.

Not until she and the girls climbed the grand columned staircase and entered their box did Elizabeth realize that she owed the notice to Kitty, whose share of it far surpassed her own. Throughout the theatre, furtive glances and open stares accompanied hushed dialogue and sympathetic head shakes. Georgiana was aware of them, too. Kitty held up her chin and did her best to ignore the attention, but something about her had captured the transient interest of the *beau monde* tonight.

"Lizzy?"

She patted Kitty's hand as she answered the unspoken question. "I do not know, Kitty. But I am sure we shall hear it ourselves soon."

Lord and Lady Chatfield entered their box, separated from the Darcys' by three others. Elizabeth nodded in greeting at the countess and privately resolved to speak with her during the interval if possible. Perhaps their friends had heard the gossip circulating about Kitty and could enlighten them as to its nature.

At the close of the first act, Elizabeth stated her intention of seeking out the Chatfields and invited the girls to join her. Kitty vacillated. Staying in their box insulated her from having to speak directly with anyone they might encounter in the corridor, but at the same time prominently displayed her to the rumormongers. Georgiana suggested that they two remain together. They would create the appearance of being too engrossed in conversation to notice the twitters, and Kitty would turn toward Georgiana so as to offer most of the house only a profile view of her face. In that posture, though she might still be observed by those who would dissect her every expression for hidden meaning, she at least would not be forced to witness their scrutiny. Kitty gratefully seized upon the solution, and Elizabeth headed off.

She encountered Lady Chatfield in the hallway behind the boxes, the young countess having left hers on the same errand. Her ladyship moved with a natural grace Elizabeth knew she herself could never hope to achieve.

"Mrs. Darcy, I was just coming to bid you good evening." Her smile at their meeting was genuine, lighting her delicate features. Her eyes, however, betrayed a hint of anxiety. "Are you and your sisters enjoying the performance?"

"It is diverting," Elizabeth responded. Similar conversations babbled around them in the busy hallway. "Though perhaps not quite enough so, tonight."

The countess drew her toward the wall, where it might be hoped that they could converse unheard. "You and Miss Bennet have heard the news, then? It must have been a terrible shock to her. I am so terribly sorry."

Foreboding swept through her. "No, we have not heard the gossip—only surmised from everyone's behavior that it had something to do with Kitty. I hoped perhaps you could tell me what is being said about her."

"Oh, dear." Lady Chatfield's smooth brow wrinkled. "I do not want to be the bearer of ill tidings."

"Better for me to hear them from a friend."

"I suppose so." They stood near a column that isolated a small pocket of the corridor from the rest. No one else lingered by it, as it would obscure from view anyone so positioned and most of the *ton* lived to be seen. The countess led her to the column, a move that made Elizabeth's chest tighten. Whatever she had to impart must be dreadful indeed. After all, everyone else in the theatre had already heard it, so Lady Chatfield sought privacy not to protect the intelligence itself from eavesdroppers, but to protect Elizabeth from being observed during the moment of revelation.

"Mr. Dashwood has taken a mistress."

Elizabeth was rendered speechless for a moment. When she recovered, she reminded herself that rumor and fact often were not closely acquainted. Her eyes roamed the crowd, seeing not individuals, but a great monster with a small mind and a thousand mouths that fed on innocent people such as her sister in its quest for entertainment and self-aggrandizement. It had seized upon Harry's recent licentiousness and invented a scandalous tale for its own amusement.

"The report cannot be true. What a horrible falsehood to spread before someone's wedding!"

The countess appeared more grave than Elizabeth had ever seen her. "Mrs. Darcy, I'm afraid it is no lie. I learned it this afternoon from my brother Phillip, who had it straight from Mr. Dashwood himself. The gossip started yesterday—rumors of a liaison between Mr. Dashwood and a nameless woman. Phillip took no heed of it when he heard it at the club. But he called upon Mr. Dashwood this morning and found him at breakfast with his paramour."

"Could not the woman he saw simply have been invited to breakfast?" Such an invitation still raised questions but offered a more palatable explanation than the alternative.

"I understand she was in a state of extreme dishabille."

"And Mr. Dashwood allowed her to be seen that way by his friend?"

"Phillip said the lady was concerned by their discovery, but Mr. Dashwood was shameless as could be. In fact, he found the whole scene highly amusing."

Elizabeth's stomach sickened. Her sister's fiancé had taken a lover. The faithless Harry Dashwood had not only broken his vows before even speaking them, he had flaunted his infidelity before his friend—and, it seemed, before all London. She recalled his recent claim of indisposition, and her discomfort gave way to disgust. Was this how he had occupied himself the past three days? Disinclined to leave his bed, indeed!

"Who is the *lady?*" Her emphasis on the last word revealed how lightly she used it.

"Phillip did not say, I did not ask, and so far the *beau monde* does not know. My brother did divulge to me, however, that she is married."

So Mr. Dashwood had managed to damage someone else's marriage, to injure another spouse, in addition to his own. No—not his own. A marriage between Harry and her sister now was out of the question. Her heart ached for Kitty.

Around them, the crowd started to file back into the auditorium in anticipation of the second act. She gazed at the entrance to her own box, dreading the conversation she must have with her sister tonight. It would not come until she'd whisked her safely out of this place, but come it must. Mr. Dashwood's association with their family was ended.

Seventeen

"Much as you suffer now, think of what you would have suffered if the discovery of his character had been delayed to a later period."

—Elinor Dashwood to her sister Marianne,
Sense and Sensibility, *Chapter 29*

I wish she would allow me to handle this for her."

Elizabeth wished so, too. Darcy would deliver the set-down that Harry Dashwood deserved. Kitty's heart still lay in too many pieces for it to have hardened against him enough to fully castigate him for his villainy, and Elizabeth feared the imminent conversation would only lead to its being shattered twice in four-and-twenty hours. She would be happier not to provide Mr. Dashwood that opportunity.

"Kitty wants to break the engagement herself." *Needed* to do so, in fact. Needed to see his expression when he issued an explanation, or uttered more lies, or brazenly mocked her naïveté—whatever response the increasingly unpredictable Mr. Dashwood might offer. Though Elizabeth's first instinct was to protect her sister from the unpleasant encounter ahead, she was glad to see Kitty taking a stand for herself. No matter what words fell from Harry's lips, the engagement was over; to that much, Kitty had committed. She would leave Pall Mall minus a fiancé but with her self-respect intact.

Elizabeth and Darcy waited in their foyer for Kitty to come downstairs. The three of them would go together to Mr. Dashwood's townhouse. He was not expecting them, but he *would* receive their call. On that point, Darcy and Elizabeth were determined. This matter would be resolved today. All that remained was to establish how much Kitty would rue ever having met Mr. Dashwood in the first place.

"Here she comes," Darcy said.

Though Kitty had risen puffy-eyed from a sleepless night, Elizabeth's maid had taken such care with her appearance that she looked every bit a young lady worth any gentleman's notice. She carried herself with dignity as she descended the stairs, and held up her chin with barely a tremble.

"I am ready."

If Harry Dashwood was still capable of regret, Elizabeth hoped it would pierce him at the sight of her sister this morning.

"This interview will go quickly, Kitty," Elizabeth said. "And should it become too unpleasant, Darcy will intervene."

Kitty merely nodded her agreement.

The ride to Pall Mall was quiet, especially in contrast to the bustle in which they found Harry's townhouse upon their arrival. Sounds of construction below and rearrangement above resonated throughout the residence. The subcellar larder project was well under way, and Mr. Dashwood apparently intended to celebrate its installation by reorganizing his furniture.

The housekeeper, a dour woman who looked as if she'd been in service forever, admitted them. Her gaze assessed them as they entered. Elizabeth instinctively disliked her.

"Did you not say a manservant turned you away when you last called?" she asked Darcy.

"Perhaps he has exchanged his salver for a shovel."

They were forced to wait in the foyer ten minutes before being shown to the drawing room, as the staircase was monopolized by the removal of a very large and—from the groans it forced from the three footmen who struggled with it—very heavy mirror. The style of its detailed gold frame suggested it might be an antique and piqued Elizabeth's curiosity. She felt at once drawn to and repelled by the looking glass; a sudden urge to gaze into it seized her, but her feet remained rooted to the floor. It was as if her body refused to follow where her mind would go, forbidding her to take close interest in anything having to do with Harry Dashwood.

As the servants wrestled the mirror down the stairs, it caught a beam of sunlight lancing the transom window. Golden arcs bounced off the varied surfaces of the gilt frame to splay upon the walls, and the glass itself reflected a fiery glow. The burst of brightness temporarily blinded one of the footmen, who cried out and stopped short. His sudden halt unbalanced his assistants, and for a few heart-stopping moments it appeared that the servants and treasure would tumble down the stairs together.

"Don't drop it, you fools!" Mr. Dashwood's voice echoed from above. "That glass cannot be damaged!"

The men somehow regained their grips and footing. Elizabeth exhaled. As they slowly continued their descent, she raised her eyes to see Mr. Dashwood monitoring the proceedings from two flights up.

"Careful!" He bounded down to hover over them as they negotiated the final few steps. When they reached the base of the stairs, they gingerly leaned their burden against the wall and paused to catch their breaths.

"Pack it up securely for the journey. I do not want it arriving at Norland in pieces." Mr. Dashwood then acknowledged Kitty and the Darcys. "Your visit is a pleasant surprise," he said. "Do come upstairs."

They followed him to the drawing room. He offered them a drink—some sort of sulfur-smelling liquor he called "brimstone"—but they declined. While he poured a glass for himself, Elizabeth noted the portrait of Sir Francis above the fireplace, as

Fanny Dashwood had described. She was struck, on this viewing, by how very much Harry resembled his ancestor not only in physical person but also in character. Their bearing at this moment was identical, their facial expressions the same, their countenances nearly indistinguishable—and their reputations more alike every day. Sir Francis may have been rich, but Harry had chosen the poorest of his relations to emulate.

"You must be feeling better if you plan a trip to Norland," Elizabeth observed. In truth, however, he did not look altogether well, and had she not learned from Lady Chatfield the real reason he'd lain abed the past three days, she would have believed his recent claims of indisposition. His complexion seemed paler, and his jaw more slack than when she'd seen him last. Dissipation was not a flattering cosmetic.

"The glass is going. I am not."

"I thought you were enamored of it?" Darcy asked.

"It has become rather too familiar to me." Mr. Dashwood tossed back his drink. He poured a second, then sat on the sofa and patted the place next to him. "Kitty, love, come sit beside me."

She instead moved one step closer to Elizabeth. "I think I shall stand."

He shrugged and rose. "As you wish. I would never deny a lady her pleasure."

"Miss Bennet has a matter she needs to discuss with you," Darcy said.

"Indeed? I am all attention."

Kitty looked uncertainly at Darcy and Elizabeth, then took in a deep breath and began. "Mr. Dashwood, it has come to my knowledge that—" Her gaze slid back to Elizabeth, who nodded in encouragement. "That is, I've been given to understand that—" She became flustered.

Amusement played at the corners of his mouth. "God's teeth, child! Spit it out before we all die of old age."

Kitty squared her shoulders. "Mr. Dashwood, do you have a paramour?"

He did not so much as blink. "Yes. Do you?"

Her eyes widened, and she took a step backward. Elizabeth caught her elbow to steady her.

Darcy approached him. "You insult Miss Bennet with the very—"

"I believe this conversation is between me and my fiancée."

"Former fiancée."

"Indeed?" He glanced from Darcy to Kitty. "Is this your wish? To break our engagement?"

She swallowed. "Can you explain why I should not?"

"So I have taken a lover. Take one yourself, if you like."

"Mr. Dashwood!"

"Mr. Dashwood!"

The first exclamation was Darcy's; the second, following hard upon, was Kitty's. Darcy appeared ready to choke the cocky youth. He opened his mouth to say more, but Elizabeth stayed him with a look. "Go on, Kitty," she said.

"Mr. Dashwood, I hardly know you anymore." Kitty repeated the words she'd rehearsed with Elizabeth this morning. "You are not the man I consented to wed. Ever since we returned from Norland, you have treated me and my family with disrespect."

"How so?"

"Through your conduct toward me and your falsehoods to me. You lied about being indisposed these past three days—"

"I said I could not rise from bed. What you inferred from that is your own misconstruction."

"You lied about not seeing me at Grafton House."

"I acknowledged you as soon as you spoke to me."

"You lied about having gone to Devonshire—"

"Devonshire? Why the devil would I go to Devonshire?"

"That is the very thing I wondered as you stood before us

insisting that you had." Her voice wavered. "Mr. Dashwood, I don't understand what has come over you. My affection for you would have enabled me to bear a great deal, but I cannot, and will not, tolerate a mistress."

"Then I hope you enjoy leading the apes."

Kitty looked as if she'd been slapped. Indeed, indignation stained her cheeks red. "I do not intend to die a spinster."

"Oh, Kitty, you are so green! That's what I found charming in you. Your husband, whoever he is, will have a lover—perhaps a dozen of them. And if you think he does not dally, that only means he is less honest about it than I."

Kitty's face contorted at the bleak portrait Mr. Dashwood painted of men's fidelity. Even Elizabeth cringed at his cynicism.

"Not all men share your dishonorable nature," Darcy said.

"Of course you would say that, Mr. Darcy. You must—your wife is present."

"I think we have all said quite enough," Elizabeth declared. She took her sister's hand. "Come, Kitty. Mr. Dashwood can add nothing worth your hearing."

Kitty stood motionless, seemingly unable to wrest her gaze from Mr. Dashwood's face. It held complete indifference. Her own exhibited an expression so full of sorrow and incomprehension and hurt and grief that Elizabeth suffered to witness it.

"Come," Elizabeth repeated gently.

They went downstairs, where Mr. Dashwood's footmen were covering the mirror in preparation for its transport to Norland. Kitty paused to cast a final look of regret toward the drawing room above.

Elizabeth put her arm around her sister's waist and directed her toward the door. "You are better off without him, Kitty," she said. "Though the broken engagement pains you today, you shall be relieved by it tomorrow."

Kitty nodded and allowed herself to be led away. Elizabeth's own gaze rose one final time to the drawing room door. Her mind's eye compared again the Dashwood on the sofa to the Dashwood above the fireplace. Their uncanny resemblance struck her. Which one of them would time prove the greater miscreant?

Her money said the one swallowing brimstone.

Eighteen

"As he required the promise, I could not do less than give it."
—*John Dashwood to Fanny Dashwood,*
Sense and Sensibility, *Chapter 2*

*Y*ou returned home early." Darcy, having himself just entered the townhouse, helped his wife remove her wrap.

"Mr. Dashwood was there."

"I see."

He had expected to arrive home to an empty townhouse but had found the ladies returning at the same time. Elizabeth had escorted Georgiana and Kitty to a ball, where all hoped the amusement would elevate Kitty's spirits. In the fortnight since she broke her engagement, Kitty had done her best to project an air of cheerfulness to those around her, but she was a poor actress. Anyone could see that Mr. Dashwood's mistreatment had left wounds that would not soon heal.

Kitty said little as she and Georgiana removed their own wraps. He'd never known a young lady to return home from a ball in such subdued spirits. Out of deference to Kitty's feelings, Darcy withheld further comment on the owner of Norland in her presence. But he gave free rein to his own thoughts. A plague take Mr. Dashwood! The scoundrel had also been the reason Darcy cut short his evening at White's.

In a span of mere weeks, Mr. Dashwood had risen to prominence as the Bacchus of the *beau monde* and had attracted to himself an entourage of like-minded new friends bent on testing the limits of how far decent society would excuse dishonor in men of fortune and rank. The Polite World was at once repulsed and fascinated by the new Pied Piper of London, scandalized by the spectacle but unable to tear away its attention. Drawing rooms and coffeehouses reverberated with tales of his exploits—speculation as to the identity of his mistress, lurid accounts of parties he'd hosted, amazed descriptions of his capacity for drink and boldness at games of chance. It was said his appetites, for everything from wine to women, were insatiable.

The Darcys were no longer the only ones drawing comparisons between Harry Dashwood and his notorious ancestor. Sir Francis enjoyed fresh renown in the discourse of the *ton,* and it was speculated that Harry would achieve even greater heights—or depths—of infamy. The Hell-Fire Club was openly discussed in gentlemen's clubs, and even ladies became acquainted with its name, if not its more salacious details. It was even said that Harry was Sir Francis reborn, his new band of merry men the former Monks of Medmenham, all reincarnated from the ashes of the underworld to fan the flames of Hell-Fire on earth once more.

That last, of course, was fiction surpassing anything Mrs. Radcliffe could write, but the gentlemen at White's Club tonight had talked of little else. Darcy had quickly become weary of the subject and departed.

Kitty and Georgiana bade them good night almost immediately and went to their own chambers. When Elizabeth's sister was out of auditory range, he turned to his wife.

"How was Mr. Dashwood this evening?"

"About the same. No—worse. Poor Kitty couldn't bear to be

in the same room with him. Fortunately, he spent most of his time at the card tables."

"He gambles so much at the clubs that I wonder he troubled himself to attend a private ball to hazard his fortune."

"He seemed to be there with his Ferrars relations. Lucy Ferrars dragged him away from *vingt-et-un* long enough to dance a set with Regina, and another with herself. Now that he is a free man once more, I think Mrs. Ferrars works harder than ever to orchestrate a match between Mr. Dashwood and her daughter. They had their heads quite close together several times."

"She is not bothered by his licentiousness? Or his mistress?" The identity of Harry's paramour remained secret, but her existence was by now generally known.

"So long as he has money, matters of character would constitute secondary considerations—if, indeed, considerations at all—regarding any gentleman who paid court to Regina. Lucy intends a profitable match for her daughter, and suitors are not exactly circling."

"They probably fear being devoured if they get too close."

"Darcy!" Despite the admonishment, she laughed. "Indeed, Miss Ferrars needs to catch a wealthy husband, for it may require a fortune to feed and clothe her. But your remark applies as much to Mrs. Ferrars as to her daughter. In many ways, she is as hungry as Regina. I almost feel pity for Miss Ferrars—she's a simple girl at the mercy of an avaricious mother to determine her future happiness."

"She is a willing participant in her own auction. Like most of society's debutantes."

"If they aspire to no better than Mr. Dashwood, they can have him."

"Did Mr. Dashwood have the effrontery to address Kitty?"

"Thankfully, no. But tonight marks the third time this week she's encountered him in public. The mere sight of Mr. Dashwood is upsetting enough to her, especially since his immoderate habits seem to be taking their toll on his physical person. You should have seen him this evening, Darcy. He looked most unattractive—his complexion red, his cheeks heavy, his new clothes already too snug. I think he's gained more than a stone in only a fortnight."

"Too much of that brimstone concoction. Or too many lemon ices from that ridiculous larder he built. Perhaps he and Miss Ferrars are well suited, after all."

"His appearance cannot help but remind Kitty of how much altered Mr. Dashwood is in character from the man she thought she knew. But beyond that, their mutual attendance at functions sends society's gossip vultures circling. Their eyes stalk Kitty relentlessly, waiting to pounce upon the slightest word, expression, or gesture that could betray her present feelings toward him, so that they can describe her suffering in minute detail to their friends the next day. How can she possibly enjoy herself under that kind of scrutiny? And even if her heart were able to accept the attentions of another admirer, what gentleman will approach her under such intense exposure? When we left, not a single partner had invited her to dance."

"If her time in London is no longer bringing Kitty pleasure, let us offer to take her home. The season is nearly over. By next spring, she will be ready to hear the addresses of a more worthy suitor, and the *ton* will be ready to let her."

"You are committing to doing this again next season?"

"If Kitty can bear it, I can." Actually, the thought made Darcy's head ache. Their months in London had been a failure all round—he had not even managed to find a suitable clergyman to fill the Kympton living. They would all have done better to stay in Derbyshire.

"I will suggest it to her. I believe she wants to go home, and would have asked us herself were it not for my mother's exhortations to punish Mr. Dashwood's wrongdoing by setting her cap for someone better."

"Mr. Dashwood is unlikely to care whom Kitty eventually weds."

"True. But marriage is my mother's solution to most problems."

The sound of a carriage arriving drew their attention. It was late for a visitor. Darcy crossed to one of the sidelights that flanked the door and looked out toward the street.

"Lord Chatfield is here."

"Are you expecting him?"

"No." He frowned. "I hope nothing is amiss." He and the earl had their regular fencing appointment on the morrow. If Chatfield sought him out tonight, he must have business that could not wait. He opened the door before his friend had so much as raised the knocker.

"Darcy!" The earl's expression revealed surprise at being admitted to the house by the master himself.

"I was in the hall and heard your horses. Do come in."

"I hope I don't disturb you too late?"

"Of course not."

The earl greeted Elizabeth, who echoed Darcy's assurances of Chatfield's welcome at any hour, then turned to Darcy. "I wonder if I might trouble you this evening to discuss a matter of business?"

Elizabeth excused herself so that the two gentlemen might speak privately. Darcy led Chatfield to the library, where he hoped his curiosity would be quickly assuaged. The earl was so well connected, Darcy could not guess the nature of business that would require his aid above that of greater men Chatfield numbered among his friends, nor that would necessitate such urgent action as the timing of this visit suggested.

As Darcy had planned to spend the evening away from home, the fire in the library had not been lit, and the air held a chill. Rather than summoning a servant, whose intrusion would delay the earl's business further, he knelt before the hearth to light the fire himself. Chatfield, meanwhile, took his customary seat but did not occupy it with ease. He leaned forward, his elbows on his knees, his hands gripping his hat rather too tightly for the long-term welfare of its brim.

"I have never known you to appear so grim, Chatfield."

"I have never had so much cause." He released a sound of disgust. "I have been these past two hours closeted with Lady Chatfield's brother Phillip. The countess and I are both deeply concerned about the company he keeps of late."

Darcy began to suspect the origin of his friend's distress. "Mr. Dashwood?"

"Mr. Dashwood." He paused, watching Darcy nurture the fledgling flames. "It appears that Sir Francis's spiritual heir has indeed restarted the Hell-Fire Club, and Phillip is one of its members."

"If you speak of these absurd tales of reincarnation—"

The earl shook his head. "I speak of facts. Since you shared that list of names with me, the authorities have maintained watch on those gentlemen. They, in turn, have led the observers to Mr. Dashwood. He is the other common link for the men on that list, is he not?"

"Yes," Darcy confessed. "I drafted the list after observing all of those men calling at Mr. Dashwood's townhouse. Pray forgive my not revealing that at the time. When I showed you the list, he was still engaged to Miss Bennet, and I did not want to cause him unnecessary trouble. Even now, I have no proof that verifies the existence of a new Hell-Fire Club."

"I do. Phillip admitted as much to me when I confronted him today. Mr. Dashwood has brought those old members together with younger ones to corrupt a new generation. He's hosted gatherings at his house and other locations Phillip would not name, to conduct activities also held in secret. Much to my frustration, Phillip will drop only smug hints about their goings-on, considering any further communication a betrayal of a leader he has come to idolize beyond my comprehension."

"I cannot myself understand the attraction of the Hell-Fire Club for any of them, Mr. Dashwood included."

"They are callow boys who play at the games of men they should revile, not revere."

Satisfied that the blaze was well established, Darcy rose but remained standing near the hearth. "Is Phillip being watched?"

"I assume so. As I told you before, there are many in Parliament and the upper reaches of the government who do not want the Hell-Fire Club influencing England's politics again." He stared into the fire. "I fear for him, Darcy. Powerful individuals are committed to stamping out this new Hell-Fire Club before it ignites into a full-blown version of its former self. I'm afraid Phillip's involvement will ruin him—politically, socially, perhaps even financially or physically, the way these fellows gamble and drink. Moreover, I fear for his soul. Surrounding himself as he is with moral corruption—" He met Darcy's gaze. "Lady Chatfield grieves to see the changes wrought in her brother already."

Darcy nodded. "We witnessed Mr. Dashwood's transformation."

"I realize that relations between you must be strained since Miss Bennet broke their engagement. But might you speak to him about this? Mr. Dashwood respects you—I could see that the day he came with you to meet Mr. Young. Can you not advise him that continuing this Hell-Fire nonsense jeopardizes his own welfare?"

"I have tried. When he was yet engaged to Miss Bennet, I attempted to explain just that. If he would not heed me then, I doubt he will hear me now."

Chatfield rose. "Then might you at least persuade him to exclude Phillip from the club? I beseech you, Darcy—if not for me, for Lady Chatfield. My wife cannot rest easy while her brother involves himself in such madness."

Darcy knew not what to say. He sympathized with his friend. He and Elizabeth had been fortunate enough to rescue Kitty from the contamination of Mr. Dashwood and his Hell-Fire Club, and he wanted very much to help Chatfield extricate Phillip. But how? Mr. Dashwood was past Darcy's ability to persuade. Indeed, Darcy suspected him past saving altogether.

Yet Darcy could not refuse the earl. Motivated by friendship alone, he would aid Chatfield in any matter it lay within his power to affect. Beyond that, he owed Chatfield several favors for which the earl had never once asked anything in return. To deny his present request, particularly one tendered in such distress, would be an unforgivable breach of honor and friendship.

Beyond that still, the Earl of Chatfield was a peer of the realm, a member of the aristocracy who wielded quiet power. He sat in the House of Lords, but it was the seat at the head of his own table, where he regularly gathered the greatest minds of the day, that invested him with the most influence. Darcy could not say no to any man who so commanded his respect.

"You have my word, Chatfield. On behalf of both you and the countess, I shall do all I can."

Now he just had to figure out what that was.

Nineteen

"*I should be undeserving of the confidence you have honoured me with, if I felt no desire for its continuance, or no farther curiosity on its subject.*"

—*Elinor Dashwood to Lucy Steele,*
Sense and Sensibility, *Chapter 23*

Delaford Parsonage
16 June, 18—

Dear Mrs. Darcy,

Edward and I thank you for your letter advising us of our nephew Harry's present circumstances. Far from considering your report officious, as you feared, we are grateful for your forthright account of recent events, and based on our acquaintance begun at Norland, trust as your motive in relating them the sincere concern for Harry's welfare that his uncle and I share. Given the broken engagement between your sister and Harry, which we grieve but concur was necessary, your continued interest in his safety bespeaks an uncommonly generous, forgiving, and noble spirit.

As my sisters-in-law apparently wished to spare us the burden of receiving such unhappy news, we had not been aware of any alterations in Harry beyond what we ourselves observed when he visited Delaford last month. That his character has undergone so material a transformation troubles us deeply.

Whilst, as you know, we had little opportunity during Harry's school years to develop a particular intimacy with him, the inclination he showed in recent months of establishing a stronger connection with his Dashwood relations leads us to hope that perhaps, as you suggest, some intervention on our part may provide a steadying influence. Perhaps also Edward's years of ministry to his parishioners may enable him to offer counsel in a manner Harry will accept. Indeed, it sounds as if any attempt on our part to redirect him cannot make the current situation worse.

We believe it best to approach Harry in person rather than by post. As fortune would have it, my sister Marianne and her family depart with my mother for Kent in two days' time. She and the colonel have offered us both transportation to London and the use of their house while in town. We expect to arrive Friday afternoon in St. James's Street, where the Brandons and my mother will stay a se'nnight before continuing on their holiday. Edward's duties shall also call him away at that time, though I will remain longer if I can be of use to Harry.

I shall call on you when we are settled to learn more about my nephew. Until then, I am—

Your most grateful servant,
Elinor Ferrars

Darcy handed the letter back to Elizabeth. Soliciting the aid of Mr. Dashwood's aunt to prevail upon Harry had been her idea, one to which he, having no better plan for fulfilling his promise to Chatfield, had readily agreed. As Elinor Ferrars had expressed, little could be lost by the effort, and they could satisfy their consciences that every possible recourse toward reclaiming Mr. Dashwood—or at least, Phillip Beaumont—had been pursued. Mrs. Ferrars's reply, however, had contained surprising intelligence.

"Mr. Dashwood visited them last month?" he said.

She refolded the note and set it beside the portable writing desk she'd been using in the parlor when the post arrived. An unfinished reply to Jane's last lay on top. "I intend to enquire after the particulars when Mrs. Ferrars calls, but apparently he indeed went to Devonshire, just as he claimed."

Darcy shook his head. "Impossible! I saw him in his own window during the period he maintains he was away."

"You saw someone in the window. Are you quite sure it was Mr. Dashwood?"

"I made no mistake."

"From two stories below? Come now, Darcy. Are you that infallible?"

"Yes." Though he made the assertion in a confident tone, he reconsidered his memory of the sighting. The figure's build, his height, his coloring—it *had* been Mr. Dashwood. "Yes," he repeated.

She regarded him skeptically.

"You do not believe me?"

"If you are certain, then I believe you." Her expression growing pensive, she tapped her quill against the blotter. "I merely contemplate that if it was, in fact, Mr. Dashwood standing in the window, we are hard-pressed to account for how he traveled to Devonshire and back so quickly. Delaford is three days' journey from here, and your call at his townhouse perfectly divided the nine days he claims to have been gone."

Confronted with the logistics, Darcy sought an explanation. "He could have traveled straight through, stopping only to change horses."

"A dangerous proposition. Visiting his relations hardly seems an urgent enough errand to warrant risking a midnight encounter with highwaymen. And even if he did travel at such a pace, the timing of your sighting means he had less than five days' time on either side to make the trip there and back again. He would have been required to turn around directly he arrived, leaving him no opportunity to conduct whatever business took him there."

"Assuming he left London and returned when he says he did."

"He claims to have departed early on Friday the fourteenth and returned late the Saturday next." She put aside her letter to Jane and pulled out a fresh sheet of writing paper. With a few dips of her pen, she sketched out a rough calendar. "You called on Tuesday at what hour?"

"Half past three."

She made a notation in Tuesday's box. "We know he returned Saturday because he came straight here, looking as if he'd just been traveling."

"He could have returned earlier and made himself appear travel-weary for his call."

"Regardless, we know he was in town by Saturday evening." She wrote as much on the page. "That's closer to four days than five between your observation of him and his appearance here—simply not enough time for him to have made the trip after you saw him."

"Then he must have left and returned before Tuesday afternoon."

"He maintains that he departed Friday morning too early to take leave of Kitty. Even if he set out at some ghastly hour . . ." She scowled at her annotations. "I simply do not see how it is possible. Besides, did not someone else claim to have seen him Friday night? That gentleman at your fencing club looking for Mr. Dashwood?"

"Longcliffe?" When Darcy had encountered him, he'd said he confronted Dashwood at the Pigeon Hole late the night before. "Yes, Longcliffe's meeting would have happened on Friday. I heard of it while waiting for Chatfield, and we meet on Saturdays."

"His testimony curtails Mr. Dashwood's travel period even

further. And we have not even considered all the sightings of Mr. Dashwood that others reported that week." She set aside her pen and rubbed her temples. "Unless Harry harnessed an eagle to his carriage, I do not know how he managed the journey."

"Mrs. Edward Ferrars arrives on the morrow. Surely additional information from her will enlighten us. If she calls as soon as she is settled, we can look for her perhaps as early as Saturday."

So intensely did his wife study her paper that Darcy was not sure she heard him.

"Elizabeth?"

She withdrew a second sheet. "I am not certain I can wait that long."

Twenty

*"She has done with her son, she has cast him off forever, and
has made all those over whom she had any influence, cast him
off likewise."*

—John Dashwood to Elinor,
Sense and Sensibility, *Chapter 41*

*E*lizabeth set out for St. James's Street within ten minutes
of receiving Elinor's communication of her arrival in London. She'd sent a note to the Brandons' townhouse begging
leave to call upon Mrs. Edward Ferrars at her earliest convenience, and in turn had been invited to come immediately. She
hoped the Delaford party would not consider her eagerness ill-
mannered, but the more she pondered the questions surrounding Harry's Devonshire visit, the more quickly she needed to
have her puzzlement abated.

Elinor greeted her warmly in the drawing room, where Edward also waited. After hearing Elizabeth's apologies for intrud-
ing on the couple so soon, and dismissing them as entirely
unnecessary, Mrs. Ferrars immediately introduced the subject of
Harry.

"The exigency of your call relates, I presume, to our nephew.
Has something further occurred since your letter to us in Delaford?"

A twinge of conscience admonished her for allowing her

own impatience to cause them undue anxiety. "Not to my knowledge. Mr. Dashwood is, however, so unpredictable of late that one can never be certain when another tale of his exploits will circulate."

"I sensed in your letter that you hesitated to disclose all the information in your possession."

"I did not know how you would respond to the intelligence. And, indeed, Mr. Darcy knows more particulars than I. Many of Mr. Dashwood's alleged transgressions, I am given to understand, are so very shocking that my husband will not describe them to me. Merely from what I myself have witnessed, I would caution anyone who takes benevolent interest in Mr. Dashwood to prepare for a distressing next meeting, for you will find him much altered from the gentleman who entertained us at Norland. But you said in your letter that you have seen him since then?"

"He called upon us a month ago," Elinor said. "It was a very sudden visit—he arrived so soon after his letter stating his intention to come that he might have saved us the postage and delivered it himself."

"Do you recall the date of his arrival?"

Elinor and Edward exchanged glances. "It was a Sunday—the sixteenth, I believe," Edward said. "I had just finished services."

"May I ask what errand brought him to you?"

"He wished to talk about Norland," Elinor said. "People and things I remembered from the period I lived there, or that I might have recalled others mentioning. He had recently explored Norland's attics and wanted to know the origin of some of the items he had discovered. Many were pieces that graced Norland's rooms until my father passed away, but that Fanny did not care for. Others I had no memory of, and referred him to my mother."

"Did Mr. Dashwood call upon your mother, then?"

"Yes, and Marianne, as well."

"On the same business?"

"Yes. He also asked numerous questions about my father and our uncle Albert Dashwood—their temperaments and deportment, their voices and manners of expression, their interests and amusements—the essentials of their characters, I suppose. He enquired, too, about Sir Francis Dashwood, and whether Papa or Uncle Albert had spoken of him."

"Had he ever expressed curiosity on these points before?"

"Not to me, but of course we have had little previous opportunity for such conversations. I do not know whether he asked my brother about any of his Dashwood relations before John's death. At the time of Harry's visit, I thought my nephew had merely developed an interest in the estate and lineage he inherited, and I was glad of it. But seen in the light of your report about this Hell-Fire business he's become involved with, I think we instead witnessed the infancy of an obsession with our notorious ancestor."

"In your letter, you said that he seemed different from what he had been at Norland just a fortnight earlier?"

"He did not look altogether well to me—tired, which I presumed to derive from the rapidity of his journey. Would you not agree, Edward?"

Her husband nodded and sat forward. "The fatigue left his nerves frayed. More than once, I startled him simply by walking into a room. I believe he also did not sleep well while he was with us. One morning at breakfast, he complained of a bad dream having disturbed his rest."

"Did you enquire into the nature of it?"

"No, nor did he offer it."

Running footsteps above drew their attention ceilingward. Several pairs of feet, small from the sound of them, sprinted across the room above. Peals of laughter followed.

Elinor smiled apologetically. "That would be Marianne and the children. They have been too long confined in carriages these past few days."

Elizabeth arched a brow. "Marianne included?"

Elinor laughed. "Actually, yes. My sister possesses as much energy as any of them, and as little natural inclination to suppress it. Though she comports herself with the dignity and temperance one would expect from a lady of her station, I think the hours when she dismisses the governess and plays with the children herself provide Marianne one of her greatest joys each day."

Elizabeth thought of the quiet, broken only by Georgiana's rehearsals on the harp or pianoforte, that encompassed the houses in which she herself lived. "It is welcome noise," she said. "Are your own children among the party?"

"No, they are with our neighbors, the Careys. With Marianne's five, we were already so numerous as to require two conveyances; to bring our own children with us seemed unnecessary, especially given the additional trouble and expense of transporting ourselves home by public coach once our business is concluded."

"We also were not certain what demands might be placed on ourselves and our time in assisting Harry," Edward said.

Regardless of what had transpired between Harry and Kitty, Elizabeth sincerely hoped Elinor and Edward Ferrars might exert a positive influence on their nephew—for the good of everyone he came in contact with, if not for himself. "You said he enquired of you about Sir Francis. Were you able to satisfy him on any particulars?"

"No," Elinor replied. "Sir Francis died over thirty years ago. By the time I reached an age where one has memories of anything, my father and Uncle Albert never spoke of him, or had any reason to. I suggested Harry ask my mother, since she would be able to recall a period when Sir Francis was still alive. I do not know the outcome of that interview, but Mama is upstairs. Shall

I call her? I am certain she would be pleased to make your acquaintance."

Elizabeth wished very much to speak with Mrs. Henry Dashwood but hesitated to impose on the older woman. "I would not wish to disturb her if she is resting following your journey."

A team of horses galloped across the ceiling.

"I somehow doubt my mother rests just now," Elinor said.

Edward left to retrieve Mrs. Dashwood. As the ladies waited, Elinor advised Elizabeth that she had not informed her mother of the extent of Harry's transformation or made any mention of the Hell-Fire Club. "I did not wish to alarm her until I had spoken with Harry myself," she explained.

"I will not reveal anything that might distress her," Elizabeth promised.

Mrs. Dashwood was a pleasant woman of about five-and-fifty, with grey hair turning silver and laugh lines around her keen eyes. She greeted Elizabeth warmly upon their introduction, expressing genuine delight at finally meeting her.

"Elinor has spoken so favorably of you, Mrs. Darcy, that I have looked forward to knowing you since Harry announced his engagement to your sister. I am sorry their marriage will not now take place."

"Unfortunately, it was necessary for Kitty and Mr. Dashwood to part ways."

"It must be of some comfort to your family that they discovered their incompatibility before the wedding vows were spoken. I was surprised to hear the news, as he talked so ardently of her when he visited. But these things do happen with young people."

Though Elizabeth and Darcy grew more relieved with each passing day that Kitty had escaped a permanent alliance with Harry Dashwood, Elizabeth had little inclination to discuss the broken engagement. She yet lamented her lapse of judgment on the point of Harry's character, and it rankled her vanity that she had allowed herself to be so deceived.

"I understand Mr. Dashwood also spoke of other matters with you during his visit to Devonshire?" Elizabeth asked.

Mrs. Dashwood smiled softly in recollection. "Yes. He wanted to hear about my husband, Henry. I was so pleased by his interest. Other than naming Harry after his grandfather, John and Fanny didn't seem to give Henry two minutes' thought before he died, and none afterward. Harry met his grandfather few times; John and Fanny visited Norland just often enough to insinuate themselves into Uncle Albert's will. That he wished to hear about Henry now encouraged me to hope that he had grown to be a man worthy of the name he bears."

"Mother, Harry asked me whether Papa or Uncle Albert had ever spoken of Sir Francis Dashwood. Did Harry pose the same question to you?"

"He did. I could not tell him much. Sir Francis was a distant relation who had been involved in some sort of scandalous affairs that became known to the public a few years before I met your father. I was only about sixteen at the time, and living far enough removed from London that I was ignorant of the details. The only time Henry ever spoke of it later was to assure me, while we were courting, that anything I might hear about his infamous relation had no connection at all to the sort of man *he* was, and that he hoped to always conduct himself in a manner that would place his honor, integrity, and respectability above question.

"That's all I ever heard of Sir Francis for years. To both your father and Uncle Albert, he was an embarrassment better left undiscussed. Then one day, shortly after we moved in with Uncle Albert at Norland, a delivery arrived quite unexpectedly from West Wycombe Park—Sir Francis's estate. It was a large mirror, with a letter from Sir Francis asking Uncle Albert to keep it for a while."

Elizabeth recalled the looking glass that Harry's footmen had struggled with when she had accompanied Kitty to his townhouse to break their engagement. "I think perhaps I have seen that mirror. Has it a Greek design?"

"Yes—with carvings of athletes round the whole frame. Uncle Albert didn't know what to think. He had never known Sir Francis well and had cut off communication altogether when the scandals broke. He was still trying to decide what to do with the mirror when we received word several days later that Sir Francis had died. The death itself came as little surprise—he was in his seventies, and by all accounts had lived an immoderate life—but it left Uncle Albert in a quandary over how to dispose of the mirror. He wrote to Sir Francis's heir to make arrangements for its return. But the heir, believing the mirror to have been a deathbed gift by Sir Francis in an attempt to polish the memory he would leave behind, exhorted Uncle Albert to keep it and sent with his reply a portrait of Sir Francis in his youth by which to better remember him. So now poor Uncle Albert had a huge looking glass and a full-length portrait to constantly call to mind a dead man he had been quite happy to forget during his life."

"What did he do with them?" Elinor asked.

"What *could* he do with them? He couldn't return them to West Wycombe without delivering an enormous insult along with them, he couldn't get rid of them, and he couldn't bear looking at them. So he stuck them in the attic, and none of us ever thought about them or Sir Francis again."

At least, not until Harry found them. It seemed that his discovery of the portrait had awakened in him some dormant predisposition to vice that he and his ancestor shared. Elizabeth remembered the conversation between Harry and Professor Randolph on the day Harry had first called upon Kitty. Would that meeting the archaeologist had never inspired Harry to explore Norland's attics! Sir Francis could have remained forever in obscurity, where he belonged.

The stampede above had ceased sometime during Mrs.

Dashwood's narration, enough so that the ladies in the drawing room were able to hear a carriage pull up. Minutes later, the arrival of Mrs. Robert Ferrars was announced.

"Lucy calls upon us already?" Mrs. Dashwood remarked to her daughter. "She must want something."

Lucy entered, sans Regina for the first time Elizabeth could recall having seen her. Free of the excess weight, she swept into the room like a cat pouncing on a mouse. She dropped herself beside Elinor and put a hand on her arm. "Elinor, I am so glad you're at home. The most— Oh!" So intent had she been on her mission, that she hadn't taken notice of the room's other occupants. "Good afternoon, Mrs. Dashwood. And Edward. Oh— And Mrs. Darcy! I didn't expect anyone but family might be here. Especially you. I mean—you know, since the sad business between Harry and Miss Bennet."

"Regardless of what has transpired between Mr. Dashwood and my sister, I continue to regard his family with esteem," Elizabeth said.

"And we think the same way of you, to be sure. Well, you all would not believe what has just happened! Elinor, I knew you were in town, and I hurried here straightaway to make sure you didn't hear the astounding news from someone else!"

Elizabeth could not help but reflect that Lucy seemed very thoughtful in this regard. Whenever bad news circulated, she could be counted upon to deliver it most expeditiously to anyone remotely interested.

"What do you think our sister Fanny has done? I'm sure you could never guess, so I'll tell you. She has disinherited Harry! Her only son! I am beside myself with shock. My heart just breaks for him." As if to illustrate the fracture, she brought her hand to her chest. "Doesn't yours?"

Elinor's face registered astonishment, but at least she and Edward possessed information about Harry's recent conduct that lent Lucy's announcement context. Poor Mrs. Dashwood appeared completely bewildered.

"Fanny has disinherited Harry? Whatever for?"

"For his profligate behavior. She has been threatening it for weeks, but today she signed the papers with the solicitors. He's still got Norland, of course, but he won't see a penny of the rest of his father's estate or Fanny's own settlement after her death. Two thousand a year, yanked right out of his grasp!"

"What profligate behavior?"

"Mother," Elinor said gently, "there have been rumors. . . . Out of fairness to Harry, I did not want to repeat them even to you, until I could determine their veracity."

"Rumors? They are more than just rumors!" Lucy exclaimed. "Why, all the *ton* is talking about his drunken soirées, and his mistress, and the Hel—"

"Yes, I am sure they are," Elinor said.

"Mistress?"

"Oh, Mrs. Dashwood, Harry's the most infamous rakehell in London right now! Why, he—"

"Our Harry?"

"Well, yes, our Harry! Who else would I be speaking of?"

"And Fanny has cut him off?"

"Utterly! Said her mother did the same thing to Edward without half so much cause, and she weren't going to allow her son to embarrass her any further. Why, she hasn't set foot outside her door these three weeks at least, 'cause she knows folks are whispering behind her back."

Edward shook his head in disbelief. "Poor Harry."

"Oh, Edward—do forgive me. I didn't even think how you must feel! Of course this must bring up dreadful memories."

Which would not, Elizabeth suspected, prevent Lucy from continuing to talk about it *ad nauseam*. She began to feel her own presence an intrusion, and pondered some means of making a graceful exit so that the family might discuss this news in privacy.

"Unlike Edward, whose younger brother benefited from his loss," Elinor said pointedly, "Harry has no siblings. On whom did Fanny settle her fortune?"

Lucy actually stopped talking long enough to catch her breath. "Well," she said slowly, "now that's the other part of the news I find so incredible, you see. As you said, Harry has no brothers or sisters, and of course Fanny wants to keep the money in the family. So she gave it to Regina."

"Regina?" Elinor said.

"I was as surprised as you, I tell you!" Again, she placed her hand on Elinor's arm. "But really, who else could she leave it to? Regina is her niece, and she and Fanny have become *so* intimate this season. Why, Fanny adores her like the daughter she never had!" She sighed dramatically and turned toward the rest of her listeners. "We feel guilty, of course, about Regina's gaining from Harry's misfortune, but what is one to do? It's better that the fortune stay within the family than go to an outsider. And if leaving it to Regina can provide Fanny with some measure of comfort to ease the pain her own son has caused her, why, it's nothing short of our duty to accept it."

"Indeed," Elinor said dryly.

"Is the bequest irrevocable?" Edward asked.

"I'm afraid so. As of this morning, Fanny retains only a life interest in it. How it pains me to say so! Believe me, I wish it were otherwise, so that she might have an opportunity to reconsider if Harry reforms. I tried to talk her out of it, of course, and urged her to at least reflect longer on her decision before signing the papers. But it is done."

Lucy's professions of conscience were as believable as they were sincere. Elizabeth had to give her credit: All these weeks, she'd thought Lucy schemed to acquire Harry's fortune for her daughter merely through the conventional means of a marriage between them. But instead she'd managed to win the money without sacrificing Regina to what would surely prove an unhappy future. And with this sizable increase to her dowry, Regina could now catch a better prize in the marriage market, thus further increasing her fortune.

"How did Harry take the news?" Mrs. Dashwood asked.

"I don't know. Fanny was on her way to Pall Mall when I left her. I'm sure he must be devastated—anybody would be." She sighed once more and rose. "Someone should offer him sympathy, even if he don't deserve it. I shall go. Better for him to be with family at a time like this. It was good to see you all, even if the occasion was the sharing of such unhappy news. Good-bye!"

With that, she blew out of the room as quickly as she had blown in, a sudden summer shower that fleetingly deluges those caught beneath it before moving on to drench another unwary party.

In the stunned silence that followed her departure, Elizabeth also rose. "I apologize to you all for having long overstayed my welcome. Doubtless, you wish to continue discussing this matter in private."

"I'm sure none of us considered your presence an intrusion, Mrs. Darcy," Elinor reassured her. "And I suspect Lucy appreciated the opportunity to play to a larger audience."

As her driver assisted her into the carriage, Elizabeth reflected anew on what a mess Harry Dashwood had made of his life in just a few short weeks. He'd lost his fiancée, half his fortune, and many of his former friends, gaining little more than infamy in their stead. Well—infamy and a paunch more at home on a man twice his age. She recalled Darcy's description of Harry preening before his elaborate mirror when they'd first met him. What did Mr. Dashwood see when he looked at himself in the glass of late? Could a man who once had taken such trouble over his appearance really be satisfied with the image now reflected?

Perhaps, she mused, that is why he'd ordered the looking

glass packed up and carted back to Norland—his vanity could no longer suffer it. And so the mirror's London season had come to as abrupt an end as Harry and Kitty's engagement, and for identical cause: Mr. Dashwood's unbecoming alteration. With Mrs. Dashwood's narrative still fresh in her mind, Elizabeth shook her head at the irony of the mirror's being returned so soon after making its escape from obscurity. The unfortunate work of art, once valued by Sir Francis and, doubtless, other previous owners, now seemed destined to languish unappreciated in Norland's attic for another thirty years or more. She wondered what Professor Randolph would think of such an obvious treasure suffering so ignoble a fate.

Halfway into the carriage, she paused suddenly. She wondered very much, in fact. Very much, indeed.

"Ma'am?" her driver said.

His prompt brought her mind back to the present. She completed her entry and settled onto the seat.

"Home, Mrs. Darcy?"

"Yes, Jeffrey. By way of the British Museum."

Twenty-one

"Are no probabilities to be accepted, merely because they are
not certainties?"

—Mrs. Dashwood to Elinor,
Sense and Sensibility, *Chapter 15*

*M*rs. Darcy! What a happy surprise! Do come in."
Elizabeth trod gingerly into Professor Randolph's
office, fearful of brushing past one of the numerous towers of
books and papers lest it topple over and bury her. Though the
archaeologist had secured his position with the museum less
than six months earlier, his workroom looked as in need of exca-
vation as any ruin. Overstuffed shelves bowed under the weight
of old manuscripts and new monographs, ancient artifacts and
modern-looking instruments. Papers littered his desk and the
floor surrounding it, stubbornly refusing to adhere to any form
of organization that may at one time have been imposed upon
them. Archaeological wonders competed with mundane tools for
dominance on every horizontal surface.

Randolph lifted what appeared to be a small statue of Hermes
from the seat of a chair. He glanced about but, finding no uncluttered surface on which to securely rest the artifact, was forced
to tuck it under his arm while he withdrew a handkerchief from

one of his profusion of pockets and wiped dust from the seat. He did not, it seemed, receive many visitors.

"Do sit down, Mrs. Darcy. To what do I owe the honor of this call?"

She gathered her skirts close about her and picked her way to the proffered chair. "I would like to say I came purely out of friendship, but I am afraid I also have need of your professional expertise."

"Indeed?" He wove past a stack of thick leatherbound volumes to sidle into his own chair behind the desk. Still lacking a safe haven for Hermes, he held Zeus's messenger in his hands. "How may I be of assistance?"

"I am wondering . . ." Where to begin? The idea that had struck her while leaving St. James's Street was still only half-formed; how to articulate it to the professor—particularly without sounding absurd in the process—eluded her.

He studied her, understanding entering his own expression. "You seek more than the appraisal of a mundane artifact, don't you?"

"Yes."

"Perhaps we should close the door."

He maneuvered past the desk again and shut the door, revealing a patch of uncluttered space on a bookcase that had previously been hidden. He set Hermes on the shelf and returned to his chair. "There. You might find it easier to speak freely now."

Only slightly. Though she and the professor had engaged in several discussions about phenomena not easily explained, she yet had trouble considering it a natural topic of conversation.

"Is it possible for an object to somehow retain the characteristics of its previous owner?"

He removed his spectacles and wiped them with the same handkerchief he'd used on the chair. At least, she thought it was the same one, though it had come from a different pocket this time. "Now that's a question I don't hear every day. But it is a very good one." He perched the spectacles back on the bridge of his nose, from which they immediately slid. "The concise answer is 'yes.' Objects, particularly items worn or carried on someone's person for a prolonged period of time, have been known to absorb their owner's aura, as it were. It's not something that would be apparent to most people, but to an individual sensitive to such things, that retained essence could be perceived even after the item has left the owner's possession."

Perhaps her theory was not so half-baked after all. "To what effect?"

"A necklace worn by your grandmother, for instance, might envelop you in her spirit when you don it yourself. If she was a bitter woman, you might experience acrimony. If she was often sad, you may be filled with melancholy. If she was brave, you might find yourself infused with courage."

"Does this hold true for larger items, as well?"

"Certainly. Houses are an excellent example. One can enter a vacant dwelling and sense whether it was a happy home. Prisons are another. I personally cannot visit the Tower of London without a sense of despair washing over me."

"How about something like a looking glass?"

He paused, analyzing her countenance the way she imagined he studied his artifacts. "How about disclosing a hint as to what these questions portend so that I may better answer them?" he said gently.

She released a heavy breath. It would be a relief to lay her suspicions before someone who might be able to make sense of them. "Do you recall Mr. Harry Dashwood?"

"The young fellow I met at your townhouse?"

"Yes."

"A pleasant gentleman. He was about to embark on an exploration of his attics, as I recollect."

"He did. There he discovered two items that had once

belonged to a black-sheep ancestor of his, Sir Francis Dashwood. One was a portrait of Sir Francis, the other, a mirror that has an antique essence to it. Mr. Dashwood brought them back to London with him and, to put it mildly, he has not been the same since."

"And you wonder if these objects have something to do with the alteration in his demeanor?"

"Precisely. Mr. Dashwood has developed a preoccupation with Sir Francis, emulating his debauchery and immoral behavior to the point where my sister, who had thought herself engaged to a kind, respectable gentleman, was forced to break all connection with the libertine he has become. While I hold Mr. Dashwood responsible for his own conduct, the coincidence of his sudden interest in Sir Francis and his discovery of the looking glass led me to speculate that perhaps something more than mere curiosity about his ancestor influenced his transformation."

She hoped she hadn't just made herself sound perfectly ridiculous. But Professor Randolph adjusted his spectacles and leaned back in his chair with a look of concentration.

"It's possible," he said. "Especially given Sir Francis's history of religious experimentation. If anyone could extend his influence beyond the grave, he would be the man."

"You have heard of him, then?"

"Quite a character, as I understand. But also quite a collector of classical antiquities. Tell me more about this mirror. Have you seen it?"

"It's a huge thing. The glass itself is almost as tall as I am, and it's surrounded by a heavy gold frame with figures standing out in relief."

"What sort of figures?"

She frowned, trying to recall. "I saw the glass only once, and I was preoccupied with other matters. But I believe the figures were young males rendered in classical Greek style."

"What was at the top of the frame?"

"A man's face."

He stood up, performed a *pas de deux* with a stack of old newspapers beside his desk, and wended his way back to the bookcase by the door. He pulled a journal off the shelf, thumbed through it, replaced it, and selected another. The second also earned a shake of his head, but a third triggered an enthusiastic nod. "Yes, yes—here it is."

He traced his finger over a page. "Mrs. Darcy, I suspect your young friend may have come into custody of an artifact known as the Mirror of Narcissus, an ancient glass said to have been brought to England shortly after the Crusades. It is a controversial piece, crafted with materials and methods so ahead of their time that some modern scholars dismiss it as a fake. Yet accounts of the mirror stretch far back in history. It has disappeared and resurfaced many times over the centuries, and was last thought to have been owned by Sir Francis Dashwood."

"Until his death, whereupon it sat in the attic of Norland House for over thirty years," Elizabeth revealed.

He snapped the volume shut and set it aside carelessly. He then scanned the bookcase, running his finger along the volumes' spines. "According to legend, it possesses supernatural properties."

"What sort of properties?"

"Those notes do not specify." He transferred his search to the next bookcase. "I know I have a book here somewhere that offers more particulars. . . ."

She contemplated the myth of the young man who pined away for love of his own reflection. "Narcissus's obsession with himself destroyed him. Could a mirror named for him somehow be fueling Harry's self-destructive indulgence?"

"It could." He shifted a large idol to access a mass of books behind it. "I seem to recall that many of its owners have met untimely ends."

The idol, which by oversight had not been placed squarely on the floor but partially on the edge of a stray pamphlet, tottered. Professor Randolph caught it in time, but in the process bumped the bookcase beside it, sending Hermes crashing to the floor.

"Oh, dear!" Elizabeth felt terrible that one of the archaeologist's treasures had been sacrificed in his attempt to perform a service for her.

"Not to worry, my dear Mrs. Darcy. I had recently determined it was counterfeit." He knelt to pick up the broken pieces. "The mirror, however, is a more serious affair. I will continue to search for my book and conduct further research into the artifact's story. In the meantime, a more detailed description may enable us to determine whether Mr. Dashwood's glass is indeed the Mirror of Narcissus. Can you obtain a better look at it?"

"He recently returned it to Norland." She retrieved one of Hermes' wings from where it had landed beside her shoe and handed it to Randolph. "But should an opportunity present itself, I'll take advantage of it."

"If you do, proceed with caution. Bring the amulet I gave you."

She'd stopped carrying the pocketwatch after Darcy had been so displeased by it the night they followed Mr. Dashwood home. "Is it necessary?"

"A safeguard. I also advise you not to look directly into the mirror."

"Why not? What will happen?"

"I have no idea." He tossed the shattered remains of Hermes into the dustbin. "But when dealing with mysterious relics, one cannot be too careful."

Twenty-two

"The time may come when Harry will regret that so large a sum was parted with."

—Fanny Dashwood to John Dashwood,
Sense and Sensibility, Chapter 2

"Have you spoken with Mr. Dashwood yet?"

Darcy winced. The moment he'd entered White's and saw Chatfield there, he knew the question would come. He'd fleetingly contemplated ducking out of the club before his friend spotted him, but to be observed by others giving Lord Chatfield the cut direct would have resulted in far worse consequences than giving the earl news he did not want to hear. Darcy had already avoided Chatfield once that day, having postponed their fencing appointment until he had developments to report, but now a reckoning was inevitable.

"Not yet." At the expression of disappointment that crossed Chatfield's face, he hastened to add, "But I have brought in reinforcements, and we launch our campaign tomorrow."

Chatfield shifted his gaze across the card room, letting it rest on Mr. Dashwood. From their vantage point in the doorway, Darcy and the earl could barely see Harry for the crowd that had gathered round his whist table. The deep play of Mr. Dashwood's party had lured others away from their own tables to observe; indeed, the stakes had risen so high that men had wandered in from elsewhere in the club, hoping to be able to say come morning that they'd witnessed a fortune won or lost.

"What sort of reinforcements?" Chatfield asked.

"Mr. Dashwood's uncle, a minister. I enlisted his aid, and he came to London as swiftly as he could. He arrived yesterday."

After Elizabeth had returned home with news of Harry's disinheritance, a note from Edward Ferrars followed that suggested a gentleman-to-gentleman talk might prove the best way to approach Mr. Dashwood. Darcy had concurred, though he thought "man-to-man" a more appropriate term, as Mr. Dashwood had not conducted himself anything like a gentleman in weeks. Darcy half wished Mr. Ferrars would undertake the mission alone, as he himself had suffered quite enough of Harry, but he wanted to be able to assure Chatfield firsthand that every possible means of persuasion had been attempted.

Raucous guffaws and whistles from Dashwood's table drew Darcy's attention to that quarter, where the betting had escalated to dizzying heights. Harry called for more wine.

"Is that your third bottle, Dashwood?" someone called.

"Fourth." He raised his glass and took a long draught.

Elizabeth was right, Darcy reflected. Harry Dashwood did look dreadful. His face had grown round and flaccid, his color bad, his girth expansive. Weeks of dissipation had wrought years of hardship on his person. But he held himself like a man without burden, someone intent to seize life's pleasures and leave the rest for others to trouble themselves over. He was confident, he was cocky, and he was having a high time.

"All right, Dashwood—you've stalled long enough," his opponent prodded. "You heard my wager. Now what's yours?"

"Norland."

His challenger laughed. "Your Sussex estate? Are you certain that's only your fourth bottle?"

Dashwood reclined in a cocksure attitude. "That's my wager,

Lovejoy. Take it or leave it, for thanks to my dear mother, I've nothing else to offer."

"And what will I do with an estate in Sussex?"

"I don't intend to lose it."

The bet was accepted, and play commenced. Dashwood and his partner won the first game of the rubber; their opponents won the second. Between honors and tricks, Harry's team was ahead by one game point. The room fell silent as Dashwood dealt the final hand.

He turned up the ace of spades as trump. "My lucky suit," he said.

"Not tonight," Lovejoy responded.

Dashwood took the first trick, his partner, the second. The third trick, trumped with the ace, went to them, as well. After the fourth trick, however, the lead shifted to their opponents.

And never returned.

Short on trump and long on liquor, Dashwood forfeited trick after trick to bad cards and worse judgment. The hand ended abysmally for the owner of Norland. Or, rather, the former owner of Norland. All waited to see how Harry Dashwood would respond to having lost the rubber—and his estate.

No one expected him to laugh.

"Ha! You have bested me, Lovejoy." He called for pen and paper. "Take this promissory note for now, and in the morning I will instruct my solicitors to draw up the proper papers regarding Norland."

Lovejoy watched Harry uncertainly as the latter dispassionately set down his debt in ink. Indeed, the victor looked more unsettled by the wager's outcome than the loser. Dashwood's hand moved rapidly across the paper, as if he couldn't sign away his birthright fast enough.

"The transfer needn't take place immediately," Lovejoy said. "I presume you shall want time to retrieve your personal effects and items of sentimental value."

"Norland holds nothing of particular meaning to me." He continued writing, then paused midstroke. "Oh—save one object. I just sent a looking glass there from my townhouse to be stored. If I might have that back?"

"Of course. Anything else?"

He shook his head and went back to writing. "Just the glass."

The crowd soon dispersed to spread the tale far and wide; the *ton* would breakfast upon it along with their morning chocolate. Harry completed his note, handed it to Lovejoy with a dramatic bow, and exited the card room.

On the way out, he passed Darcy and Chatfield. Darcy could not help feeling that he'd just witnessed a tragedy.

"I am sorry for your loss, Mr. Dashwood."

"Whatever for, Mr. Darcy?" He grinned. "'Things won are done; joy's soul lies in the doing.' It has been a tremendously entertaining evening, has it not?"

"I cannot fathom what my own feelings would be upon losing Pemberley," Darcy said to Elizabeth the following morning, "but nonchalance—nay, *amusement*—would not number among them."

"You never would have risked Pemberley for so ridiculous and irresponsible an end."

She had heard his account of Mr. Dashwood's latest exploit with all the amazement he'd still possessed while delivering it. The loss was as stunning as it was stupid, not at all what she would have predicted from the master of Norland who had eagerly led them about his house. The whole business supported her conjecture that perhaps another influence was at work upon Harry—if not the Mirror of Narcissus, at the very least too much brimstone.

She poured water into the basin, splashed her face, and blindly reached for the towel. Darcy handed it to her.

"I dread our call today," he said. "I do not know what Mr. Ferrars and I shall say to him that has not already been said, and a man who has just lost two fortunes in two days will be unlikely to appreciate advice from any quarter."

"Perhaps the losses will sober him—literally and figuratively."

He made a sound of disgust. "I doubt anything can do that."

"Are you quite certain I cannot persuade you to let me accompany you?" Since yesterday's conversation with Professor Randolph, she had tried to devise some means of obtaining a second look at Mr. Dashwood's mirror. Darcy's report that it was now on its way back to London lent her hope that she might get a glimpse of it yet.

"I dislike the idea of your being in his house at all, even with me." He washed his own face and accepted the towel from her. "He is ungentlemanly, unpredictable, untrustworthy, and unfit for the company of a lady—nay, any respectable person. Rejoice in avoiding further exposure to him. I wish I myself did not have to go."

She supposed the morrow was too soon to expect the mirror's return anyway. She would wait a few days to invent some pretext to call upon Mr. Dashwood. Out of respect for Darcy's concerns, she would not visit Pall Mall alone, but she did not plan to reveal to her husband the true reason for her errand. Darcy would consider her entire discussion with Professor Randolph nonsense and utterly dismiss the possibility that the mirror was anything more than a dusty old artifact. She did not want to hear his criticisms until she'd had an opportunity to evaluate it herself.

"Then let us hope your sortie succeeds—and quickly, for Elinor Ferrars and I shall be waiting most impatiently for the two of you to return with news of your conquest."

"After subjecting myself to Mr. Dashwood, I shall be impatient to reclaim your superior companionship."

She took back the cloth and dabbed a few stray droplets on his temple. "Are you certain? You and the reverend won't find yourselves tempted to prolong your visit and stay for one of Mr. Dashwood's notorious parties?"

He pushed damp locks from her forehead. "I have temptation enough here at home."

They kissed, then broke apart to continue dressing. He selected a shirt that she had recently made for him. She was pleased with the way it had turned out; it fit him well across the shoulders and its sleeves extended the perfect length. A second shirt was halfway to completion. In the weeks following Kitty's broken engagement and the abrupt end it had brought to preparing her sister's trousseau, Elizabeth had sought substitute employment for her needle. She'd tried to return to work on Jane's layette, but found herself unable to muster enthusiasm for it.

At breakfast, Elizabeth heard with restlessness the clock chime announcing that hours yet stood between the present time and the one that had been fixed upon for Darcy and Mr. Ferrars's call in Pall Mall. She would accompany her husband as far as St. James's, where Elinor had invited her to meet the Brandons while they awaited the results of the gentlemen's errand.

"You and Mrs. Ferrars seem to have formed a congenial acquaintance," Darcy observed.

"I like her very much," she replied. "She is an easy person with whom to converse. Had Kitty's marriage taken place, my sister would have been fortunate in her connection to Mrs. Edward Ferrars."

"And what of her connection to Mrs. Robert Ferrars?"

"Conversation with Lucy Ferrars is easy, as well. No one else in the room need speak at all."

The designated hour at last arrived. She and Darcy drove to the Brandons' townhouse, where Elizabeth was shown to the drawing room and Edward Ferrars took her place in the carriage.

Elinor's mother, sister, and brother-in-law were gathered in the room when Elizabeth entered. Mrs. Ferrars introduced her to Colonel and Mrs. Brandon, who welcomed her graciously and apologized for having been otherwise occupied when she called the previous afternoon. Elizabeth judged the former Marianne Dashwood to be perhaps two-and-thirty, and her husband nearly twenty years older. Five minutes' observation of the couple declared that they had married for an affection that the intervening years had not diminished.

They spoke the pleasant nothings that fill the conversations of people first meeting, until Mrs. Brandon grew obviously weary of empty chatter and cut to the subject on all of their minds.

"I understand your husband accompanies Edward to try to save our nephew from himself," she said.

Elizabeth appreciated her directness and returned it. "I am afraid we cherish little expectation of prevailing upon him. Mr. Darcy attempted to guide Mr. Dashwood while he and my sister were still engaged, without success, and their acquaintance has become less cordial since. With Mr. Ferrars's aid, however, perhaps Mr. Dashwood may be worked upon. We can but hope, especially following last night's debacle."

Marianne and the others regarded her in ignorance. "Something more occurred last night?"

Elizabeth felt the blood drain from her face. She had assumed someone would have informed Harry's relations by now that he had lost the estate they had once called home. She certainly did not want to be the bearer of tidings that would so shock and grieve these good-hearted people.

Fortunately, she was spared the unpleasant office by the timely arrival of Mrs. Robert Ferrars, who did not even allow the housekeeper to finish announcing her before bursting into the room with exclamations of astonishment and condolence.

"My dear Elinor and Marianne! Dear Mrs. Dashwood! I came the moment I heard about Norland. How devastated you must be!"

Had anyone else appeared so conveniently, Elizabeth would have marveled at the coincidence. But Lucy Ferrars was like the herald of a Greek tragedy, invested by her creator with the ability to enter a scene just when her communication could provide its most dramatic result. If only she would then exit as quickly, instead of staying on like a chorus to comment on her revelations, her dedication to performing the office might earn her more appreciation.

All the room regarded her with dread—most in apprehension of what they were about to hear, Elizabeth in anticipation of its effect.

"We have received no news of Norland today," Elinor said. "Be so kind as to enlighten us."

"Why, I can't believe you haven't heard! Harry lost Norland! Gambled it away in a card game to Lord Lovejoy. The whole estate!"

Marianne gasped. "Norland—gone?" She looked to her mother. "I cannot conceive of it. Strangers in our home?" She turned her gaze back to Lucy. "You are quite certain? There has been no mistake? You know how the *ton*—"

"Oh, I'm certain! I had it from Harry himself."

Elizabeth wondered what occasion Lucy would have had to see Mr. Dashwood already today, but given the magnetic pull between her and tidings of misfortune, some meeting between them in the wake of Harry's ill-fated whist game had probably been inevitable.

Mrs. Dashwood looked as if she'd been struck. "I am thankful Henry and Uncle Albert are not alive to witness this," she said quietly. "What an ungrateful child John and Fanny raised."

"Yes, poor Fanny!" said Lucy, oblivious to the fact that Mrs. Dashwood had been ascribing some of the responsibility to Harry's parents. "As a mother, my heart just breaks for her. Don't all of yours? Well—not yours, Mrs. Darcy, since you don't have any children. But if you were in the family way like your elder sister, I'm sure you'd understand."

Elizabeth smiled thinly and said nothing. The last person from whom she cared to hear observations about her family state was Lucy Ferrars.

"Thank heavens Fanny disinherited him before he could gamble away her fortune, too," Lucy continued. "Mrs. Darcy, your younger sister is well rid of Harry. I'm relieved that Regina avoided connection with him. I suspected he was developing an attachment to her, but obviously that will be most soundly discouraged now. Besides, she has so many gentlemen pursuing her that she hardly need settle for her own cousin."

Elizabeth, still vexed by Lucy's earlier remark, could not let this one pass unchallenged. "Indeed? I don't recall Miss Ferrars ever mentioning a suitor."

"Why, we had so many callers yesterday we could paper the parlor with their cards."

Fanny's bequest had evidently transformed Regina into a more eligible commodity in the marriage market. Elizabeth wondered if her newly enhanced dowry would prove enough to make up for inheriting Lucy Ferrars as a mother-in-law.

"Had you not better return home soon, then," Elinor suggested, "in case a caller appears whom Regina would like to receive?"

Elizabeth knew there was a reason she liked Elinor.

"No. I've told her a gentleman must come three times before we'll admit him—to prove he's serious." She rose. "But I do need to supervise her toilette. We are going to Almack's tonight."

She made as dramatic an exit as possible given that no one in her audience took interest in watching it. Her departure did, however, occasion a collective expression of relief on the part of those remaining.

"Norland—lost!" Marianne said as the curtain fell on Lucy's

performance. "I still can scarcely comprehend it. I hope Edward is soundly lecturing Harry this minute. Though what further evil our nephew can commit, I cannot imagine."

"Nor can I," Elinor said. "But I am sure that if he gets himself into any more trouble, Lucy will most thoughtfully keep us informed."

Twenty-three

*When people are determined on a mode of conduct which they
know to be wrong, they feel injured by the expectation of any
thing better from them.*

—Sense and Sensibility, *Chapter 36*

*M*r. Ferrars and Mr. Darcy." Mr. Dashwood repeated his
servant's announcement. "Come to call on me together. How congenial."

Harry received them in his dining room, where he sat behind
a large dish of ice cream. Though the *glace* looked appealing on
this warm June afternoon, Darcy begrudged Mr. Dashwood the
simple pleasure of it. In sacrificing his estate so capriciously, he
had injured not just himself and his family, but all those who
relied on Norland for their livelihoods. One ought not, it seemed
to Darcy, taste anything but remorse on the day following a dere-
liction of duty and honor such as he had committed.

"Your uncle and I share a common purpose this afternoon."

"I would invite you to sit," Harry said, "but that would suggest that I want you to stay. Which I do not." He swallowed a
spoonful of ice cream. "You are come, I suppose, to admonish
me once more for my wicked ways? You should have saved
yourselves the trouble. I have heard enough already from you,
Mr. Darcy, and from your wife, Mr. Ferrars."

Edward appeared puzzled. "Elinor has been in contact with you?"

The spoon paused halfway to Mr. Dashwood's mouth. "Forgive me, I meant my other aunt Ferrars. One loses track of them."

Darcy noted the full glass and half-empty bottle beside him and deduced the nature of Harry's genealogical impairment.

"Harry," Edward began, "all your family is very concerned about you."

Mr. Dashwood swallowed more ice cream. "This is splendid stuff. I cannot decide which I prefer—water ices or cream ices. I shall have to order Cook to stock both in the new larder."

"Harry," Edward continued, "I did not come to lecture you about Norland, or about your mother's fortune. Those losses cannot be restored. But the rest of it can be mended."

Harry tossed back his wine, or brimstone, or whatever it was he drank, and refilled the glass. "The rest of what?"

"This 'Hell-Fire Club' in which I understand you have immersed yourself."

Irritation flashed across Mr. Dashwood's face. "I do wish everyone would cease calling it that. I have never called it that."

"What do you call it?"

He shrugged. "The Monks of Medmenham, the Friars of Saint Francis, the Knights—choose whichever you fancy. I prefer the Knights of late. But it has never been the Hell-Fire Club. That's an old name the ignorant persist in using."

Darcy's patience ebbed. He had many words to describe Mr. Dashwood, his companions, and his activities, none of which he expected Harry would care to hear. "Whatever its name, your continued promotion of and involvement with the organization threatens more than your fortune."

"What else do I risk, Mr. Darcy? My life? It will run out in due course. My sacred honor? In their day, many great men associated with the Knights."

Darcy regarded Mr. Dashwood with contempt. Naught but his respect for Lord Chatfield could compel him to carry this mission any further.

"You are not a great man, Mr. Dashwood. Great men consider the influence they bear on those around them. If you will not check your behavior for your own sake, at least do not ruin others' futures along with yours."

"My Knights are grown men who make their own choices."

"To the grief of those around them." Darcy leaned on the table, so that his eyes were level with Harry's. "Mr. Dashwood, when you broke faith with Miss Bennet, you also betrayed the friendship I extended to you. My wife and I accepted you into our home, into our family circle, and into our lives. When you came to me seeking guidance, I gave it willingly. I regarded you as my brother."

Mr. Dashwood sighed, his expression bored. Darcy swallowed both his scorn and his pride, and continued.

"In remembrance of that former esteem, I ask one boon of you. Grant it, and I will trouble you no further."

The petition seemed to amuse him. "The righteous Mr. Darcy begs a favor from the fallen Mr. Dashwood? I am all attention."

"Lord Phillip Beaumont."

"What of him?"

"Drop him. From your Knights, from your acquaintance, from your memory."

Dashwood studied him. "What is Beaumont to you?"

"He has friends who wish to avoid hearing his name linked with scandal."

A sardonic smile twisted Harry's lips. "And who, in turn, pressure you to intercede." He laughed coldly. "I am afraid, Mr. Darcy, you will simply have to bear their displeasure at your failure, for I choose my own society, and so does Beaumont."

He emptied his glass again and reached for the bottle. "You may both leave now, for I have done with you."

Darcy and Edward stared at the rude dismissal. Mr. Dashwood waved them away. "That's right. 'Stand not upon the order of your going, but go at once.'" He returned to his ice cream, now half-melted in its dish. Darcy hoped he choked on it.

"I am astounded," Edward said when they reached the hall. "I thought your description had prepared me for his degeneration, but I had not comprehended its extent. He conducts himself in this manner all the time now?"

"Not always. He is often worse."

Mr. Ferrars shook his head. "He looks terrible. I have seen men whose health was ruined by drink or gluttony, but I have never witnessed an appearance deteriorate so quickly. And his eyes—his gaze is wizened, as if he possesses knowledge best left unknown."

"Candles that burn all night dwindle faster."

A knock at the door summoned the housekeeper, who answered it to admit, of all people, Phillip Beaumont. Providence had created a final opportunity for Darcy to fulfill his pledge to the earl. Darcy greeted Lord Phillip and presented Edward to him.

"Lord Phillip," Darcy said, "I wonder if I might speak to you about a matter of some concern."

Mr. Ferrars, recognizing his presence as superfluous and likely detrimental to the achievement of Darcy's objective, excused himself to wait in the carriage. Once he departed, Beaumont regarded Darcy expectantly.

"Lord Phillip—" Darcy considered his words, conscious that he had but moments to form an argument to which Beaumont might prove receptive. If the earl's entreaties had gone unheeded, how could the cautions of a near-stranger expect to find audience? Chatfield had already appealed to Phillip's sense of honor, family duty, and safety. But Beaumont was young, too young to believe himself or his reputation vulnerable to harm.

Harry Dashwood had believed himself similarly impervious, and look at him now.

Yes—look at him. Darcy would appeal to Beaumont's vanity.

"Lord Phillip, I have just come from Mr. Dashwood. As his friend, I desire your opinion. Does he seem much altered to you in recent weeks?"

"Of course. He's more lively and amusing. And he throws much better parties than he ever did at Oxford."

"But do you not think his pursuit of pleasure has taxed his physical person?"

"Perhaps a little."

The housekeeper hovered, obviously impatient to announce Lord Phillip to her master so she could get on with her other duties. A look from Darcy induced her to retreat a few steps.

"Only a little?"

"Well, all right—Dashwood is hardly cutting a dash these days. But what of it? He is seizing life."

"Do you not fear that participating in his dissipation will work similar effects upon you?"

He shrugged. "It hasn't thus far."

From the dining room, Mr. Dashwood summoned his house-keeper. Harry probably wanted to know who had knocked on the door. Darcy had at most a minute more with the countess's brother.

"Lord Phillip, it is not my business, but I urge you to take care in your intercourse with Mr. Dashwood."

"You are correct, Mr. Darcy. It is not your business."

Darcy accepted the rebuff without answer. This trip to Pall Mall had soundly thrashed his dignity. Having been curtly dismissed by both Dashwood and Beaumont, he would not tarry long enough to be run out by the housekeeper, as well. With a nod of farewell to Lord Phillip, he departed. His obligation to the earl had been discharged.

Twenty-four

*Her thoughts were silently fixed on the irreparable injury
which too early an independence and its consequent habits of
idleness, dissipation, and luxury had made . . . The world had
made him extravagant and vain—Extravagance and vanity
had made him cold-hearted and selfish.*

—Sense and Sensibility, *Chapter 44*

*E*lizabeth called in St. James's for what she expected would
be her last visit to the Brandons' townhouse. Elinor had
written that morning to report that, given the failure of Darcy
and Edward's meeting with Mr. Dashwood, the Ferrars saw little reason to continue their stay in town and would depart for
Devonshire on the morrow. Darcy, too, had expressed his desire to get Kitty and themselves out of London by week's end.
So Elizabeth set out to take proper leave of Mrs. Ferrars and
assure her that, whatever had transpired between Elinor's
nephew and Elizabeth's family, the Darcys valued their acquaintance with Mr. and Mrs. Edward Ferrars, and desired its
continuance.

To her disappointment, she arrived to find Elinor just going
out.

"You shall have to excuse me," Mrs. Ferrars said, "but I am on
my way to see Harry, and this is my only opportunity to do so."

Elizabeth accepted this announcement as good news. Perhaps Edward, upon review of yesterday's interview, had struck

upon a novel strategy to reclaim Mr. Dashwood. She did not, however, see Elinor's husband anywhere about.

"Does Mr. Ferrars accompany you?"

A guilty expression crossed Elinor's features. "Edward does not know—he is out with the Brandons and my mother. From what he told me of his encounter with Harry, I suspect he would not approve of my going. But I could not come all this way to London only to leave without so much as a glimpse of my nephew—without attempting myself to prevail upon him, even though others have been unable to do so."

"I could not either, were I you. How did you intend to get to his townhouse?"

"By hackney."

"I will take you."

Elinor gratefully accepted Elizabeth's offer, and soon the Darcys' carriage headed toward Pall Mall. Elinor seemed anxious, a mood Elizabeth jointly ascribed to apprehension over her imminent meeting with Harry and unease over the perceived deceit of making this call without Edward's knowledge. The former, at least, Elizabeth could attempt to mitigate, and perhaps the latter.

"As I have mentioned previously, Mrs. Ferrars, you should prepare yourself for a great alteration in your nephew," she said. "But take hope in the possibility that as a Dashwood yourself, you may succeed where others have failed in convincing him that your ancestor's legacy is not one to be admired."

"I pray you are correct," she replied. "I thought I would try evoking his memories of my father and Uncle Albert—forebears more worthy of his esteem. I only hope I do not get the reception Edward and Mr. Darcy did yesterday. One hopes Mr. Dashwood retains enough civility to treat a lady with more courtesy."

"One hopes." Elizabeth recalled his conduct toward Kitty, and doubted it. But she kept the opinion to herself, seeing little value in amplifying Elinor's trepidation.

"Mrs. Darcy, might I impose upon you to call on him with me? You have been in his company recently and might discern better than I an opening in the conversation that could be used to our advantage. And when I tell Edward of this visit—as tell him I must—the fact that I called with a companion might lessen any displeasure the news occasions."

"Of course I will accompany you." Elizabeth would have done so simply for friendship's sake, but Elinor's invitation also offered the potential for a glimpse at Mr. Dashwood's looking glass— provided it had arrived from Norland, and that she could locate it within the townhouse. She didn't imagine the Mirror of Narcissus was something likely to be left lying around the front hall.

She recalled Professor Randolph's caveat to refrain from looking directly into the glass, and to bring his amulet with her. Unfortunately, she could not heed all of his advice. She did not have the amulet on her person at present, nor could she justify to Elinor the need to stop at her own home en route to Pall Mall so she could retrieve a pocketwatch. She would simply have to go without it, for this would likely prove her only opportunity to obtain a look at the mirror.

As they arrived and disembarked from the carriage, a woman emerged from Mr. Dashwood's townhouse. At first, Elizabeth wondered if they beheld Harry's mystery mistress, but then she recognized the lady as Lucy Ferrars. Lucy stomped down the steps in such a state of vexation that she did not hear Elinor's salutation and almost strode right past them without recognition. A second greeting from Elinor slowed her.

"Elinor!" Lucy appeared startled. Her gaze darted toward her carriage as if she contemplated continuing into it without pausing to talk to them. Her sharp features tensed with impatience as the demands of common courtesy defeated the impulse. "Whatever are *you* doing here?"

"I was about to ask the same of you," Elinor said. "Mrs. Darcy and I hope to implore Harry to come to his senses."

"Well, good luck to you! Harry Dashwood is a knave and a scoundrel and I don't know what else! He can go to the devil, for all I care!"

"Good heavens, Lucy. What has happened?"

"He's lost all sense of honor, that's what. He'll take advantage of anybody." Her cat eyes narrowed as she struggled to check tears of anger. "I declare, Elinor, he has completely lost his conscience! Take my advice—get back in your carriage, go home, and forget you ever considered coming here. I wish I had."

With that, she threw herself into her gig and left.

"Well!" Elinor pulled her gaze away from the receding vehicle to face Elizabeth. "That certainly makes one want to proceed, does it not?"

"It makes me wish we had arrived a quarter hour earlier." Harry had probably grown weary of Lucy circling his townhouse to scavenge for gossip, and told her so in terms Elizabeth might have found diverting.

The housekeeper kept them standing outside while she ascertained whether the master was at home. Knowing quite well he was within, the ladies wondered whether he might refuse them entry following his row with Lucy. But the servant returned and admitted them.

There, resting in the last place Elizabeth expected to see it, was the mirror. Mr. Dashwood had indeed left it lying about the front hall—at least, temporarily. It leaned against the wall, still wrapped in the heavy blankets that had protected it during its journey from Norland. The blankets prevented Elizabeth from examining its detail, but given its size and dimensions, the object could be none other than Harry's antique looking glass. Three footmen, the same three who had struggled with it the last time Elizabeth called, prepared to move it once more. They looked for all the world as if they would be overjoyed to never lay eyes on the massive thing again.

Wineglass in one hand and pipe in the other, Mr. Dashwood directed their efforts from the landing above. "Simply stash it somewhere convenient for now—one of the spare bedchambers, perhaps. Lord Phillip says he will come retrieve it on the morrow."

"Yes, sir," replied one of the men, who appeared of the opinion that lifting the mirror up two flights of stairs for a single day's residence did not constitute his definition of convenience.

Elizabeth caught Mr. Dashwood's last statement with interest. Why was Lord Phillip taking possession of the looking glass? Had he, like Albert Dashwood, been asked to "keep it for a little while"?

"Mrs. Darcy, you and your friend may join me in the drawing room." Without waiting for Elizabeth and Elinor, he turned round and entered that room himself.

The ladies climbed the staircase before it became occupied by the looking glass. Elizabeth had hoped to observe the mirror's relocation so as to determine the exact chamber to which it was being consigned, but she would have to settle for listening to the movers' weighted footfalls from the drawing room and making her best guess.

As they entered, Mr. Dashwood refilled his glass with amber liquid that smelled of sulfur. He poured two more and held them toward the women. "Care to join me in a glass of brimstone?"

Elizabeth could scarcely stomach the odor of it. The thought of swallowing the vile brew made her nauseated. She declined, as did Elinor.

He laughed. "Probably too strong for your delicate palates anyway." He drained one of the glasses, then the other, and set them on the table beside the empty bottle. He took his own glass in hand once more and came toward them.

Elinor gaped at Mr. Dashwood as he neared, causing Elizabeth to assess his person anew. Weeks of heavy drinking, all-night gambling, and God knew what else had corrupted his form into that of a man over twice his age. Grey touched his hairline, and his cheeks had developed into jowls. Wrinkles framed his blood-shot eyes, and a slight tremor in his hand threatened the security of the glass he held. For Elizabeth, who had witnessed his deterioration gradually, his appearance was distressing enough; she could only imagine Elinor's shock at seeing it all at once. Colonel Brandon, at more than fifty, appeared in better health than her nephew.

And the impression did not even take into account Harry's moral corruption. She was reminded of Milton's Satan, whose outward appearance declined in pace with his spiritual fall until the former angel Lucifer was as ugly without as within. This was no epic poem; this was real life. Yet Harry, too, had made a hell of heaven and a heaven of hell, pushing away the fiancée, friends, and family who loved him to rule over his own profane domain.

Mr. Dashwood assessed them both with a lascivious gaze. "Mrs. Darcy, your visit today renders me all curiosity—particularly since Mr. Darcy does not accompany you. Tell me, does your husband know you are here?"

"Of course." The lie came out smoothly.

"Truly?" He smirked. "I would have guessed him ignorant on the subject of your coming."

"Mr. Darcy knows me well."

"I'd like to know you well."

Her pulse quickened, like that of prey realizing a predator lurks. Mr. Dashwood made no move toward her, but she nevertheless retreated a step.

He laughed, a scornful sound that went straight to her spine. "Is it I who threatens you, Mrs. Darcy? Or your own repressed desires?"

"Harry Dashwood!" Elinor exclaimed. "I rejoice that my father cannot hear your wicked address!"

"And who is he to me?"

"You may not have inherited your grandfather's noble character, but you do bear his name. Perhaps you could cease dragging it through the sewers of London."

He appraised her for a minute before finally saying, "Can I anticipate any more aunts arriving to lecture me today, or shall you be the last?"

"You should be ashamed of your behavior to Mrs. Darcy."

He mocked them both with a bow. "I beg your pardon, Mrs. Darcy." He gestured at his glass. "'That which makes others drunk hath made me bold'—"

She acknowledged his apology with a curt nod, but every muscle remained tense. She wanted to get away from him.

"—'and hath given me fire' . . . which I would be most obliged if you would quench."

An audible gasp escaped her. She thought she'd previously borne witness to objectionable behavior in him, but his conduct in her home had been nothing compared to what he now displayed in his own. She could not even formulate a reply sufficient to express her revulsion. Still nauseated, she now believed it was not the smell of his brimstone concoction but Mr. Dashwood himself making her sick.

"Mrs. Ferrars," she said, "if you do not object, I think I would be more comfortable waiting in the hall whilst you visit with your nephew."

"I understand," Elinor replied. "I shan't be long."

"Take as much time as you need. I shall be quite all right."

A sardonic smile contorted Mr. Dashwood's lips. "I hope it wasn't something I said, Mrs. Darcy?"

She left the room, shut the door, and leaned against it. She'd hoped the nausea would abate once she was outside Mr. Dashwood's presence, but it did not. Her heart, however, stopped pounding in her ears enough that she could think clearly. Conscience pricked her for leaving Elinor alone with Harry, but she thought Mrs. Ferrars would be fine. As Elinor was his aunt, Elizabeth doubted she would suffer anything worse than incivility from Harry—certainly nothing approaching the insult she herself had just endured. Besides, if Elinor's mission were going to succeed at all, it was probably best attempted without a third party present.

Her withdrawal, meanwhile, presented an ideal opportunity to obtain a glimpse of the mirror. While Mr. Dashwood's inappropriate overtures in the drawing room had diminished her motivation to try to help him, her own curiosity over whether he indeed possessed the Mirror of Narcissus—combined with a lack of anyplace better to go for the next few minutes—proved sufficient incentive to climb the stairs.

She found the looking glass in the bedchamber most proximate to the staircase, its bearers evidently having determined it the most convenient to their interests. She shut the door behind her, in case any servants wandered past, and went about unveiling the mirror.

The process involved a good deal of exertion. Removing the coverings required her to lift the heavy frame away from the wall and support it with one hand while tugging the blankets with her other. Fortunately, the mirror had been positioned so that when the wrap at last pooled on the floor, the glass faced outward.

She stepped round the front of the mirror. Keeping Professor Randolph's caution in mind, she diverted her gaze from the glass and focused on the frame. Exquisitely sculpted ancient athletes stood out in relief from a background of intertwined laurel leaves. Each champion, whether gripping a javelin, launching a discus, or racing on foot, was as flawlessly formed as the last. Elizabeth's eye roamed from one to the next, awed by the display of physical perfection, until her gaze reached the top of the frame.

There, at the mirror's crown, she beheld the most ideal male visage she'd ever seen. It was the face of youthful vigor, its noble cheekbones, strong jaw, and expressive eyes enhanced by Apollonian curls. The beauty of it overwhelmed her. Surely, this was the image of Narcissus.

She looked upon the mythical youth she knew not how long, unable, like he himself in legend, to tear her gaze away. The mirror itself possessed a quality of timelessness, creating the sense that it was not the product of any one age but of eternity, and Elizabeth could well have spent eternity studying it had not a sudden noise in the hall wrenched her attention toward the door. She held her breath in anticipation of discovery, but released it when no one entered. The sounds must have come from a passing servant.

She turned back to the mirror, but the interruption had distracted her. She forgot, just for a moment, Professor Randolph's warning.

It was a moment too long. She looked full into the glass.

'Twas not her own reflection it returned. It was Harry Dashwood's.

Twenty-five

No time was to be lost in undeceiving her, in making her acquainted with the real truth.

—Sense and Sensibility, *Chapter 37*

*E*lizabeth whirled around to confront Mr. Dashwood. She fought down panic at having been caught prowling where she did not belong. How had he sneaked in without her awareness?

He hadn't.

She was alone in the room. The door remained shut. Nothing had been disturbed—except her ease of mind.

Had the vision been only her own projection? She spun back around.

"Oh!" She caught her breath.

Again, Harry Dashwood gazed back at her.

Repeated glances over her shoulder confirmed that he was not behind her. She stepped back, struggling to make sense of what she saw.

He stood slumped, dejected, watching her with a resigned air. Though his gaze followed her, it was detached, as if he observed a stage actor delivering a performance in which he did not take part. Despite the events of recent weeks, somehow this sight of him caused an overpowering wave of sadness to engulf her.

Why she should experience pity for a man who had behaved so reprehensibly toward her sister, herself, and everyone else who cared about him, she could not comprehend. Then she realized that this image of Mr. Dashwood was not that of the degenerate rake she'd left downstairs with Elinor, the man suffering disfigurement wrought by his own dissipation. It was that of the earnest young man who had wooed Kitty, the handsome gentleman who'd earned the respect and admiration of them all. Erased were the effects of excess. In his mirror image, Harry was restored to health, vigor, and—from outward appearance, at least—himself.

How was this possible? If Mr. Dashwood was not present in the room, whom—*what*—did she behold?

"Mr.—Mr. Dashwood?"

His eyes widened. He stood up straight and moved toward her, stopping when he reached the glass barrier between them. He regarded her eagerly.

Mrs. Darcy, he mouthed. *Mrs. Darcy, can you hear me?*

His expression implored her to say yes. But she could not. The only sound she could hear was the pounding of her own heart.

She shook her head. "Can you hear me?"

He nodded vigorously.

She had no idea what to say. Or to whom she would be saying it. Was this Harry Dashwood? A devil in his guise? A figment of her imagination?

"Mr. Dashwood, what—" She gestured toward the empty chamber. "You are not present in the room with me. How is it that I can see you in the mirror?"

He started talking, but she could not hear a syllable.

"I cannot comprehend you. More slowly, Mr. Dashwood."

He nodded and took a deep breath, then tried again. Though

he moved his lips with deliberate slowness, she still could not make out his words.

She shook her head helplessly. "Mr. Dashwood, I'm afraid I still cannot understand you."

He ran his hands through his hair, even more disheartened than she at their inability to communicate. She wanted to know what was transpiring, and he clearly wanted to tell her. She searched her mind for some means by which he could make himself heard, but turned up naught.

She glanced at the door. Could someone else help them? She doubted Elinor could, and even so, how would she ever get Harry's aunt to this chamber without the knowledge of—

She froze.

Of whom? If Harry Dashwood was in the mirror, whom had she left downstairs? And if Harry Dashwood was downstairs, who or what was in the mirror? She didn't know which thought disturbed her more. Of only one thing was she certain: The Mirror of Narcissus was indeed cursed. She needed to find Professor Randolph. If anyone could explain this extraordinary situation, he could.

She turned back to the figure in the mirror. "I—I have to go," she said.

He shook his head vehemently. *No! Please—no.* He pressed his hands against the glass.

"But Mr. Dashwood, or whoever you are—"

Help me.

Though the words had no sound, they reverberated in her mind. His haunted expression beseeched her. Compassion seized her, yet the fact remained that she hadn't the power to grant his plea.

She held up her palms. "How can I aid you if I cannot understand you?"

His jaw and fists clenched in frustration. He broke their gaze and brought his hands up before him. He looked from his fists to the glass as if contemplating punching the barrier. He seemed about to try when his gaze shifted to her palms, still raised.

He opened his hands and studied them. Then he raised his head and met her eyes.

He gestured to her hands. He held his own up and pressed them to the glass. Then he nodded toward her hands again.

Elizabeth hesitated. If Professor Randolph had warned against looking directly into the mirror, pressing one's hands against it to commune with some image that had no original present seemed like a very poor notion, indeed. She did not know upon whom or what she gazed. Man or ghost? Benign entity or demonic creature? If she did as he bade, what would be the consequence? *I seem to recall that many of its owners have met untimely ends,* the archaeologist had said. She did not even have the amulet with her for protection.

She should leave this instant. Turn her back and walk away. Retrieve help—or perhaps never return. She owed Mr. Dashwood nothing. He had ceased being an object deserving her concern the moment he first mistreated Kitty.

If that transgressor had, in fact, been Mr. Dashwood.

She could not ignore the nagging impression taking hold of her, that somehow she presently gazed upon the true Harry Dashwood. Nor could she ignore the desperation in his countenance.

Elizabeth said a swift, silent prayer. Then lifted her hands to the glass.

She is in a great, drafty room, cluttered with trunks and shrouded furniture. A large, rectangular object leans against one wall. A slightly smaller and thinner parcel rests against it. She reaches out to the smaller object. Her hands are not her own. They are larger— a man's hands. She unwraps the item. It is the portrait of Sir Francis. She unveils the mirror. Harry Dashwood gazes back at her. But he moves as she moves. His reflection is hers. She is Harry, discovering the mirror at Norland. Experiencing his memory with dual consciousness—her own and Harry's.

She is in a well-appointed dressing room now. Pall Mall bustles outside the window. Her valet helps her tuck her shirt into her trousers, then offers a cravat. She approaches the mirror to tie the neckcloth and is startled to see someone else's face instead. Not her own—not Harry's—but one very like his. The vision lasts but an instant.

She is in the dressing room again. She—Harry—straightens her waistcoat before the mirror. Behind her hangs the portrait of Sir Francis, brought from Norland. She sees the face in the mirror again. It matches that in the portrait. It speaks. Come closer, Harry. *Then the face is gone again.*

It is dark. She is in bed, alone. Exhausted but afraid to sleep. A voice whispers in the night. Trust me, Harry. *She crushes a pillow to her ears and prays for sunrise.*

She is in her own house—her and Darcy's townhouse. Darcy is speaking to her in the hall. Mr. Dashwood, if you would but confide in me, perhaps I can help you out of this scrape. *She shakes her head.* I have to go home. *She returns to Pall Mall and heads straightaway for the mirror.* Show yourself, Sir Francis! *Nothing happens. She keeps vigil. No matter what, she cannot allow herself to fall asleep. But fatigue overtakes her, and she nods off as the candle sputters out.*

———

She awakens with a start. Twelve white-robed figures surround her bed, chanting. She at first takes their song to be a Gregorian chant, but soon realizes that the Latin words hold a profane undercurrent. She tries to rise from the bed, but the rhythmless song holds her immobile. One of the monks parts the curtains to admit the light of the full moon. The shaft illuminates the mirror. Sir Francis appears. And steps out.

He stands over her. He laughs ominously, a sound that leaves her hollow. He offers a blasphemous incantation and reaches toward her. His voice rises steadily, repeating the same words until they engulf her. Reddet animam pro anima.

He touches her chest. Her heart stops. Excruciating pain rips through her. She is rent in twain, her spirit torn from her body.

For an instant, all goes black. Then, from the side of the room, she sees her body—Harry's body—on the bed. It sits up and looks at her with Sir Francis's eyes. He raises an exultant shout. I am flesh once more!

She releases a cry of her own and charges forward. She strikes glass. She sinks to her knees, her hands sliding down the invisible barrier between herself and her self.

The curtain is drawn. Sir Francis and his disciples file from the room, and sounds of celebration soon echo below.

Only she remains: the newest prisoner of the mirror.

Twenty-six

She was mortified, shocked, confounded.
—Sense and Sensibility, *Chapter 22*

*E*lizabeth fell to the floor, the force of Harry's memories literally knocking her from her feet. She curled in a ball,
gasping for breath, clutching her head, willing the ache that
pierced her mind to stop. She shut her eyes against the horror
of what she'd witnessed.

Gradually, the pain diminished. She opened her eyes and
raised herself to her knees. She did not dare look at the mirror
again. She stared at the floor, resting on all fours as she struggled
to regain command over herself—to comprehend the knowledge she'd just received.

Harry Dashwood was trapped inside the Mirror of Narcissus, and had been for weeks. While she and Darcy had maintained surveillance outside, suspecting Harry of wrongdoing,
the old Hell-Fire Club had released its leader and imprisoned
Harry in his stead. And while Harry's spirit was trapped, Sir
Francis roamed free in his shell.

It was Sir Francis, then, who had hurt Kitty, who had insulted
her and Darcy. Who led London's bloods in new explorations of

debauchery. Who had alienated Harry's friends and family to the point of losing his maternal inheritance, then gambled away his estate. It was Sir Francis whom Elizabeth had left in the drawing room with Elinor, and who would come looking for her if her absence was realized.

She pushed herself to her feet. From the corner of her eye, she detected Harry attempting to capture her attention. She averted her gaze, fixing it instead upon the door. She prayed Sir Francis would not come through it while she deliberated what to do.

Harry must be released from the mirror. But how? His body and soul had been separated through some unholy ritual enacted by Sir Francis and twelve others—all of them practiced communicants. What could she, ignorant of their rites, unprepared for the test of spirit, accomplish alone? She regretted again the lack of Professor Randolph's amulet. She needed its protection. She needed the archaeologist's knowledge. She needed a plan. She needed Darcy.

"I am leaving to summon assistance, Mr. Dashwood." She did not know how he responded to the statement, for she yet avoided sight of the glass. "But I shall return. I give you my word."

She descended to the drawing room, wondering how long she'd been gone and what had transpired in the interim. Thankfully, she heard Elinor's voice, indicating that Harry's aunt and Mr. Dashwood—Sir Francis—were yet in conference. God willing, they remained unaware that she'd been anywhere but waiting in the hall.

She entered to find Sir Francis well into a new bottle of brimstone. The smell of the liquor made her stomach roil, and the sight of him filled her with revulsion. She concentrated on maintaining a steady countenance so as not to betray her new knowledge of him.

"Mrs. Darcy." Sir Francis greeted her. "Have you elected to rejoin us?"

"I am afraid that I feel indisposed and would like to return home. Mrs. Ferrars, if you have not completed your call, I would be happy to send my carriage back to convey you whenever you are ready."

"You do look rather peaked," Sir Francis observed.

She realized belatedly that in having so studiously avoided looking into the mirror, she had no idea whether her ordeal had left any telltale effects. But if her appearance made her look even more ill than she felt, so much the better.

"Let us leave at once, Mrs. Darcy," Elinor said, "for my business here is finished."

"Yes, my aunt was taking me to task for my irresponsible behavior, until I informed her that I shall soon be settling down. I am engaged to be married, you see."

Elizabeth blinked at the unexpected news. "May I ask who the lady is?"

"My lovely cousin Regina."

"Congratulations." She did her best to mask the speculation his announcement occasioned. Was this, she wondered, the subject of his earlier row with Lucy Ferrars? With Norland lost and Regina in possession of Fanny's fortune, the match Regina's pushy mama had once so aggressively pursued was now of advantage only to Mr. Dashwood. "I wish you better success in reaching the altar this time."

"Oh, I shall reach it. We plan to wed as soon as a special license can be procured."

Having sacrificed Harry's estate to the pursuit of pleasure, Sir Francis would thus secure the remainder of Harry's rightful fortune. Meanwhile the unsuspecting Regina would be trapped in a marriage with the devil in disguise.

"That is little time to prepare for a wedding. How does Miss Ferrars feel about such a brief engagement?"

"She is flattered by the intensity of my ardor."

Of course she was. The green girl had never received a second look from any man until Fanny settled her fortune upon her, and by then she'd been groomed by her mother to covet Mr. Dashwood's addresses above all others.

Her head yet ached, and this new intelligence only worsened it. Repeating her plea of indisposition, she departed with Elinor. She wanted nothing more than to get away from this place, to consult Professor Randolph and to confide in Darcy.

Twenty-seven

"You will tell me, I know, that this may, or may not have hap-
pened; but I will listen to no cavil, unless you can point out any
other understanding of this affair as satisfactory as this."
    —Mrs. Dashwood to her daughter Elinor,
    Sense and Sensibility, *Chapter 15*

*D*arcy glowered at Julian Randolph. "If my wife has endan-
gered herself as the result of a conversation with you—"

"I'm sure she has not," the professor said hastily. "I've called
today only as a precaution."

Darcy was little satisfied. Until Elizabeth returned home
from her leavetaking of Elinor Ferrars and promised to not so
much as muse about Mr. Dashwood or his mirror, he would
hold Randolph culpable for every moment of his own uneasiness. The archaeologist had called at their townhouse following
a discussion he and Elizabeth had had several days ago, a meeting Mrs. Darcy apparently had not felt the need to mention to
her husband. When Darcy learned its nature, he guessed why.
Randolph had been filling her head with his supernatural nonsense again.

He listened impatiently for sounds of Elizabeth's return and
had left the drawing room door open to aid his hearing. He was
not angry with her, but he wanted very much to discuss this
business with her directly. Elizabeth tended to place too much

credence in Professor Randolph's preposterous notions, and Darcy wanted to counter his influence.

"So I am to understand that based on some half-remembered tales of an old Greek mirror, you have convinced my wife that Mr. Dashwood's glass is a legendary artifact known as the Mirror of Narcissus? And further, that after persuading her to obtain another look at this object, you have since come to believe it is cursed?"

"I speculated that it *might* be the legendary mirror, and suggested that a better description would provide more certainty. Mrs. Darcy then told me that the mirror had been returned to Sussex, making it doubtful that she'll come into contact with it again. As it turns out, that is a fortuitous circumstance." He tapped the cover of the book he had brought with him, a worn volume with tattered pages. "Since speaking with her, I have further researched the mirror's history. Based on my findings, I came here to urge her to stay away from the glass altogether in the unlikely event that an opportunity to view it should arise."

"On that point, you and I are united. Though it is the artifact's owner that I wish her to avoid. The mirror itself cannot possibly be the one in question—its craftsmanship is too modern for it to have been fashioned in ancient times."

"That may not necessarily be true."

Darcy heard a carriage arrive, followed by the front door opening. The welcome sound meant Elizabeth had returned, for Kitty and Georgiana had gone to spend a few days with the Gardiners before leaving London and thus were not expected home. He relaxed in anticipation of momentarily laying eyes on his wife and putting an end to this whole discussion.

When she entered the drawing room, however, his disquiet increased rather than diminished. She seemed pale and looked as if she'd just come in out of a strong wind. She also moved more slowly than usual and had an air of anxiety about her.

He rose and went to her immediately. "Are you well?"

"I am fine. Though I have just returned from a distressing meeting and am glad to find you at home." She turned to Randolph. "Your being here is also most fortunate, Professor, as we are going to want your assistance."

"It shall be given most willingly."

Darcy took her hand and led her to a chair. "What is the trouble? Did you find Mrs. Ferrars unwell?"

"Mrs. Ferrars is quite well. Her nephew, however, is in grave danger."

"No doubt of his own making," Darcy declared. "I cannot pity Mr. Dashwood."

"You will, Darcy, when I tell you what was happened to him."

Thereupon she commenced a tale he could not have countenanced the telling of, had it come from anyone but his wife. Only the vision of her sitting immediately before him, safe now, enabled him to attend her in patience. He heard with displeasure her confession that she had gone to Dashwood's townhouse, with foreboding the news that the mirror had arrived just before her, and with incredulity her account of what had transpired after that.

Mr. Dashwood's spirit, imprisoned in his mirror? The very idea was beyond absurd.

"Mr. Dashwood must have practiced some deceit upon you," he pronounced when Elizabeth finished her narration. Grateful that she had escaped the ordeal unharmed, he sought a rational explanation of it. Harry Dashwood was a man without honor or conscience; morally, Darcy considered him capable of anything. What he had not yet determined was how the rogue had created a ruse elaborate enough to convince Elizabeth. His wife was an intelligent woman; mere sleight of hand would not suffice.

"How, Darcy? How could he have embedded an old image of himself in the mirror?"

"There—you have struck upon it exactly. It is an old image.

He used his birthday portrait; he secured it in place of the glass. That is why you could not see your own reflection, because it is no longer a mirror. In fact, perhaps that is why the mirror was out of his possession recently. He sent it to Norland, where he had left his birthday portrait, and a cohort performed the modification."

"I could believe that if the image had been fixed," she said. "But it was animated. It spoke to me—or tried to, at least. How could Mr. Dashwood accomplish that?"

"I am still working that out."

"Well, while you ponder, poor Mr. Dashwood remains trapped in the glass."

"Elizabeth, people do not become trapped in looking glasses."

Randolph cleared his throat. "Perhaps in this one, they do." He pushed his spectacles up and opened his book to a page with several illustrations, including one Darcy had to admit looked familiar, even from his vantage point. "Mrs. Darcy, is this the mirror you saw today?"

She studied the drawing. "Yes. It's not an exact rendering, but there's no mistaking it."

"The artist never saw the original; he sketched it from description." He offered the book to Darcy. "Mr. Darcy, does the picture match your recollection of Mr. Dashwood's mirror, as well?"

Darcy accepted the volume, discovering as he did so that it was older than he had realized. Its leather cover was worn smooth; many of its pages were mottled and warped. The metal lock that once guarded its contents looked to have lost its clasp long ago. From the style of the illuminations and hand-lettered text, he judged the book to be at least three or four centuries old. He handled it with reverence, appreciating its age and artistry.

"What is this book?"

"*Mysteries of the Ancients,* a text that describes numerous artifacts from Italy, Greece, and Egypt thought to have found their way to Britain."

Darcy examined the illustration Randolph had indicated and grudgingly conceded its similarity to his memory of Harry's looking glass. While he had the book in his hands, he skimmed its words. The text itself was Latin; annotations in multiple hands and languages covered the page margins.

The writers offered an explanation for the mirror's anachronistic construction, but one in which Darcy could not invest any credence. Apparently, however, many others had. He gave the original myth only a cursory glance and skipped to later accounts of the glass. The legendary Mirror of Narcissus had already earned a deleterious reputation by the time of the book's authorship, one amplified by successive owners of the volume.

"The text and notes speak of the mirror's owners meeting untimely deaths," Darcy said, "yet also state that they died of old age. How is such an end unanticipated?"

"If you read more closely, the authors indicate that those owners lived few years. They were young men and women who died elderly."

Elizabeth regarded the professor in puzzlement. "I do not understand."

"Let us start at the beginning." Randolph accepted the book back from Darcy. "According to legend, the Mirror of Narcissus was created for a vain king who could not bear to see the changes time naturally wrought upon his face and form as he aged. He commanded his best craftsman to design a mirror that would reflect him as he had appeared in his prime. The craftsman, unable to follow this order, turned to Aphrodite for aid. He prayed to the goddess of beauty to enable him to create the most beautiful mirror in Greece.

"After weeks of supplication, the goddess granted his request. Through her power, the artisan crafted a mirror unlike any ever seen before. When he had finished, he brought the mirror to the Temple of Aphrodite, made an offering of gratitude to the goddess, and begged one last petition: that she invest his creation with the power his master demanded.

"The goddess appeared to him. She praised his work and blessed the hands that had produced it. But she denied his request, explaining that eternal youth, even in image only, was a privilege reserved for the gods.

"The craftsman thanked her and returned to the palace with the mirror. He presented it to the king and related Aphrodite's words. The king was angry. As he raged at the craftsman, he caught sight of himself—old, bent, and ugly with wrath—in the glass and grew still more furious. He cursed the mirror and ordered the craftsman's hands cut off as punishment for his failure. The guards acted immediately and severed the hands that Aphrodite had blessed.

"As they led the maimed craftsman away, the king pointed to the mirror and started to order it destroyed. But then he saw his reflection. In the glass, he was a young man once more. He instructed his servants to move the mirror to his private quarters and retired to gaze upon his image uninterrupted, as Narcissus had gazed into the water. In the morning, they found him dead, still staring into the glass."

Darcy listened with the interest he accorded any engaging story. "That is a good cautionary tale against the evils of vanity," he pronounced when the archaeologist had finished, "but like any myth, hardly something to be accepted as fact."

"Subsequent tales support it," Randolph replied. "According to this book, many of the mirror's more vain owners through the centuries have undergone radical disfigurement in their final days. Young or old, they died ravaged by extreme effects of age."

What little color had been in Elizabeth's face drained from it. "Are all its gazers cursed?"

It bothered Darcy to witness distress in her. "Nobody is

cursed," he asserted. "The glass is an artifact whose history inspires embellishment—nothing more."

Randolph closed the book. "I don't believe you are in any danger yourself, Mrs. Darcy, for having looked into the glass today. But I disagree with your husband. The Mirror of Narcissus is indeed cursed, and how the curse functions has been a subject of mystery and speculation for centuries."

Darcy found himself unable to sit still. Harry Dashwood's transformation had been caused by his own excesses—not a looking glass, and certainly not a curse. He rose and went to the window, needing to distance himself from the discussion or risk responding uncivilly to the archaeologist. He looked out onto the street, with its buildings, carriages, people—tangible things, things that were real.

"Until now, no one has been able to satisfactorily explain the nature of the curse," Randolph continued. "However, based on your account of Harry's memories, Mrs. Darcy, I have a new theory."

"Do let us hear it," Darcy said.

"I submit that the mirror's original owner, the king, died because his spirit was absorbed by the glass. He wanted to become the image that he saw, and the mirror granted his request. His body, an empty shell, remained behind. As the mirror passed from owner to owner, those equally possessed by the same desire were also entrapped."

"It must be growing rather crowded in there," Darcy scoffed.

"Not at all," Randolph replied. "Mrs. Darcy, kindly repeat what Sir Francis said when his followers released him from the glass."

"I believe it was *'reddet animam pro anima.'*"

"From the Book of Exodus: 'Thou shalt give life for life.' In this case, it could also be interpreted as 'soul for soul,'" Randolph said. "The glass can hold only one life, or soul, at a time. The king's essence remained incarcerated only until the next victim took his place. When his spirit left the mirror, it entered the new prisoner's discarded body. But the unnatural reincarnation could not last long—the king's soul was by then so old that the new body could not sustain it. The host suffered rapidly accelerated aging as the body's clock strove to catch up with the spirit's, until it ultimately burned out."

"And this cycle repeats itself with each new victim?" Elizabeth asked.

"Yes, and is at work upon Harry Dashwood now."

Darcy stared out the window, unable to reconcile the image of the modern, mundane London before him with the mystical events Randolph imagined had taken place within it. Something strange was happening in Mr. Dashwood's townhouse—having witnessed some of the goings-on himself, he could not refute that much. But he firmly believed Dashwood the perpetrator, not the victim, of deception. Even if he willingly suspended his disbelief, accepted for the sake of argument some of the professor's premises, he still could not agree with Randolph's conclusions.

He turned from the window but remained beside it. "There is a flaw in your theory. Assuming my wife, through Mr. Dashwood's memories, indeed witnessed this theoretical trading of souls between Sir Francis and Harry Dashwood"—an assumption Darcy could hardly voice, much less believe—"it required twelve others and a secret ceremony to effect the transfer. I find it hard to believe that each previous victim was involved in such a ritual."

"The other victims were willing participants in their own entrapment," Elizabeth said. "Harry Dashwood was not."

"Precisely," Randolph said. "The king and his successors were drawn in because they could not resist the sight of their former selves. Harry Dashwood, however, was in the full bloom of youth. He was not yet vulnerable to the mirror's temptation and would not be for some time. I suspect that Sir Francis, already incarcerated for more than thirty years, grew impatient and forced the exchange."

Darcy remained unconvinced. "If he was trapped in the glass, how did he gather his former Hell-Fire Club together to perform the rite?"

"That I don't know."

"And if Sir Francis was a victim of the mirror," Darcy pressed, "why do no accounts of his death mention the accelerated aging suffered by the others?"

"If he was already elderly and very close to the end of his natural life, the effects may have gone unnoticed. His body might have died within hours or even minutes of the mirror's previous occupant taking possession of it."

"So short a time?" Elizabeth's brow creased with worry. "Sir Francis has occupied Mr. Dashwood's form for a month now. How much time do you think he has left?"

"How old is Harry's body supposed to be, and how old did he look when you saw him today?"

"He is one-and-twenty, but he appears fifty at least."

"Do we know how old Sir Francis was when he died?"

"In his seventies."

Professor Randolph withdrew a handkerchief from one of his many pockets and wiped his spectacles. "It sounds as if Harry Dashwood's body is aging rapidly, indeed, and to compound matters, I understand Sir Francis has not been the most gentle tenant. I would guess your friend has perhaps a fortnight, if that, to reclaim himself."

"He is *not* our friend," Darcy said. "And he has made it very clear to me that he does *not* want our assistance or interference in his affairs."

Elizabeth stared at him a long moment. His wife's gaze made him uncomfortable, and he shifted under the weight of her disapprobation. When she rose and came to the window, came to him, he looked away. On the sofa, Randolph replaced his spectacles and consulted his book once more.

"Darcy," she said, speaking in tones so soft that they reached his ears alone. "It is Sir Francis, not Harry, who has behaved so uncivilly toward us."

He sighed heavily. "Elizabeth, this is all too far-fetched to be believed. At least by me. I can barely listen to it, let alone acknowledge it as possible."

"If you had seen what I saw, you would think otherwise."

"But I did not."

He at last faced her. Sadness spread across her face, and he disliked himself for having caused it. Worse, her eyes, normally bright with exuberance, dimmed with disappointment. In him.

"Darcy, when we were last at Netherfield, we both stumbled into danger because you believed in reason more than you believed in me. I know what I experienced today. Will you not this time trust my perceptions?" She laid a hand on his arm. "I am certain that the Harry Dashwood we first met, the Harry Dashwood who won Kitty's heart, whom you considered as a brother, still exists. He desperately needs our aid, and how I shall live with myself if we fail him, I do not know. If you will not act for Mr. Dashwood's sake, will you do so for mine?"

She had struck upon the only argument she could have used to win his cooperation. For a worthless rakehell he would do nothing. But to prevent the blackguard from causing his wife a moment's further anguish—and to remove that expression from her eyes—he would do anything.

"Professor Randolph, what must be done to release Harry?" He cast her a meaningful look. "Hypothetically?"

She smiled.

"The mirror will demand a soul for a soul," Randolph replied, "and if Harry is to get his own body back, that soul must be Sir Francis's. We must therefore trick Sir Francis into gazing at Harry's reflection long enough to effect the exchange."

"The person presently answering to the name Harry Dashwood is many things, but he is not a fool. You said that without such a ceremony as Sir Francis arranged, a victim must be complicitous in his own entrapment. Sir Francis will never allow himself to risk reimprisonment," Darcy said.

"In fact," Elizabeth added, "he schemes to rid himself of the mirror altogether. I heard him say that Lord Phillip Beaumont would retrieve it tomorrow."

Lord Phillip? Darcy suppressed a groan. Why the countess's brother, of all people? Despite his skepticism over the whole enterprise and his recent rebuff from Lord Phillip himself, Darcy now felt himself obligated by his friendship with the earl to at least keep the mirror—whatever it might or might not be—out of Beaumont's possession.

"Why does Sir Francis not simply destroy the glass?" he asked.

Randolph pushed his spectacles back to the bridge of his nose. "There is no account of any previous owner attempting to do so. Perhaps once released into a new body, a victim's continued existence yet depends on the mirror's enchantment. Or the victim may merely fear it does. However brief his new life may be, the newly freed prisoner is unwilling to risk it ending any sooner than it must."

The archaeologist shrugged. "Whatever his reasoning, let us be grateful for Harry's sake that Sir Francis has not destroyed the glass in all the time he's had to do so. But with Lord Phillip planning to take ownership of it, we now must devise a strategy quickly, as our task becomes far more difficult if the mirror leaves Sir Francis's proximity. We also need to rescue Harry before Sir Francis wears out his body. If Sir Francis dies, Harry could be trapped inside the mirror indefinitely. He would be forced either to wait until another unsuspecting victim fell prey to the mirror's curse, or to ask us to destroy the mirror with him in it, putting an end to the cycle."

"Let us formulate a plan, then, and go directly," Elizabeth said.

"*I* will go," Darcy corrected. "You will stay here, out of danger and well away from anyone named Dashwood."

She appeared about to object, but Professor Randolph did it for her. "Mrs. Darcy's participation may prove critical to our success. From her description of her encounter with Harry's reflection, it sounds as if he was surprised that she could see him. Indeed, I expect most people can't, or surely the servants would have noticed him by now, the way the mirror's been moved around lately. Mrs. Darcy may possess a sensitivity to her environment which surpasses that of the average person."

Darcy disliked the reminder of a fact he preferred not to contemplate too often. If he acknowledged to himself that his wife's perceptions were legitimate, he must also acknowledge that there were forces in the world that he could not himself perceive and therefore could not protect her from. It was far easier to deny the existence of cursed mirrors than to admit his own powerlessness.

He felt the gentle press of her hand on his arm. "I promise to be very careful," she said. "And you shall be with me."

He did not like this, any of it. Supernatural issues aside, the Mr. Dashwood who moved freely in the world—whichever Dashwood he might be—was an unpredictable rogue. Darcy would not put it past him to become violent if sufficiently provoked, and should that happen, he wanted Elizabeth nowhere near. Indeed, he would rather himself not be anywhere near. But somehow it had fallen upon them to make one final attempt to reclaim his soul—either from the mirror or from perdition itself.

He took his wife's hand and went to sit near the professor again. "All right," he conceded. "How do we do this?"

Randolph tapped the page he'd been studying. "I have just thought of a strategy."

Twenty-eight

*B*ut my business with Mr. Dashwood is most urgent," Elizabeth insisted to Harry's housekeeper. "I would never call upon him at this hour were it not." She hoped she sounded convincing. Her errand was indeed urgent, though did Sir Francis know its nature he might hold a different opinion. Releasing Harry from the Mirror of Narcissus and becoming reincarcerated himself probably did not top his priorities this morning. "Tell him Mrs. Darcy calls."

"Oh, I know who you are, ma'am. The master is not at home."

As Elizabeth pulled her wrap tight against the light rain, her hand brushed Professor Randolph's amulet, which she wore on a chain round her neck. She resisted the urge to steal a glance at her carriage, where the archaeologist and Darcy concealed themselves. Seeking admission alone had been her suggestion, one Darcy had resisted until the moment the coach stopped in Pall Mall. He had not wanted her to enter Mr. Dashwood's townhouse without him—and she had not even told him about Sir

Francis's indecent advances yesterday. But relations between Darcy and Sir Francis had become so strained that she feared Darcy might no longer gain entrée any time of day, and she hoped that Sir Francis might be sufficiently intrigued by her calling unaccompanied so early in the morning that he would receive her. Unfortunately, he had not yet been given that choice—first she had to pass Cerberus.

"May I please at least step in from the rain while you ask whether he will receive me?" While the housekeeper was thus occupied, Elizabeth would let in the gentlemen, who would make their way to the room with the mirror and wait for her to lead Sir Francis there. That was the second part of the scheme Darcy disliked. Actually, he disliked all parts of it, particularly those that involved her.

To be honest, she was not bubbling with enthusiasm over the plan herself. Nervous about today's events, she'd gone to bed nauseated, woken up nauseated, and probably would remain so until the situation was resolved. She hardly looked forward to being once more in proximity to Sir Francis, the source of her indisposition.

"I'm telling you truly, ma'am, the master is not at home. He's not in his chamber, nor anywhere in the house—"

A woman's scream resonated somewhere deep in the house.

"Beg your pardon, ma'am!"

The housekeeper hurried off, swinging the door behind her. Before it shut, Elizabeth caught it and stepped inside. The hall was empty, and she could hear a commotion belowstairs. She went back to the door and beckoned Darcy and Professor Randolph to come quickly.

"The housekeeper claims Mr. Dashwood is not at home," she said when they joined her. "The servants are all below—someone just screamed."

"The scream came from downstairs?" Darcy asked.

"Yes," she said. "Go up to the chamber with the mirror, as

we planned. You will never have a better opportunity to reach it unseen. I will determine whether the scream warrants our concern."

Darcy shook his head emphatically. "You stay here with Professor Randolph while I investigate the scream."

"And how will you explain your presence in the house?"

"That is immaterial."

"Mr. Darcy, I must concur with your wife," the professor said. "If you reveal yourself now, our whole scheme falls to pieces. We cannot risk failure over a scullery maid spying a rat."

Darcy released an exasperated breath and cast his gaze about the hall. It came to rest on the dining room door, which stood open. "We will wait for you in there," he said. "If someone is screaming, I do not want to be three stories away from you. Tell us what you learn, and we will proceed from there."

"But how will I report back to you without the servants noticing?"

Her husband looked at her confidently. "If I know you, Mrs. Darcy, you will find a way."

It was not difficult to determine how to reach the lower level; she simply followed the noise. Nor was it hard to overhear the cause of the excitement and return to the dining room undetected by the preoccupied staff.

"We no longer have a need for subterfuge," she announced to Darcy and the professor. "Sir Francis is dead."

"I just knew those ices would be the end of him." The cook shook her head sadly. "Only, I thought he'd *eat* himself to the hereafter. I never expected this."

"I doubt anyone did." Elizabeth tried to sound sympathetic, but her mind was only half engaged in the conversation. The other half wondered what they were going to do about Harry now that Sir Francis had died. A glance at Darcy and Professor Randolph revealed that they didn't know, either.

"The master was in that larder every night, don't you know, dipping into the ices. Usually after all of us had gone to bed. Lemon was his favorite. I think his lady friend preferred strawberry. Liked to sneak down there himself, instead of waking a servant—made it seem like more of a guilty pleasure, I think. I'd get up in the morning and find the empty pans." She dabbed her eyes with her apron. "This morning, I found *him*."

The cook had discovered Sir Francis in the subcellar larder, his body as cold as the ices of which he was so fond. It was her scream that Elizabeth had heard and that had summoned the whole staff. The servants were in such a state of shock over their employer's demise that when Elizabeth had returned to the scene with Darcy and the professor in tow, no one had looked askance at their sudden appearance. In fact, many of them recognized Darcy from previous visits and gratefully looked to him, a gentleman, as some sort of authority figure who could provide direction.

"How did you come upon him?" Darcy asked.

"After I started breakfast, I went down there to get ice cream for the master's strawberries—"

"Ice cream at breakfast?" Elizabeth could not help but interrupt.

"He used to simply have ordinary cream, but since he built that larder, now he wants ice cream. So I give him ice cream." She shrugged. "That was nothing. Gentlemen have all sorts of peculiar tastes—if you'll pardon my saying so, sir—but the master had more than anyone else I've ever worked for."

"Continue," Darcy said. "You went down to the larder?"

"Yes. When I opened the door, there he was on the floor. All huddled up, like he'd been trying to keep warm."

"Was the door locked?"

"Bolted, sir."

"And that is normal?"

"Well, of course, sir. The door must stay shut to keep the cold in."

"Would Mr. Dashwood have closed the door behind him when he entered?"

"Oh, I doubt it, sir. Though he was well into his cups last night, and you never know what a man what's been drinking might do."

Elizabeth recalled Sir Francis's state when she'd seen him the previous afternoon. He'd still seemed in possession of his faculties, but if he'd continued to consume brimstone at the rate she'd observed, he would have been pickled by midnight.

"The bolt can be operated only from the outside?"

"Yes, sir."

"Might someone have seen the open door and closed it, not realizing Mr. Dashwood was inside?"

"No one else was about. I'm always the last of the kitchen staff to retire. Last night I left a fresh pan of lemon ice in the larder before I went to bed. This morning, I was the first person with any cause to go down there. The lemon ice was still there—along with the master."

Darcy raised his gaze to Elizabeth's, and she saw that they had both reached the same conclusion. Someone had murdered Sir Francis.

Further conversations with the staff confirmed as highly unlikely the chances that their master's death was accidental. Sometime between midnight and five o'clock, when the cook had retired and risen, an intoxicated Sir Francis had descended to the larder to indulge his sweet tooth. Someone had either followed him or happened upon him, bolted the door, and left him to die of cold. His mind muddled by drink, he quite possibly had not even heard his captor or realized his peril until it was too late. The room was so well insulated and so deep in the house that with the door sealed, no one would have been wakened by a shout.

When Darcy dismissed the last servant, who joined her fellow domestics in hovering outside the drawing room waiting for instruction, he shut the door. Elizabeth was glad to finally have a chance to discuss the situation privately.

"Have you learned enough to identify a suspect?" she asked.

"All London."

"Splendid. I was afraid we would be unable to narrow the field."

"Apparently, Sir Francis had instructed the staff to leave a back entrance unlocked at night so that his paramour might come and go as she pleased in anonymity. Though no one can say with certainty whether she visited the house last night, neither can anyone say she did not. That unlocked door, meanwhile, offers easy ingress to anyone who might harbor less than amiable feelings toward the house's owner. The way Sir Francis had been conducting himself, that list includes everyone from jealous husbands to government officials."

"There is plenty of motive within the house, as well," Elizabeth said. "From what I was able to learn, it sounds as if he seduced half the female staff."

Professor Randolph entered. He had gone downstairs to have a look at the corpse.

"The body is as they describe," Randolph said. "Very cold, very stiff, and from the smell of liquor, very well preserved. His hands are quite bruised—I expect from beating against the door, trying to escape."

"We should summon the authorities," Darcy said.

"Not yet," countered Professor Randolph. "Once they arrive, we'll lose all opportunity to help Mr. Dashwood."

"I think he is beyond help."

"I meant the one in the mirror."

"So did I," Darcy said. "Assuming Harry's soul is indeed trapped in the glass—an assumption about which you know I still harbor doubt—with Sir Francis dead, we have no spirit to exchange for Harry's. His has fled this earth, we certainly are not going to offer one of ours, and allowing anyone else to fall victim to the mirror is unconscionable."

Darcy had voiced the conundrum that had weighed on Elizabeth's mind since the moment Mr. Dashwood's lifeless body had been discovered. Without Sir Francis, what were they to do? The murder had left them with a horrible dilemma: They could not sacrifice an innocent party to release Harry, but neither could they abandon him to an eternity of imprisonment within the glass. The whole situation had her stomach in knots.

"Professor, is there not some way we can yet rescue Mr. Dashwood?" she asked.

"I have been pondering that question. Sir Francis's death profoundly complicates matters. I must say, his murder occurred most inconveniently."

"Murder usually does," Darcy said. "At least to its victims."

"We are fortunate, however, in the manner of Mr. Dashwood's death, as I believe the circumstances have left his body still viable. Between the cold and the liquor, it has not yet started to deteriorate. If we can release Harry's essence very soon, his body might yet sustain life."

The weight on Elizabeth's chest eased. Her heart had grown heavier as the morning passed, but now she rejoiced that there was any hope at all for Harry.

"Very well," Darcy said. "His spirit has a place to go. But how do we transfer it there?"

"That is the more difficult part. However, one account of the mirror suggests that it may be possible for a spirit to leave the glass and roam incorporeally for limited periods. It was a passing mention—an unsupported speculation, really. But the notion caught my attention, as it could explain how Sir Francis

261

gathered his former associates to conduct the ceremony that imprisoned Harry."

"It could also explain all those occasions when people observed him in places he later claimed he had not been," Elizabeth said.

Randolph regarded her keenly. "What occasions?"

"There were so many of them." She looked to Darcy for help. "He was seen in Bond Street, and outside Boodle's . . ."

"At the Pigeon Hole and other gaming establishments . . ."

"All over town the week he was in Devonshire."

"Yes, I saw him myself that week in his window."

"Indeed?" Randolph asked. "Did these incidents occur before or after the night of the transference ritual?"

"Before," Elizabeth said. "We all went to Norland for Mr. Dashwood's birthday, and the *on-dits* started shortly after we returned."

"Is this when he first brought the mirror to London?"

"No," said Darcy. "He brought it with him on a previous trip."

"He did, however, return at that time with this portrait of Sir Francis." Elizabeth pointed to the painting that still hung above the fireplace.

Professor Randolph pondered that intelligence, and the portrait. "This image of Sir Francis looks remarkably like the young Mr. Dashwood I met in March. The people who saw Mr. Dashwood about town, after this portrait arrived—they were quite sure it was Harry?"

"They were all positive," Elizabeth said. "Though he ignored those who knew him best, and many thought they saw him in costume, as his clothes were quite out-of-date."

Randolph nodded at the portrait. "That far out-of-date?"

Elizabeth started at the sudden realization. Darcy, deep in contemplation, stared at the portrait.

"Think back, Mr. Darcy. Are you certain you saw Harry

Dashwood in the window?" Randolph asked. "Or could it have been Sir Francis?"

"Until this moment, I would have sworn it was Harry Dashwood," Darcy said. "But now—" His eyes met Elizabeth's. "Perhaps it *was* Sir Francis."

She held his gaze a long moment, knowing what it had cost him to concede that.

"It sounds as if Sir Francis's spirit was indeed able to leave the mirror before the exchange," Randolph said. "So there is hope that Harry's might as well, if we can determine how Sir Francis managed to liberate himself. I suspect his freedom had something to do with this portrait. Has it hung here since its arrival?"

Elizabeth recalled one of Harry's memories. "No. In the first memory I experienced of Sir Francis speaking to Harry, the portrait hangs behind me—him. I could see it in the glass."

"Aha." Professor Randolph leaned back to better study the portrait. "Harry Dashwood unknowingly hung this portrait where Sir Francis could see himself as he was in life—no doubt triggering the same sense of loss and yearning that caused him to become entrapped in the mirror in the first place. Just as his spirit once flew toward his reflection, it now went outward, toward the portrait. But without a body, it could not remain outside the glass for long. Or perhaps Sir Francis simply wasn't satisfied with a ghostly existence and wanted more. Either way, he decided to make his freedom permanent."

"At terrible cost to his own kin," Elizabeth declared.

"Just one in a litany of moral transgressions, from what I understand," the professor said. "Now, if only we had a portrait of Harry Dashwood, we might use it to free him."

"What about the birthday portrait?" Elizabeth said.

"It is at Norland, which means it now belongs to Lord Lovejoy," Darcy reminded her. "And we have not time to send for it anyway."

"Norland was filled with portraits of Harry," Elizabeth recalled. "Perhaps his mother has one in Harley Street. It would not be as recent—"

"The particular image should not matter," said Randolph. "It is the same soul."

A secretary stood in the corner of the drawing room. Elizabeth went to it and found a pen, ink, and paper. She got no farther than the salutation before she realized she had no idea what to say. *Dear Mrs. Dashwood—Though you never liked my sister and you have not spoken to your son in weeks, I need to borrow a portrait of him to release his soul from a cursed mirror and restore it to the recently vacated body his lecherous ancestor stole from him. Yours most sincerely—*

"Perhaps I would do better to call in person," she said.

"Go immediately," Randolph urged. "While you are gone, we will have Mr. Dashwood's body moved to the room with the mirror."

"You truly believe this can work?" Darcy's skepticism remained obvious.

"We must hope so. If it does not, I have one last idea, but it is far more dangerous."

"And what is that?"

"You might call it a false exchange. Essentially, we deceive the mirror. One of us poses as a new victim and gazes into the glass to release Harry. At the very moment of transference, just as Harry emerges but before the new soul is drawn in, we break contact with the mirror. The importance of precise timing cannot be overstated—a second too soon or too late, and Harry could be lost, or a new victim claimed."

Elizabeth shuddered. "I'll go retrieve that portrait."

Twenty-nine

"I approached her with a sense of guilt that almost took from me the power of dissembling."

—Mr. Willoughby to Elinor,
Sense and Sensibility, *Chapter 44*

W hat is he, six?"

"Four. It was the only one she had."

Elizabeth sank onto the sofa, having returned victorious from her deployment to Harley Street. Fanny Dashwood had loaned them a small portrait of a very young Harry, which Darcy now held. He was proud of his wife—he could never have charmed Harry's mother into cooperating, let alone in the mere half hour Elizabeth had required. She had spent more time traveling there and back than in the call itself.

"How did you justify our need for it?"

"Good heavens, I told so many falsehoods that I shall never be able to remember them all. And when those ran out, I flattered her in a manner that would put Mr. Collins to shame. You can imagine how much I enjoyed begging a favor of her—she was exceedingly condescending the whole while. Before I escaped, I had agreed to sponsor her membership in the Rose Garden Club and make a donation in her name to the Ladies' Benevolent Aid Society. Oh—and I hope you have no plans for Friday?"

"I do not believe so."

"Good. You are engaged to polish her silver."

The door opened to admit Professor Randolph. He appeared pleasantly surprised to find Elizabeth in the drawing room. "You have returned already, Mrs. Darcy? And with a portrait, I see. Capital!"

"Is Mr. Dashwood in place?" Darcy asked.

Relocating Harry's body had proven more awkward than anticipated. He was so stiff from cold that his limbs were stuck in their huddled position—knees up, arms wrapped around legs—until he had an opportunity to thaw. The servants had carried him thus curled from the subcellar to the upper spare bedchamber.

"He is. With the portrait now here, we can begin any time."

"We should start immediately, then. I overheard the servants questioning why no one else has been summoned. I announced that Mrs. Darcy had gone to inform Mr. Dashwood's mother, which seemed to satisfy them, but now that Elizabeth has returned, they will start to wonder what we are about."

"Let us say that Mrs. Dashwood is so overcome with shock that she cannot leave her bed, but requested the authorities not be called until she could lay eyes upon her son," Elizabeth said. "Say further that I promised we would sit with him until she came, and we would like to commence our mourning undisturbed."

Darcy regarded her with admiration. "I had no idea you could spin tales with such facility."

"Nor did I," she responded. "I think I am still recovering from my call upon Fanny Dashwood."

Once they were upstairs, the mood became heavier. The light rain that had been falling at breakfast time had grown stronger throughout the day, and now dark grey clouds cast the chamber in gloom. Darcy had hardly noticed the weather earlier, so preoccupied had he been with the business of Mr. Dashwood's death, but as they prepared to challenge the Mirror of Narcissus for Harry's soul, the steady patter of raindrops seemed an appropriate prelude.

Or perhaps requiem. Mr. Dashwood's balled-up body lay on its side on the bed, his face toward the mirror. Darcy watched Elizabeth's countenance. He expected her first sight of the corpse to disturb her, but she only regarded it sadly.

"Poor Mr. Dashwood," she said. "Even if we succeed, he will never be the same."

Indeed, at one-and-twenty, Harry would inhabit a body he should not have had until his mid-fifties, and a very roughly used one at that.

"It is not a form I would wish to bear at this time of life," Darcy admitted.

"But it is life," she said.

Professor Randolph entered with a lit candelabrum and the portrait of Harry. The candles he set on a side table, where their flickering glow illuminated the room just enough to keep their party from stumbling in the dark as the sky rumbled outside. He shut the door.

"Are we ready?"

Elizabeth continued to gaze at the lifeless form on the bed. "Let us proceed."

"I'm sure I need not remind either of you to avoid looking directly into the glass," said Randolph. "Mrs. Darcy, do you still wear the amulet?"

"Yes."

"Can you see Harry in your peripheral vision?"

"Yes. He is trying to get my attention again."

Darcy interposed himself between her and the mirror. He did not want Elizabeth glancing into the glass again, accidentally or intentionally. Nor did he want her close to the artifact if anything unusual *did* happen. Not that anything would.

"Mr. Darcy, can you perceive Harry?"

He stole sideways glances at the mirror, but detected nothing but an ordinary-looking glass. "No," he said. And the fact troubled him. What he could not see, he could not defend against.

"Nor can I," said Randolph. He walked to the bed and propped the portrait against Mr. Dashwood's body so that the likeness faced the mirror. "What is Mr. Dashwood doing now, Mrs. Darcy?"

She leaned backward, trying to see around Darcy while using her side vision to answer the professor's question. Darcy knew he was making her job difficult, but he felt better standing between her and the glass.

"He is staring at his body on the bed."

"I would, too," Randolph said. "Probably quite a shock, seeing oneself displayed in such a state. Can he hear me?"

"I think so."

"Good." He crossed to the mirror and stood beside it, offering a three-quarters profile. "Mr. Dashwood, we are going to try to release you from the glass. I would like you to concentrate very hard on this portrait of yourself."

"He is listening," Elizabeth said.

Randolph nodded. "Mr. Dashwood, imagine yourself as that child again. Before all this happened. Before the weight of worldly cares settled upon you. You are that child. Those are your innocent eyes. Those are your soft curls . . . ."

Randolph continued in a slow, soothing voice, weaving mesmerizing words until Darcy was almost ready to believe *he* was the boy in the portrait.

"Now, Mr. Dashwood, I would like you to step out of the glass and into your body there on the bed."

Darcy fought the urge to look at the mirror and see whether anyone emerged. He suspected the temptation was worse for Elizabeth. He took her hand and gripped it, willing her to look at him instead. Their gazes met.

And then, from the corner of his eye, he saw a small figure dart across the room.

It was the boy Harry—the child of the portrait. Or rather, the ghost of a boy. Darcy could at once see him and see through him as he climbed onto the bed. The bed did not respond to his movement. He added no weight; he made no impression on the counterpane.

The child crawled to his lifeless adult body and threw himself over it. He lay on top. He pushed himself down. He passed through it and out. He tried again.

And again. Spirit and shell would not merge.

He moaned, a wail of desperation and anguish. "What do I do?" He spoke in his own voice, not a boy's. Yet the image was that of a tormented child, a little boy in dire need of aid and protection. It was a sight heartbreaking to behold.

Randolph raised his hands helplessly. "I do not know."

Harry looked up at Darcy. "Mr. Darcy?" His round child-eyes regarded him imploringly. "Can *you* help me?"

Darcy was suddenly reminded of Harry at Norland, Harry as he had been just hours before all these terrible events were set into motion. Harry had been a fatherless boy seeking guidance as he matured and accepted his adult responsibilities. He had turned to Darcy then, just as he turned to Darcy now, and Darcy had tried to teach him through example how a gentleman takes care of those dependent upon him.

Whatever had transpired in the intervening weeks, this child, this man, this spirit now before him was *that* Harry. Until this moment, Darcy had not believed he existed any longer. And once again, Harry was depending on him.

The young Harry jerked as if tugged. "The mirror! It pulls me back!"

Before Darcy could respond, Elizabeth tore herself away and rushed to the bed. "Fight it, Harry! Fight it!" She extended her hand to grab his. Harry reached toward her.

But her fingers closed around air, and the little boy was gone.

"Oh!" Elizabeth took a shaky breath and stared at her empty hand. "Oh, Harry . . ." She choked back a sob.

Darcy approached from behind. He put his hands on her shoulders. He consoled her thus—consoled himself—a moment, then bent his head to her ear.

"Give me the amulet."

She turned, her face full of confusion. Her hand went to the silver watch that hung round her neck, her fingers brushing the symbols engraved upon it. She looked at him searchingly. "The amulet? Why?"

He gazed into her eyes, which held the only reflection of him that mattered. He reached for the chain and gently lifted it over her head. Then he slipped it around his own neck.

"Professor Randolph," he said, his eyes never leaving his wife. "Tell me more about this idea of a 'false exchange.'"

Thirty

The very circumstance, in its unpleasantest form, which they
would each have been most anxious to avoid, had fallen on them.
—Sense and Sensibility, *Chapter 35*

*E*lizabeth held her breath as Darcy walked to the Mirror of Narcissus. She would not look directly at the glass—'twas especially reckless to do so now that she no longer wore the amulet—but she would not take her gaze off Darcy if Hades himself sprang from the mirror.

"You are certain?" Professor Randolph asked.

Darcy nodded.

"Bear in mind that the amulet lends some protection but does not make you impervious."

His lips crooked into a wry half-smile. She knew he doubted the silver watch possessed any powers of protection at all. "I understand."

"All right, then. Help me move Mr. Dashwood's body to the foot of the mirror."

The two men lifted Harry's huddled form and sat it upright in front of the glass. Still stiff with cold, the body held its position. Mr. Dashwood hugged his legs; his forehead rested on his knees.

"Stand behind Harry's body so that when his spirit emerges

from the glass, his own shell is the first available receptacle he encounters, and he enters it instead of attempting to enter yours."

"Harry would not steal Darcy's form," Elizabeth asserted.

"Perhaps not intentionally," said Randolph. "But he may have little or no ability to control the transfer. Remember—we actually know very little about the mirror's workings. Most of this is conjecture."

Rather than remember that uncertainty, she wanted to forget it. Just now she shared Darcy's preference for hard facts and indisputable truths. She wanted a detailed chronology of every incident that was about to unfold, with annotations, illustrations, and an index. She wanted a guaranteed outcome, assurance that when this ordeal ended, Darcy would still be Darcy—safe, and whole, and hers.

She knew Darcy was not nearly as concerned. He thought his skepticism would grant him immunity to whatever power the mirror might indeed hold. If Elizabeth's willingness to believe enabled her to see into the glass, his disbelief would protect him from its hazards. Or so he had assured her. She prayed he was right, that his trust in his own invulnerability would not prove misplaced. That on this day, at least, pride would not go before a fall.

Darcy moved into position. He stood about three feet from the mirror, just behind Harry's curled form. He turned to Elizabeth and regarded her as if committing to memory every nuance of her countenance. "Naught will happen to me," he insisted once again. "I am not about to become trapped in the glass."

"Take care that you don't." She tried to smile. "It does not match the décor at Pemberley."

He held her gaze a moment longer before Professor Randolph coughed self-consciously.

"Shall we begin?"

Darcy nodded and turned to face the professor. Randolph

took up his position at the mirror's side and moved the artifact slightly away from the wall.

"As we discussed, when the moment of transference approaches, I shall tilt the mirror toward Mr. Dashwood's body on the floor to further focus his spirit's destination," he said. "For now, however, I'll hold it upright. Gaze into the mirror whenever you're ready."

Darcy looked into it immediately. His stance was relaxed, his expression calm—just now he seemed more unflappable than Beau Brummell himself. Merely an ordinary English gentleman looking into an ordinary glass.

"What do you see in the mirror?" Randolph asked.

"Myself."

"Harry?"

"Only the one at my feet."

Elizabeth could discern Harry moving in the glass, his still-childlike image crossing that of Darcy. One moment Darcy stood out more strongly; the next, Harry did. 'Twas frustrating to observe by indirection. She kept her gaze on Darcy—the real Darcy.

"Do you see anyone or anything else?"

"Elizabeth."

"Of course! I had not considered that the glass would capture the whole room, depending upon the angle of the viewer. Mrs. Darcy, come stand on the other side of the mirror. You can help me hold it."

She repositioned herself so that she flanked the glass along with Professor Randolph. Though she gripped the frame, he supported most of the mirror's weight. From her present angle, she could no longer see images in the glass at all.

"Mr. Darcy, do your best to block us from your thoughts and focus only on your own reflection. As you look into the glass, hold in your mind an image of yourself as you would like others to see you. The mirror should respond by reflecting that image back at you."

"Must it be an image different from what I see now?"

"I believe so. The mirror preys upon those who are discontent with themselves."

"But I am not discontent."

"Everybody wants something, Mr. Darcy."

Thunder rumbled outside. The rain fell harder, its patter the only sound in the room.

Darcy gazed into the mirror. She wondered what image he had conjured, what desire as yet went unfulfilled.

"Concentrate on that ideal," Randolph said. "Allow yearning for it to envelop you. It will shimmer and tease; it will offer a tantalizing vision of what was or could be. Let it tempt you."

The drumming of the rain increased, competing in volume with the sound of Elizabeth's own breathing. Tension raised the temperature of the room. She wanted to open a window, to admit cool mist and fresh air.

Darcy did as the professor bade. His expression at first exhibited his natural resistance, but the longer he gazed into the mirror, the more he yielded. She wondered again what vision held him transfixed.

"Let the image lure you. Let it whisper its promises."

She grew warmer. Her muslin dress stuck to her chest and back. Moisture beaded her upper lip. She longed to wipe it away, but held still lest she distract Darcy. He appeared warm, as well; damp locks clung to his forehead. But he seemed oblivious to discomfort.

The rain cascaded now, pounding on the cobblestones and splattering the windows. Gusts of wind shook the panes of glass that revealed a sky as black as night. The candles flickered, their dim offering barely sufficient to combat the darkness. Shadows skipped like dark elves in the corners of her vision, illusory representations of her own foreboding.

"The image will beckon. Answer its call—but for only a moment."

The room grew unbearably hot. Droplets ran down her temple. She wiped her brow—she could not help herself; it was either that or be blinded by her own perspiration. The movement went unnoticed by Darcy. The mirror held him completely in thrall. At his feet, Mr. Dashwood's body slumped over. Thawed by the intense heat, it now lay on its side in a state of repose.

The wind howled, and a huge thunderclap shook the house. The candles sputtered and died, but a glow brightened the room.

It came from the mirror.

The glow illuminated Darcy, curling around his contours, grazing every muscle and sinew. It danced across him, bathing him, caressing him, dancing and wavering like—

Flames.

A powerful sensation of evil assailed her with such force that she nearly collapsed under its magnitude. She let go of the frame and staggered forward, weaving to the side to avoid tripping over Mr. Dashwood's body. The mirror tugged at her mind, inviting—directing—demanding that she look. She need only turn her head.

She turned.

Mr. Dashwood, still bearing the image of a child, clawed the glass in silhouette. The fires of hell were behind him.

She looked to Darcy. He remained enthralled, transfixed by something she could not see.

"Mrs. Darcy, stand back!" Professor Randolph cried. He spread his feet wide and began to tilt the mirror.

Thunder boomed. The room was so hot she could hardly breathe.

Darcy shifted. Or appeared to. Then she realized he had not moved at all, but had developed a double profile. The narrow gap between outlines slowly widened, the fainter one moving toward the glass.

It was Darcy's soul.

Why did Darcy himself not move? It was time! He must break contact now, or the false exchange would become true.

The gap increased. The Mirror of Narcissus summoned, demanding its tithe. But she'd be damned before she allowed it to take Darcy's soul. That belonged to God. And to her.

With a cry, she hurled herself against her husband, knocking him to the floor. She held him, and her breath, while she waited in agonizing helplessness to see whether she also held his spirit. Its outline remained separated from that of his body for what seemed an eternity until, blessedly, they merged.

Darcy's gaze, however, found the glass once more and locked upon it.

"Darcy?" she shouted. "Darcy!"

She could not command his attention, nor, she discovered, could she physically turn his face from the glass. Professor Randolph abandoned his post. He pushed the mirror upright and rested it against the wall, where it continued to bathe the room in the glow of hell-fire. He rushed forward and dragged Darcy out of the mirror's range. She stood and tried to follow.

The mirror would not permit her.

It held her in its sight. Invisible claws raked her, rent her, trying to claim her soul for the one she had denied. She felt a tear, a grasp, as the mirror prepared to consume her spirit. The flames leapt in anticipation of their feast.

Still on the floor, Darcy pushed himself to a sitting position. He moved groggily, as if awakening from slumber. She could not even see his face. With a swift prayer that this would not be her last vision of him in this lifetime, she steeled herself against the mirror's imminent pull.

She felt its grip—strong, overpowering, cold for all the heat of its fire. Then, suddenly, it released her.

The wails of every soul the Mirror of Narcissus had ever held flooded the air, centuries of tormented shrieks and cries that had gone unheard in their glass prison. The flames burned blue, then black. Mr. Dashwood's image had disappeared, no doubt consumed by the raging inferno.

The mirror's surface wavered, losing solidity, threatening to send molten glass oozing across the floor. The wails grew so loud she had to cover her ears or go mad. As they reached a crescendo, a mighty roar sounded. The mirror shook violently. Elizabeth feared it would come away from the wall and topple over to crush her. But it did not.

It imploded.

Thirty-one

"Thank Heaven you are what you always were!"
—*Marianne Dashwood to Edward Ferrars,*
Sense and Sensibility, *Chapter 35*

*T*he sudden silence was almost more disturbing than the howls of the damned.

Only the sound of the rain, falling gently once more, penetrated the stillness. No one spoke. No one moved. All simply stared at an empty gold frame. The glass had collapsed in on itself, disappearing into whatever plane of hell it had occupied and leaving nothing but a tarnished shell behind.

Elizabeth shuddered—from horror or chill, she knew not. Probably both. The room had returned to a normal temperature, leaving her cold in her perspiration-drenched gown.

Darcy came to her. He pulled her into his arms and held her tightly enough to assure her that he was, indeed, her Darcy—unscarred, if not untouched, by their ordeal. His whispered enquiries and her murmured responses reassured him of her own wholeness.

Though the dimness of the room granted them partial privacy, they soon grew conscious of their audience and separated. Professor Randolph had crossed to the table, where he was tactfully taking his time relighting the candelabrum. When he finished his task, the tapers emitted a gentle glow, comforting in contrast to the blaze just extinguished.

Randolph assessed them. "You both appear all right."

"We are," Darcy confirmed.

"Then I think we must consider the end result of this enterprise a success, even if we failed to rescue Mr. Dashwood."

Dread washed over Elizabeth at the mention of Harry. She glanced at his body, still lying on the floor. "Is he lost forever?"

"The mirror is destroyed. I can only assume that his spirit perished along with it."

She swallowed a lump in her throat. Sadness settled upon her as she thought of the lost potential Harry's death represented. How extraordinarily unfair it was, that he should have the simple pleasures of one life stolen from him, so that Sir Francis could indulge in the guilty pleasures of a second.

Darcy, noting her distress, touched her cheek. "Perhaps instead of being destroyed along with the mirror, his spirit found rest."

She released a heavy sigh and turned to look at Harry's body once more. "I shall hold out hope of that."

Viewing Mr. Dashwood now, she could believe he had, indeed, somehow found rest. He posed as if in slumber, his limbs having fallen into more natural positions when his body warmed. He lay on his side, his knees slightly bent, his left arm tucked under him and his right gently draped. She imagined his chest lightly rising and falling in the steady rhythm of sleep.

She caught her own breath. 'Twas not her imagination.

"Darcy, Mr. Dashwood is breathing."

Incredulous, they all gathered round Mr. Dashwood's form. Elizabeth extended her hand, but Darcy captured it and instead felt Mr. Dashwood's chest himself.

"His heart beats, and he is as warm as you or I."

She pressed Darcy's hand at the news but hesitated to celebrate. She raised her gaze to Professor Randolph. "Is he Harry—or Sir Francis?"

"Harry," Mr. Dashwood murmured.

His eyes opened. He slowly rolled to his back and blinked, trying to focus his gaze as it shifted among the three of them.

"I'm afraid I've been a neglectful host today," he said. His voice was feeble, but he sounded more like himself than he had in weeks. "Do forgive me—I've been away for a while."

The rain had ceased, and a ray of evening sunlight slanted through the window. Elizabeth smiled.

"It is good to have you back, Mr. Dashwood."

A quarter hour saw Harry sufficiently recovered to transfer from the floor to a chair, and another quarter hour beyond that brought his request to remove from the chamber altogether. Though only the mirror's frame remained, the sight of it distressed him far more than the exertion of changing rooms. His own chamber having also been the scene of unpleasant memories, Mr. Dashwood chose to relocate to the drawing room.

They assisted him downstairs, where they found most of the servants milling around, speculating about what had transpired above. Elizabeth supposed a little curiosity was the natural result of all the wailing and roaring they must have heard issuing from the spare bedchamber. At the sight of Mr. Dashwood—whom they had last seen stone-cold dead—all gasped, a few crossed themselves, and one maid fainted.

"Mr. Dashwood has recovered from his indisposition," Elizabeth announced.

The four of them ignored the servants' bewildered gazes and continued to the drawing room, where they settled Harry in a comfortable chair. Mr. Dashwood's ordeal had left him weak, but he showed signs of steady improvement. In fact, Elizabeth thought his visage already looked better than it had when she'd last spoken to Sir Francis. Confident that some nourishment would further speed his revival, Elizabeth called for a light supper to be brought up.

"Shall I also send for something fortifying to drink?" she asked Harry. "Wine, perhaps?"

Mr. Dashwood grimaced. "Tea. I think in recent weeks this body has taken in quite enough spirits, in every sense of the word."

The tea arrived first. Its delivery required two maids—one to carry the tray, the other to look busy while casting furtive glances at Mr. Dashwood.

"Will your servants speak of this outside the house?" Darcy asked when they departed.

"They are not my servants. Sir Francis replaced my staff with his own, and paid them well to keep silent about anything they might observe. Startling as my apparent resurrection is, I'm afraid it's not the most shocking thing that has taken place in this house."

Elizabeth poured tea and placed the first cup in Mr. Dashwood's hands. Then, still feeling a bit indisposed herself after their ordeal, she poured a cup of her own and swallowed a sip. "What *did* happen?" she asked. "I know what you revealed to me when I discovered you in the glass yesterday—" Good heavens, had that been only yesterday? "But all the rest?"

A shadow passed across his countenance, and she immediately regretted the query. "Do not speak of it, if doing so will cause you distress," she hastened to add.

"No, I—I want you to know," he said. "I want to assure you that whatever indignities you or anybody else suffered, they were not my doing."

"We understand you are not to blame."

"Oh—I accept the blame as my own. It was I who brought

the glass here, I who brought the portrait. Had I not wanted to show off with the former and insult my mother with the latter, none of this would have happened."

"Until some other unsuspecting person stumbled upon those objects in the future," Professor Randolph said. "Cursed artifacts seldom allow themselves to remain in obscurity forever. Had you not found the glass, your son, or his son, might have become the mirror's next victim. Let it bring you some measure of peace to know that you have spared your progeny the misery you endured."

"All the same, I wish I had invited you to examine my attic discoveries, as I had promised," he said. "I almost did solicit your assessment of the glass, but I feared you would think me mad. Heavens, *I* thought I was mad—hearing a voice coming from the glass, seeing a face that was mine and not mine. Sir Francis haunted me awake in the mirror and asleep in my dreams. Then people started seeing me in places I had not been, and I wondered if he'd found a way to roam about while I slept. Even when I was in Devonshire, if I so much as dozed, his spirit wandered London free."

"And eventually he grew dissatisfied with that?" Elizabeth asked gently.

"After more than thirty years of imprisonment, he was like a child on holiday. He sought pleasure, but his lack of substance limited his enjoyments. He could not hold cards, consume food or drink, or satisfy his . . . more carnal interests." A hint of red crept into his cheek, and his teacup became a sudden subject of rapt attention.

The arrival of Harry's supper broke the awkwardness. Two different servants, probably having won at straws the privilege of ogling Mr. Dashwood up close, delivered the repast. When they had served the food and retreated, Harry continued.

"After the—after Sir Francis and I exchanged places, he gave free rein to his hedonistic impulses. You cannot imagine my torment! To have not only lost my freedom, but to watch help-lessly as my relationships, reputation, fortune, and physical person suffered irreparable damage!"

"You know the extent of his transgressions?" Darcy asked.

"I probably do not," he said. "But I know a good many of them. He would gloat to me about his exploits—found my hor-ror and dismay exceedingly amusing. And what went on in my own bedchamber, where he relished the presence of a captive audience, defies description. I would turn away, cover my ears, and retreat to the mirror's farthest recesses."

"Could none of his"—Darcy cleared his throat—"visitors see you in the glass?" Darcy asked.

"Until Mrs. Darcy saw me yesterday, none but Sir Francis ever detected me. Believe me, I tried to draw attention to my-self! Every servant, every woman who entered inspired shouts and frantic waving, but for naught. Once I thought my aunt Lucy had noticed me. She gazed into the mirror a terribly long time, but it turned out she was only admiring herself. The inci-dent unnerved Sir Francis enough, however, that he shipped the mirror back to Norland the next day."

Elizabeth, who had been refilling Harry's teacup, paused to regard him closely. "Mrs. Robert Ferrars was in your—Sir Francis's—bedchamber?"

"Mrs. Robert Ferrars was Sir Francis's mistress."

"Oh, my!" Elizabeth required a moment to absorb that intelli-gence. "I suppose that explains how she was always in posses-sion of the latest news about you—I mean, him. Sir Francis must have taken her into his confidence, for surely Mrs. Ferrars would not have entered into an affair with her own nephew."

"Unfortunately, she was quite of the belief that it was I who seduced her. I shall never be able to hear my name on her lips without the sound giving rise to memories I would much rather forget."

"As someone who knows you well, she did not find Sir

Francis's actions so contrary to your nature as to make her question them?" Darcy asked.

"My aunt is not possessed of the strongest perception," Harry said. "Indeed, she was flattered by his advances."

"It is little wonder Miss Ferrars's engagement so enraged her."

"My cousin Regina is engaged?" Harry asked. "To whom?"

Elizabeth hesitated. "To you, I fear."

Mr. Dashwood looked a little ill. "I knew I had lost Miss Bennet. I saw the three of you arrive at the townhouse as the mirror was being prepared for transport to Norland. I caught a glimpse of Kitty—what a blessed gift that was! But I feared for her. When I heard you speak of the broken engagement as you left, I rejoiced that she had escaped Sir Francis's taint." He poked at his food, apparently having lost his appetite. "To now find myself engaged to my cousin—well, it is most surprising news. I am not certain what attraction she held for Sir Francis."

Elizabeth exchanged glances with Darcy. If Harry had been at Norland since Kitty ended the engagement, he had been absent when Sir Francis gambled away his estate and Fanny settled his remaining inheritance on her niece.

"Mr. Dashwood, I'm afraid we must advise you of additional unpleasant occurrences," Darcy said.

Harry bore with dignity the news that Sir Francis had left him penniless. He became very quiet, and the others allowed him the privacy of his own thoughts. At last he said, "I am glad he has left this world, for otherwise I might have killed him myself."

"Someone did," Elizabeth said. "The servants found him trapped in the larder this morning."

"Indeed? I had wondered at his odd position when you brought him upstairs. Will there be an investigation?"

"Unfortunately, there is nothing to investigate," said Darcy. "With you here, there is no corpse, and hence, no murder. I would guard my back, however, were I you, for Sir Francis managed to offend a great many people in your name."

"After what you all endured to restore my life, I do not intend to lose it easily. Mere words can never express the measure of my gratitude. When I consider what you almost sacrificed—"

"Almost," Elizabeth emphasized. "All turned out well in the end." She looked to Professor Randolph. "Though, Professor, I do not understand what happened in the final moments. A soul for a soul—was that not the mirror's price? Obviously, Mr. Dashwood's spirit was released. In exchange, I saw the glass try to steal Darcy's, and I felt it try to snatch my own. What caused it to destroy itself instead?"

The archaeologist pondered her question a moment. "Maybe the mirror tried to take too much at once."

She shook her head. "No—Darcy was out of its range in the end. I was alone before it."

Professor Randolph regarded her, his expression inscrutable. Finally, he said, "I have no other explanation to offer at present. Perhaps in time you'll find the answer within yourself."

They were interrupted by a voice rising from below, where someone sought admittance. Mr. Dashwood rose and opened the drawing room door to better hear the visitor. Her voice was familiar to them all.

"What dreadful news about my nephew! I came as soon as I heard. . . ."

Mr. Dashwood winced. "I do not think I can cope with my aunt Lucy just yet."

After what she had learned today, Elizabeth did not know whether she would ever again be able to greet Mrs. Robert Ferrars with a placid countenance. She was curious, however, as to the nature of the news to which Lucy alluded. To Elizabeth's knowledge, word of Mr. Dashwood's supposed demise had not traveled outside the house.

"Will you allow me?" she asked.

"By all means."

Elizabeth left to receive the visitor. As she headed down the stairs, Lucy's voice continued to resound in the hall.

"As his kin, I wonder that you did not send me word immediately," Lucy admonished the housekeeper. "I will, of course, handle all the arrangements, in consultation with his mother." She tried to push her way past the servant.

"Good evening, Mrs. Ferrars," Elizabeth greeted her. The housekeeper looked as if she had every intention of staying, but Elizabeth dismissed her. "What arrangements would those be?"

"Mrs. Darcy." Lucy opened her mouth to speak, then closed it. It was the first occasion Elizabeth could recall of her being at a loss for words. "I did not expect to find you here," she said finally.

"I did not expect to be here myself today, but necessity required it."

Lucy nodded sympathetically. "It was good of you to come. Those senseless servants obviously didn't know who to summon. But I'm here now. Where is the—where is poor Harry?"

Mr. Dashwood's aunt had hardly referred to him as "poor Harry" the last time Elizabeth had seen her.

"In the drawing room."

"The drawing room?" She appeared puzzled. "Well, I suppose that's as good a place as any. Is he—is he quite dreadful to look at?"

Actually, Elizabeth reflected, Harry's appearance had continued to improve dramatically since he'd regained consciousness. At present, he didn't look a day over fifty.

But to Lucy she said, "How did he look when you last saw him?"

An expression of guilt flashed across her face. It lasted the merest fraction of a second, but it was long enough. "Oh, you know . . ." Lucy shrugged.

Yes, she did.

Thirty-two

"Tell her of my misery and my penitence—tell her that my heart was never inconstant to her, and if you will, that at this moment she is dearer to me than ever."

—Mr. Willoughby to Elinor,
Sense and Sensibility, *Chapter 44*

I came to bid you farewell," Mr. Dashwood said as he entered Darcy's library.

Darcy greeted Harry, though not the cause of his call, with genuine pleasure. In the three weeks since Mr. Dashwood had been restored to himself, Darcy had come to hold him in esteem surpassing that of their earlier acquaintance. His ordeal in the mirror had purged him of those flaws of character Darcy had previously defined as a want of seriousness, leaving him instead a sober young man mature beyond his years. In fact, both Elizabeth and Darcy worried that he had grown a little too serious and hoped that eventually the passage of time would lighten his spirits.

He invited Mr. Dashwood to be seated. "You look very well today."

"I am, thank you." In physical appearance, Mr. Dashwood had remarkably improved. The effects of premature aging that Sir Francis's tenancy had wrought upon his person had receded beyond anyone's expectation. He had appeared gradually younger each day for a fortnight, until settling into the form of a man perhaps in his mid-thirties. Professor Randolph theorized that when his soul reentered his body, it had yet borne the image of a child, and that this fortunate circumstance had somehow countered the years Sir Francis had added. He still looked considerably older than he ought, and probably always would, but his appearance was superior to what could have been.

"I understand you leave on the morrow?" Mr. Dashwood asked.

"Yes." The Darcys had extended their London stay to see Harry through his initial recovery, but now they headed back to Pemberley. They would stop en route at Longbourn to return Kitty. "But I expect it is not I to whom you particularly wished to say good-bye."

"I hoped to see Mrs. Darcy, too, of course."

"And no one else?"

·Mr. Dashwood had enquired after Kitty at every opportunity, but the two had not yet met in person. Though free of his obligation to Regina—breaking the engagement between the cousins had seemed best for all involved—the awkwardness of seeing Kitty again, after the hurt Sir Francis had inflicted upon her, had deterred him from calling at the Darcys' townhouse.

"She is out with Mrs. Darcy and my sister at the moment but should return soon," Darcy said.

"I do not know what to say to her—how to begin to apologize, or even explain."

"Mrs. Darcy told her you have been unwell but are on the mend. What you reveal beyond that is your own choice."

"Do you think she could ever possibly believe the truth?"

"I suspect she still wants very much to believe in you."

Mr. Dashwood avoided Darcy's gaze. "I am unworthy of that faith."

"Do you still care for her?"

His ardent expression said that he did, but it quickly transformed to one of misery. "I have nothing to offer her. My fortune is gone, my friends alienated, my reputation blackened beyond redemption. My very body is so changed I don't yet feel entirely comfortable in my own skin." He held up his hand before him. "I cannot tender her a hand I don't even recognize as my own and a name everyone recognizes as infamous!" He slumped against the chair back and shook his head. "I have nothing to recommend me."

"Nothing but yourself."

"That is not enough, and you know it even better than I."

Unfortunately, Darcy did know it. Even if Miss Bennet could overlook the alteration of Harry's form, and her family the damage Sir Francis had done to Mr. Dashwood's reputation, no one could ignore the loss of his fortune. Love alone could not sustain a couple, nor could the interest on Kitty's one thousand pounds.

Mr. Dashwood rose. "I think honor requires me to distance myself from Miss Bennet, so that her heart is free to bestow itself on a more deserving gentleman. I shall leave now, before she returns."

"Where do you go?" Darcy asked. "I speak not merely of the present moment, but of your future. Without your inheritance, how do you plan to maintain yourself?"

"During my captivity, I spent a great deal of time contemplating my life and its value—not just to myself, but to others. I concluded that I had been a rather selfish creature, though I hoped I had started to mend that deficiency under the influence of Miss Bennet's regard. I resolved that should I ever be so blessed as to escape my prison, I would endeavor to prove a more useful human being. I have been granted salvation; I believe it now my duty to help others reach it."

"You intend to enter the church?"

"As soon as I can take orders. I think quitting town for a quiet life as a country vicar, such as my uncle Edward Ferrars enjoys, is the very thing for me. By some miracle, he and my aunt Elinor are still speaking to me, and I plan to solicit his assistance in getting ordained and finding a modest living—provided the reputation Sir Francis left me with does not prejudice one and all against my serving as a clergyman. I hope perhaps, in some place far removed from London, there may exist a potential patron who has not heard the tales."

A life devoted to the church, if Harry served well, could go a long way toward restoring his respectability. Darcy studied Mr. Dashwood, not in the light of the summer sun streaming through the window, but in the light of the trial he had just endured. The idle young buck Darcy had first met at the Middletons' soirée would never have made a good minister; the gentleman who entertained them at Norland might have, but lacked any motive for entering the profession. This man before him, however—this chastened, reborn Mr. Dashwood, baptized in the mirror's fire—he would make a very good clergyman, indeed.

"I know of a living in Derbyshire that will become vacant soon. In Kympton, a pleasant little village."

"Indeed?" Mr. Dashwood's interest was evident. "Do you think its patron might be prevailed upon to consider me?"

"The living is mine to grant. And yours if you want it."

He was silent a moment. "Mr. Darcy, I hardly know what to say. I am humbled by your generosity. You have already done so much for me and are one of the only friends I have remaining. I most gratefully accept, and pledge to devote myself wholeheartedly to the parishioners in my care."

"Do you not even wish to know the living's value?"

"It is immaterial, but tell me if you like."

"About four hundred a year, enough to support in comfort a man of moderate habits—" Darcy paused. "And his wife, if he happened to have one."

Hope illuminated Mr. Dashwood's face, but he quickly fought it back, unwilling to give himself over to it. "Do you think she would have me?" he whispered.

Below, the front door opened, filling the hall with the sound of ladies returning.

"That, Mr. Dashwood, is up to her. And to you."

He left Harry in the library and went to the balcony. Miss Bennet was in the hall below, with Elizabeth and Georgiana. Kitty laughed at something her sister said, and Darcy reflected that during the period of Mr. Dashwood's recovery, she, too, had begun to heal from the injuries Sir Francis had inflicted. He captured her attention.

"Miss Bennet, there is someone in the library who wants very much to speak with you."

Curiosity crossed her countenance but did not erase her smile. She came up the stairs. "Who is it?"

He took her arm and led her into the library, closing the door behind them. "Receive him only if you wish."

Mr. Dashwood gazed out the window, lost in thought, his back to the door. In his altered form, which Kitty had not seen in weeks and which had undergone still more changes since, it took her a moment to recognize him. When she did, she gasped.

"Mr. Dashwood."

He turned round. Darcy had never seen a face exhibit such a range of emotions in so short a span. Joy. Regret. Hope. Grief. Longing. Sorrow. Tenderness.

"Miss Bennet."

He went toward her. She took an involuntary step back and leaned closer to Darcy. He stopped.

"You are afraid of me." The fact clearly wounded him, but he bore it with acceptance.

"No." She withdrew her arm from Darcy's supportive grasp and walked to Mr. Dashwood. Raising her chin, she looked him in the eye. "No, Harry," she said quietly. "I am not afraid of you."

"I cannot blame you if you are, after all that has transpired."

Darcy retreated toward the door to grant them some measure

of privacy, but he would not leave until assured that Kitty was easy in Mr. Dashwood's company.

She studied Harry a long time. "My sister says you have been ill."

"I was not myself when we last saw each other, and had not been for weeks."

"And now? Are you once more the gentleman I knew at Norland?"

"No," he said. "I fear that, like Norland itself, that man is gone forever. But I hope I am a better one."

Her gaze darted about the room, as if she were afraid to let it rest on him too long. His, however, never left her. He drank in the vision of her, cherishing each expression, each gesture, even those unfavorable to his suit. He had not seen her in over two months, and, depending on the outcome of this meeting, might never see her again.

"Mr. Dashwood, why have you called today? Surely you realize how difficult this interview is for me. The horrible things you said at our last meeting—the wicked things you did—" Her voice broke.

"Miss Bennet, I—"

"We were engaged to be married, and you took a mistress!" She shut her eyes against the sight of him and turned her head. A deep, shaky breath followed. When she opened her eyes once more, she looked away from him, at the floor.

The anguish that crossed his countenance at the sight of her distress at least equaled hers. "Miss Bennet—"

"A mistress," she repeated quietly. "Have you any idea how much that hurt me?"

He swallowed hard. "Yes."

His own hands trembling, he reached for hers. She let him take them, but she would not meet his eyes. He dropped to his knees so that he could look up into her face.

"Miss Bennet, I have no right to beg your forgiveness, to hope that somewhere in the heart that suffered so on my account is a corner that does not utterly despise me. But Miss Bennet, if there is—if any chance exists that you might one day look upon me without revulsion—that I may someday regain your respect, if not your love—" He drew in an unsteady breath of his own. "Oh, God, Kitty—if I could but take your pain upon myself, how willingly, how gratefully, how humbly I would bear it!"

She withdrew one hand from his grasp, to wipe tears from her eyes.

"Oh, Harry, I want to believe you. . . ."

Neither of them heard Darcy open the door and close it behind him. Miss Bennet and Mr. Dashwood still had a great deal to talk through, and they did not need an audience. Darcy believed, however, that they eventually would find their way back to each other.

Elizabeth waited just outside. "You are most mysterious this afternoon." She nodded toward the door. "Who is in there?"

"The future vicar of Kympton."

"You filled the living? That must be a relief—I know how the vacancy has plagued you. Whom did you find?"

"A promising gentleman who plans to take orders soon."

"He must be a younger person, then. I am glad—there is less likelihood of your having to fill the benefice again right away. How old a man is he?"

Darcy's brow furrowed. "At present, I am not altogether certain."

"Well, never mind. I am just pleased we can leave London with that objective satisfied." She headed back to the staircase and started to descend. On the second step, however, she stopped and turned around. "But Darcy, whatever does the new vicar want with Kitty?"

"I believe he wants to marry her."

She regarded him in puzzlement. Then sudden understanding lit her expression. "Mr. Dashwood is in there?" she whispered excitedly.

"He is."

"And you've left them alone together? Shame on you, Darcy—'tis most improper." It was an empty admonishment—her eyes danced with delight as she returned to his side. "What is he saying to her?"

"I am not privy to that information."

"All right—as a fellow gentleman, what do you *think* he is saying?"

He looked into her face and took her hand. "I think he says that if she will grant him the opportunity, he will spend the remainder of his life proving himself worthy of her." He raised her hand to his lips and kissed it. "I think he says that if she can content herself to live on a clergyman's income, he will treat her like a duchess." He kissed the inside of her wrist. "I think he says that—" He whispered the last in her ear.

"Mmm. I had no idea Mr. Dashwood was such a romantic fellow." She allowed him to lead her away from the library door. "And what do *you* have to say, Mr. Darcy?"

"That I pray your sister consents, for I do not think I could endure another London season such as this."

Epilogue

"Think only on the past as its remembrance gives you pleasure."
—Elizabeth to Darcy,
Pride and Prejudice, *Chapter 58*

*E*lizabeth gazed out the window, momentarily distracted from her needlework by the beckoning landscape of Derbyshire in late summer. The flower gardens called, the majestic trees beckoned, and the warm afternoon sun tempted her to abandon her needle for her best pair of walking shoes.

But she wanted to finish the infant gown today, and so would postpone her walk until later. On the desk, a note to Jane also wanted completion. Elizabeth thought of her sister often these days, wondering how her sister fared as the time of her confinement neared.

Darcy entered, a letter in his hand. "I have just received word that the old vicar of Kympton passed away yesterday. The living is now Mr. Dashwood's as soon as he is eligible for ordination."

"That is sad news for the vicar's family, but Kitty will be glad to hear it. She and Mr. Dashwood can now fix upon a wedding date."

"Do you think they will wed as soon as he takes orders?"

"I imagine so. After all, Mr. Dashwood is not getting any younger."

She added several stitches to the bedgown. The mundane task, undertaken in the comfort and security of Pemberley, made their encounter with the Mirror of Narcissus seem as though it occurred long ago. However, one had only to recall Mr. Dashwood's matured countenance to remember that awful day vividly. She raised her eyes to her husband, grateful for the thousandth time that she had not lost him to the mirror's curse.

"You have a distant expression," he observed.

"I was thinking about the Mirror of Narcissus," she said. "I have often wondered what image held you spellbound. When Professor Randolph bade you imagine yourself as you wanted others to see you, did you create a younger representation of yourself, as had so many victims before you?"

"No, older."

"Older?"

"Not advanced in age, so much as in understanding," he explained. "I pictured myself the kind of man my father was, a teacher with wisdom to impart."

"To someone like Harry?"

"To my own son. Or daughter."

She pushed the needle through the muslin and brought it up again. Darcy sat down beside her, observing.

"That is a handsome dress—I think the finest of all you have made for Jane. Your sister will treasure it, I am certain."

"This one is not for Jane."

"It is not?"

She met his gaze and smiled softly. "No, it is not."

He did not speak, only gently took the dress from her hands and set it aside so he could pull her close. As he gathered her into his arms, she looked forward to seeing him as he had seen himself in the glass—a father to the child who had been the cause of the mirror's destruction.

A soul for a soul. That had been the mirror's price, and all it could contain. But in that terrible moment when it had tried to claim hers, unknown yet even to herself, her body had held two.

Author's Note

*She would, if asked, tell us many little particulars about the
subsequent career of some of her people. In this traditionary
way we learned . . . that Kitty Bennet was satisfactorily married to a clergyman near Pemberley.*

—James Edward Austen-Leigh,
A Memoir of Jane Austen, 1870

Dear Readers,

While Suspense and Sensibility *is a work of fiction, Sir Francis
Dashwood (1708–1781) was a real person who indeed founded a
secret society that came to be known as the Hell-Fire Club. As many
of my readers are interested in history, I thought those unfamiliar
with Sir Francis might want to know a little more about him.*

*The two centuries since Dashwood's death have left us with
conflicting accounts of what Sir Francis was like in life. Some
historians sympathize with him; others demonize him. Well
traveled and widely read, he pursued varied interests with zeal.
These included antiquities, art, architecture, and landscape
gardening; he spent enormous amounts of money in building
projects at his West Wycombe estate and nearby Medmenham
Abbey. He served in Parliament for forty years and held the offices
of Chancellor of the Exchequer and joint Postmaster-General. He
was an intelligent man who gathered around him many of the
leading minds of his day, from John Wilkes to Benjamin Franklin.*

In founding the so-called Hell-Fire Club (a name its members did

not use themselves), Sir Francis Dashwood brought together his
fascinations with religion, sex, and politics. The specific activities of the
group, which met over a period spanning three decades, are shrouded
in legend and mystery but share a common theme of debauchery
and dissipation. History charges the "Friars of Saint Francis" with
crimes of conduct ranging from drunken revels, mockeries of
Christianity, and orgies, to incest, Satan worship, and black magic. Yet
many of its alleged members wielded considerable political influence,
and some historians credit the Friars with contributing to the
development of democracy in England and America.

I first heard of Sir Francis Dashwood after many readings of
Sense and Sensibility, and immediately thought of Jane Austen's
Dashwood family. Wouldn't it be interesting, I thought, if the
shocking Sir Francis were somehow related to Austen's Dashwoods?
Talk about two worlds colliding! Just the image of him in the same
room as Austen's characters inspired so many possibilities that
the premise proved irresistible. The seed that eventually became
this book was planted.

Sir Francis, however, died well before the events of Austen's
Sense and Sensibility unfold—a somewhat inconvenient fact if he
was to interact with the Dashwoods of Norland. Though Austen's
book was published in 1811, it takes place in the mid-1790s: some
fifteen years after Sir Francis lived, and even longer after his
heyday. Meanwhile, Austen's Pride and Prejudice, and my own
Pride and Prescience, last left Mr. and Mrs. Darcy in late 1812.
Aging the S&S characters to bring them into contact with the
Darcys was no problem, but what to do about Sir Francis? Well, if
ever there was a figure whose activities in life lent themselves to a
return appearance, it was he.

The actual Sir Francis Dashwood was a complex man, and I
leave it to his biographers to draw his full character. The Sir
Francis you meet here is an imaginary construct based on the real
man, but altered by thirty years of imprisonment in a cursed
mirror. An ordeal like that is bound to change a person and affect

how he would respond to newfound freedom of such limited
duration as he experiences in the novel. Bear in mind also that his
portrayal here is filtered through the eyes of Elizabeth and Darcy,
whose own beliefs, values, and morals influence their impressions.

Sir Francis's dialogue and actions within my story are, of course,
purely fictitious. Whatever history may accuse him of, he died of
natural causes in 1781 and (one presumes) stayed dead. But I like to
think that given the opportunity for a second run at life's pleasures,
Sir Francis was a man who would seize it. I hope you enjoyed his
reincarnation in the pages of this book as much as he did.

I also hope you enjoyed the further exploits of Austen's
characters. If you had not been previously introduced, you can find
the Darcys and Bennets in Pride and Prejudice, and the
Dashwood, Ferrars, Brandon, and Middleton families in Sense and
Sensibility. Austen herself imagined the continuing stories of many
of her creations; her nephew wrote in his memoir of her that she
entertained her family with additional details about her characters'
lives. Though I believe Harry Dashwood's decision to enter the
church is a natural result of the events he experiences in the story I
have told, it is also a choice that dovetails with Austen's statement
that Kitty Bennet eventually married a clergyman.

Where will the Darcys go from here? Most assuredly, more
adventures await them. You can visit my Web site located at
www.carriebebris.com for clues about what lies ahead and other
information about the Mr. & Mrs. Darcy mystery series. While
you're there, do drop me a note, as I love to hear from readers.
I thank all of you who have already so thoughtfully shared your
impressions of Pride and Prescience, and look forward to
your comments on Suspense and Sensibility.

I am—

Your obliged and faithful servant,
Carrie Bebris